THE SAMURAI BANNER OF FURIN KAZAN

風
林
火
山

THE SAMURAI BANNER
OF FURIN KAZAN

by
YASUSHI INOUE

Translated by Yoko Riley

TUTTLE PUBLISHING
Tokyo • Rutland, Vermont • Singapore

First published in 2006 by Tuttle Publishing, an imprint of Periplus Editions (HK) Ltd., with editorial offices at 364 Innovation Drive, North Clarendon, VT 05759.

First published in 1959 in Japanese as *Furin Kazan*.

Library of Congress Control Number: 2005930470
ISBN: 0-8048-3701-5

Distributed by
North America, Latin America & Europe
Tuttle Publishing
364 Innovation Drive
North Clarendon, VT 05759-9436
Tel: (802) 773-8930
Fax: (802) 773-6993
info@tuttlepublishing.com
www.tuttlepublishing.com

Japan
Tuttle Publishing
Yaekari Building, 3rd Floor
5-4-12 Ōsaki
Shinagawa-ku
Tokyo 141 0032
Tel: (03) 5437-0171
Fax: (03) 5437-0755
tuttle-sales@gol.com

Asia Pacific
Berkeley Books Pte. Ltd.
130 Joo Seng Road
#06-01/03 Olivine Building
Singapore 368357
Tel: (65) 6280-1330
Fax: (65) 6280-6290
inquiries@periplus.com.sg
www.periplus.com

First edition
09 08 07 06   10 9 8 7 6 5 4 3 2 1

Designed by Meg Coughlin Design
Printed in Canada

TUTTLE PUBLISHING ® is a registered trademark of Tuttle Publishing.

Contents

Acknowledgments   *vi*

Main Characters   *vii*

The Takeda Domain ca. 1572   *vii*

The Takeda Domain ca. 1572, detail   *ix*

The Battle of Kawanakajima   *x*

Foreword   *xi*

Chapter 1 The Demise of Aoki Daizen   *1*

Chapter 2 Yamamoto Kansuke Joins the Takeda Clan   *12*

Chapter 3 The Conquest of Suwa   *25*

Chapter 4 Kansuke Convinces Princess Yuu   *39*

Chapter 5 Love and Hate   *50*

Chapter 6 I Have to Kill Her…   *75*

Chapter 7 Nagao Kagetora Threatens   *91*

Chapter 8 Princess Ogoto   *106*

Chapter 9 Renounce the World   *121*

Chapter 10 Princess Yuu Goes Home   *140*

Chapter 11 Kaizu Castle   *153*

Chapter 12 Prepare for Battle   *169*

Chapter 13 Cry of Victory   *184*

Epilogue   *199*

Notes   *201*

Chronology of Key Events   *208*

Japanese Hours of the Day   *209*

Acknowledgments

There are many people to whom I would like to offer my appreciation, but all cannot be named. The following made special contributions and offered assistance in key areas without which I could not have completed the translation of *Furin Kazan*.

My many thanks and heartfelt appreciation should go to:

Yasushi Inoue who provided such powerful material to work with.

The University of Calgary students in my many Japanese civilization classes over the years who complained that there are few, if any, any interesting books to read on the Japanese Warring era and gave me the idea, and the motivation, to translate this book.

The Department of Germanic, Slavic, and East Asian Studies of the Faculty of Humanities of the University of Calgary, which supported me all through the years of my study giving me the opportunity and support to complete this work. Also to the two very supportive Department Heads that lead the Department during these years, Nick Zekulin and Xiao-jie Yang.

My brother, Hirano Takashi, who drove me to the related historical areas in Japan, including to the house where Yamamoto Kansuke's descendents live and where his grave stone is located. I thank him for his knowledge of Japanese history and for communicating the details of that history to me.

My son, Patrick John Riley, who reluctantly helped me to read through the textbook and provided advice on the appropriate use of masculine expressions. My daughter, Maureen, who constantly supported me and encouraged me to complete this translation.

My neighbor, Jean Hamel, who read an early translation, offered me some advice and encouraged me that this book was worthwhile publishing.

And, last but not least, my husband, Mike Riley for his brutal attention to detail. As challenging and as difficult as it is to accept detailed criticism of one's own work, it is a necessary part of the creative process.

To all of these people, I am very grateful as I see this dream go to the bookstores.

—YOKO RILEY

Takeda Shingen's Heritage

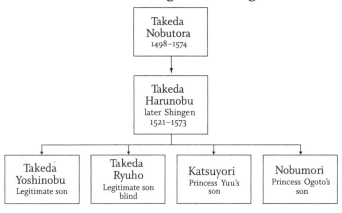

Takeda
Nobutora
1498–1574

Takeda
Harunobu
later Shingen
1521–1573

Takeda Yoshinobu	Takeda Ryuho	Katsuyori	Nobumori
Legitimate son	Legitimate son blind	Princess Yuu's son	Princess Ogoto's son

THERE WERE OTHER CHILDREN, BUT THEY DO NOT APPEAR IN THE BOOK.

Takeda Shingen's Samurai

Yamamoto Kansuke	Itagaki Nobukata	Obu Toramasa	Amari Torayasu
	Hired Kansuke Died at the battle of Uedahara		Died at the battle of Koseki

Takeda Nobushige	Oyamada Nobushge	Yokota Takatoshi	Takeda Gyoubushoyu Nobukado
Younger brother of Harunobu Died at the battle of Kawanakajima		Died at the battle of Koseki	Shingen's illegitimate brother

TAKEDA SHINGEN HAD TWENTY-FOUR FAMOUS SAMURAI UNDER HIM.
ONLY THESE APPEAR IN THE BOOK.

Takeda Shingen's Key Enemies

Suwa Yorishige	Murakami Yoshikiyo	Nagao Kagetora later Uesugi Kenshin
Married to Shingen's Sister Nene, father of Princess Yuu who is a daughter of Yorishige's concubine	Daimyo who lived in Katsurano castle. Loses great generals in the battle of Murakami	Young sophisticated general. The strongest enemy encountered by Shingen

The Takeda Domain c. 1572

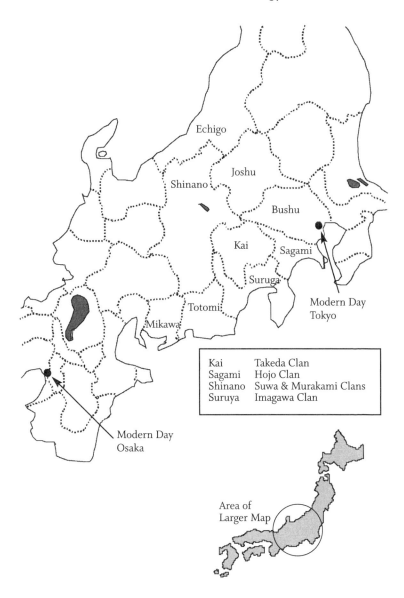

Echigo

Joshu

Shinano

Bushu

Kai

Sagami

Suruga

Modern Day
Tokyo

Totomi

Mikawa

Kai	Takeda Clan
Sagami	Hojo Clan
Shinano	Suwa & Murakami Clans
Suruya	Imagawa Clan

Modern Day
Osaka

Area of
Larger Map

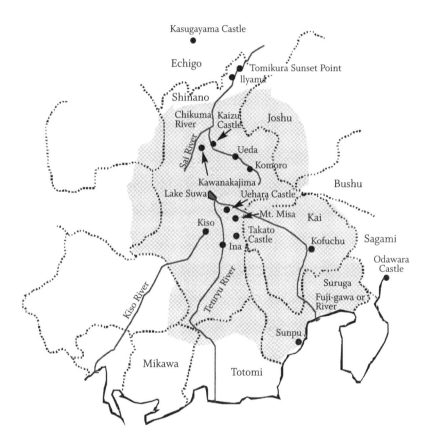

The Takeda Domain c. 1572 *detail*

Kasugayama Castle

Echigo

Tomikura Sunset Point

Ilyama

Shinano

Chikuma River

Kaizu Castle

Joshu

Ueda

Komoro

Sai River

Kawanakajima

Bushu

Lake Suwa

Uehara Castle

Kiso

Mt. Misa

Kai

Takato Castle

Kofuchu

Sagami

Ina

Odawara Castle

Kiso River

Suruga

Tenryu River

Fuji-gawa or River

Sunpu

Mikawa

Totomi

The Battle of Kawanakajima
Troop movements in the battle in Chapter 13

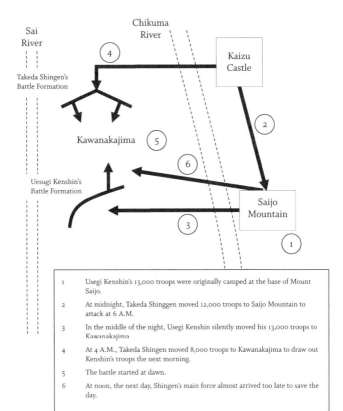

Sai
River

Chikuma
River

4

Kaizu
Castle

Takeda Shingen's
Battle Formation

Kawanakajima

5

2

6

Uesugi Kenshin's
Battle Formation

Saijo
Mountain

3

1

1   Usegi Kenshin's 13,000 troops were originally camped at the base of Mount Saijo.

2   At midnight, Takeda Shinggen moved 12,000 troops to Saijo Mountain to attack at 6 A.M.

3   In the middle of the night, Usegi Kenshin silently moved his 13,000 troops to Kawanakajima

4   At 4 A.M., Takeda Shingen moved 8,000 troops to Kawanakajima to draw out Kenshin's troops the next morning.

5   The battle started at dawn.

6   At noon, the next day, Shingen's main force almost arrived too late to save the day.

FOREWORD

THIS BOOK, ENTITLED *Furin Kazan* in the original Japanese, was written by Inoue Yasushi in the year 1958.

This book is about Takeda Shingen (1521–1573), *Sengoku daimyo*¹ of the province of Kai (Yamanashi Prefecture). A celebrated statesman and military commander, Takeda Shingen was exalted as the strongest warrior of the Sengoku period. A series of battles he fought against Uesugi Kenshin, Oda Nobunaga, Tokugawa Ieyasu, and other powerful daimyo have been taken up in many novels and motion pictures as the most dramatic events of the Sengoku period.

A seemingly trivial conflict named Onin no Ran drove Japan into a warring period of over one hundred years. The centralized government, under the strong control of the military leader called a *Shogun*, lost its power. During the period from 1480 to 1590, a previously united Japan crumbled and was divided into many small fiefdoms, the leaders of which tried to expand their power by conquering neighboring territories.

It is hard to tell how many of these local warlords appeared and disappeared during this era. A new phenomenon in the country was emerging: the hierarchical order, once very restrictive unless one was born to high samurai rank, was beginning to break down. This emerging phenomenon was called *Gekokujo*, which means that the lower defeats the upper, and anyone who had the ability and power could ultimately aspire to lead. This was the classic shift from an absolute hereditary monarchy model to a meritocracy.

As the order crumbled during the warring era, the people faced a time of cruelty and treachery and of death and survival. The strong and powerful daimyo swallowed up their weaker neighbors without mercy.

The Samurai Banner of Furin Kazan is the story of the strategist who served one of the strongest warlords in this era. Takeda Shingen, the warlord of Kai district, first appeared in Japanese history in 1541 at the age of twenty-one, when he exiled his father to a neighboring territory.

Furin Kazan is a story of Takeda Shingen, as assisted by his one-eyed, crippled strategist Yamamoto Kansuke, and how he explored and extended his territory. A new history of the east was about to be created by three young powerful leaders, Takeda Shingen, Imagawa Yoshimoto, and Hojo Ujiyasu. If these three had clashed, they would have destroyed each other. Cooperation among these rivals was essential.

Yamamoto Kansuke's love toward his master and concubines and his brilliant strategies inspired by his passion for war and his admiration for his enemies' war tactics are brilliantly expressed throughout this book.

The army of Takeda Shingen carried a standard on which four Chinese characters, fu-rin ka-zan, were printed. These characters aptly represented Shingen's way of fighting. Thus, translated, the title of this book means:

風	fu	Be as swift as the wind
林	rin	Be as silent as the wood
火	ka	Attack as fiercely as fire
山	zan	Be as composed as the mountain

I completed the translation of *The Samurai Banner of Furin Kazan*, historical fiction from the feudal era of Japan written by Inoue Yasushi, as input to the Japanese Civilization course that I teach at the University of Calgary, to enhance students' understanding of the social situation of an era for which very limited documentation exists in English. This translation provides detailed reference materials for the study of pre-twentieth century Japanese civilization with a focus on the samurai culture, which is the base of modern Japanese civilization and its way of thinking and societal, economic, and organizational structures.

Although all of Japanese history has contributed to the complex mosaic that Japan is today, samurai philosophy, the *Bushido*[2] ethic, and this particular period of history have had a particularly formative effect on Japan today and, in particular, the present Japanese business and bureaucratic culture.

Teaching Japanese civilization for the last nine years, I found that large numbers of students showed a high level of interest in the samurai culture as a subject for essay assignments. However, feudal documents dealing with the life of the samurai are very limited, although reference materials referring to theories of Bushido (the way of samurai, samurai disciplines, self-control etc.) are available.

Historical fiction using contextually and historically accurate daily life and events can fill this void by providing a depiction of the life of the samurai, women's position in the samurai culture, traditions and social values as they really were.

In this foreword, I have followed the traditional Japanese convention of placing the surname first and the first name last. Thus, the author's surname is Inoue and his given name is Yasushi and he is referred to here as Inoue Yasushi.

The existence of the hero of this story has been argued over and discussed by historians for a long time. Recently a discovery of a letter purported to be written by Yamamoto Kansuke brought special attention to this book, written in 1958.

Furin Kazan was written by Inoue Yasushi, first published in 1958 and reprinted sixty-four times until, at least, 1988. Inoue Yasushi (1907–1991) was born in Asahikawa, Hokkaido, graduated from Kyoto University, and became a journalist at the *Mainichi Daily News* before becoming a very successful author. His first novel, *Togyu* (A Bullfight), was published in 1949 and received the revered Akutagawa Literary Prize. He was known as Japan's master of historical fiction for his many popular novels, such as *Tempyo-no-iraka*, *Hyoheki*, and *Fighting Guns*. Some of Inoue's works that have already been translated into English are *Tun-Huang*, *Lou-Lan*, *The Counterfeiter*, and *The Hunting Gun*.

—YOKO RILEY

Chapter 1
THE DEMISE OF AOKI DAIZEN

NO ONE KNEW MUCH about Aoki Daizen's background or early life. The thirty-year-old *ronin*³ was quite a mystery. It was known that he originally was a vassal of the Hojo family in Sagami, a position that he lost due to scandalous misconduct. He was an extremely skilled swordsman, but his school of swordsmanship was unknown. His movements were unbelievably fast and his skill was quite evident. During battle he seemed to thirst for blood, and he always killed his opponent with a single blow.

It had been a year since he had last entered the castle town that belonged to the warlord Imagawa Yoshimoto in Sunpu.⁴ Most of the Imagawa vassals avoided Daizen whenever they encountered him on the street. He seemed to represent something evil and unpleasant. He had a pale complexion and a thin white scar between his eyes. His lips were thin, and he lifted his left shoulder slightly when he walked. Although he was rather good-looking, he had a somewhat cold and ruthless appearance.

The same spring of his return to Sunpu, there was a tournament in the square of the castle town. Even ronin were allowed to participate. Nobody could compete with Daizen's skill with the sword. Many experienced and skillful samurai⁵ fell under his blows. In every case, Daizen's *bokuto*⁶ was thrust straight into their chests, and they were thrown onto their backs. One opponent vomited blood as a result, and the rest were injured in similar fashion. That was the day the name Aoki Daizen became famous. In spite of this, the Imagawa family sent no offers of service. Although he was a talented swordsman, he seemed to generate an aura of distrust, and people were warned to stay away from him.

The evening of the tournament, Daizen left the samurai residence in Ogata where he had been staying.

At the gate, a servant said something to him, but, as usual, he did not answer. The servant mentioned something about the return of the master of the house, but whether or not Daizen heard the servant was uncertain. He walked slowly, in a sullen manner, toward the back gate. Judging by the fact that Daizen left through the back gate to avoid a possible encounter with the master of the house, it was assumed that he had heard the servant.

An hour later, Daizen was walking along the Abe River. Eventually he went down to the riverbank at a large bend in the river. He passed the back gate of several farmhouses and entered a rustic temple at the edge of the bamboo forest.

At the threshold of the gate, Daizen called out in a low voice "Are you there?" When he heard no answer, he opened the wooden gate and entered the narrow backyard. Some trees were planted in the yard, and stepping-stones were placed randomly on the ground.

"Are you there?" He whispered again. Sensing somebody was there, he sat down on the veranda.

"Who is it?" a rather hoarse voice answered.

"Aoki Daizen." He answered arrogantly. Silence emanated from the room.

"It is Aoki Daizen." Daizen repeated. His eyes were fixed on one of the trees, which were shining under the cold sun.

Then, a slight noise came from beside him as something hit the ground. A gold coin fell on the veranda beside his knee. He picked it up and glanced at it. On the coin there was a pattern like a straw mat, the hallmark of a *kiri*[7] tree and the character of Suruga.[8]

"One gold piece!" Daizen snorted scornfully. "You fraud!" he said with hatred in his voice, "It's amazing that you are boasting about your training in Bushido! Traveling the provinces, learning their customs, studying fortresses, and acquiring an excellent knowledge of geography! Ha!" Then Daizen laughed in a much lower voice. It was a nasty laugh, which truly revealed his insulted ego. Normally he was known to be a silent person; however, it was he who was doing all the talking here. "You deformed bastard! How can you talk about the art of war! Scholar of the secret knowledge of capturing castles and capturing battle camps! You know all about the art of war? Ha! Furthermore you say you are a skillful swordsman of the Gyoryu School of swordsmanship! I would love to see what this Gyoryu is that you boast about. I, Aoki Daizen, would challenge you anytime!"

The person inside remained silent. Then Daizen shouted furiously. "Give me one more piece of gold! Although you are a ronin such as I, you swindle the general public; therefore you fare much better than I do. Give me another coin!"

Another gold coin fell on the veranda with a small, barely audible sound.

"I will wait ten days before I find out who you really are." Then, he stood and yelled out again. "I am busy. I must meet the Takeda's high vassal and negotiate my employment. I've had enough of Sunpu Castle." With that, he started to walk away.

"Wait!" the hoarse voice followed him through the door.

"What?"

"You said Takeda's high vassal. Who is it?"

"Oh, you are curious. Itagaki somebody, one of the chief vassals of the Takeda Clan. I don't know the rest of his name."

After some hesitation, the hoarse voice asked. "Is it so easy to be hired?"

"How do I know? I have to try."

It was after Daizen had walked two more steps down the walkway that the paper door opened. The person who came out, sliding on his knees, was very small. His face and body were eerie looking.

"What do you want?" Daizen asked as he turned around.

"I will give you a clue. Listen! You said 'Itagaki.' He must be Itagaki Nobukata. For generations, the Itagaki family has been playing an important role as vassals of the Takeda. Today, Amari Torayasu and Itagaki Nobukata are considered to be the Takeda's key vassals. He will not listen so easily to a ronin asking for a position. There is only one way. Listen. You should attack Itagaki Nobukata."

"Attack!? Why?"

"It's obvious. You attack him, and I will save Itagaki from danger."

Daizen did not understand. The small man continued.

"Then Itagaki and I will have some kind of bond. No human being would feel more obligated to help me than someone who had his life saved. I also want to serve his lord, Takeda. When I am given a position with the Takeda, I shall recommend you to him."

"A trick?" Daizen spat and stared malevolently at Kansuke.

"There is no other way."

"You deformed bastard!"

"If you don't like my idea, just leave."

Daizen stood in thought for a minute, then came back to the veranda and said, "You've revealed your true nature finally, you one-eyed fraud!"

The man who sat on the veranda had a wandering eye, and it was difficult to tell where he was looking. When Daizen returned to the veranda, the man put his right hand down and lifted his hip. His middle finger was missing. Though he rose to his feet smoothly, he was extremely short. He was not even five feet tall. The short man went back to his room.

Daizen laughed contemptuously, but the man who entered the room did not even acknowledge the ridicule. From inside the rather dark room, the man's face was fixed on a red chrysanthemum. He remained this way, totally ignoring Daizen.

"It is rather difficult to attack a person without wounding him. I, Aoki Daizen, have never done something like that before."

But the man inside the room said nothing.

"Say something, Yamamoto Kansuke!" shouted Daizen with a rush of emotion. His face suddenly contracted in anger and emotion

From inside the room, the hoarse voice finally emerged, "You can injure him, but I don't want him to be killed. It would be meaningless."

Daizen disliked Yamamoto Kansuke. He had met Kansuke only half a year ago, but from that time on he hated this man. Whenever he heard Kansuke's voice, he could not help wanting to bully him and abuse him to the point that Kansuke totally surrendered. To beg for money was one reason he came, but fundamentally he had a stronger motivation to harass Kansuke.

The name ronin Kansuke was well known among the three territories of the Imagawa Clan, Suruga, Totomi, and Mikawa. He was a masterless samurai from Ushikubo, of Mikawa Province, which was one of the Imagawa Clan's territories. It had been nine years since he had come to Suruga. For those nine years, he had been asking the Imagawa to employ him. For unknown reasons, he had never been offered any position. During these nine years, he had been protected and fed by the chief retainer of the Imagawa, Iohara Tadatane. It was rumored that the reason Iohara had been providing Kansuke's supply of rice and salt for such a long time was that he and Iohara were related.

It was also rumored that Kansuke had mastered his swordsmanship in the school of Gyoryu and no retainer of the Imagawa Clan could defeat him. However, nobody had actually seen him draw his sword, nor heard any stories of his prowess on the battlefield; nor were there any stories of him having killed or wounded anybody at all. His gruesome face might have played a large role in this rumor.

His height did not reach five feet, he had a dark complexion, one eye was blind, and he had a limp; he also had no middle finger on his right hand. He must have been close to fifty years of age.

Whenever he left his house and walked the castle town, which was not very often, children turned around to look at him, but the adults ignored him. His appearance was both gruesome and painful to look at. Although the children turned around to stare at him, they never followed him, most likely out of fear.

It was said that since he was twenty years old, he had traveled all over Japan, had excelled in planning military strategy, had great knowledge of the old and new arts of war, and was known as an expert on battle formation and the capturing of castles. The fact that he had not been hired for nine years, in spite of his military acumen, helped fuel his fame. Most felt that there was someone powerful near Lord Imagawa who was jealous of Kansuke's intelligence, experience and talent, therefore this officer prevented the hiring of Kansuke. It was then rumored that the jealous officer was actually his protector, Iohara Tadatane, himself. People rarely visited Kansuke, even the Imagawa's vassals. His house was always quiet.

Only Daizen did not believe the rumors surrounding Kansuke. Deformed fraud! This was how Daizen thought of him. It was not that he analyzed every possible achievement of Kansuke; his opinion of him was based solely on his intuition. It was impossible for him to imagine Kansuke standing with his sword in his hands. If he forced the image into his mind, he did not appear to be a dashing or brave samurai, rather a pathetic one.

It was some six months ago that Daizen had met Kansuke, but from the very moment of the meeting, he did not trust him. He thought a master of the sword should not be like him. He wished to challenge him with his sword once and peel off his deception. Several times he tried to entice him into drawing his sword, but Kansuke never responded to the temptation; every time Kansuke tactfully escaped from Daizen's challenge.

Daizen occasionally visited the house of Yamamoto Kansuke to verbally abuse him. Kansuke always remained silent. Daizen started to accumulate feelings of disgust and hatred toward Kansuke. His existence was the only entertainment in Daizen's unemployed, impoverished daily life. When it came to the art of war and the information about many fiefdoms, Daizen himself had no knowledge, therefore he could not test or judge Kansuke, but he thought that this was probably quite similar to his ability with the sword. It was probably all a fraud. How could he talk about battle formation and capturing castles without a single retainer of his own?

It was doubtful that he had traveled abroad. Once Daizen asked him about the geography of the Odawara area where Daizen was born, but Kansuke did not reply. He assumed Kansuke knew nothing.

Today, Daizen was pleased with the fact that Kansuke had revealed his nature as a fraud. He was walking faster than usual along the Abe River. Even if Kansuke's idea of attacking Itagaki Nobukata was a trick, at least it excited Daizen. "You deformed bastard, although you have been deceiving the world, you cannot deceive me!" he thought.

Daizen was walking along the pebbly shore of the Abe River, from where the fallow fields spread out along the horizon. No rice would be cultivated this year! This idea darkened his mind. When it came to rice, it was a serious matter. Many peasants had abandoned their land and had become itinerants. Consequently, there were hardly any people who cultivated their fields. On top of that, it had rained heavily this year, for ten consecutive days. East of Kyoto, everybody was suffering from the terrible flood. Even in the Imagawa's land, countless houses were washed away along the Abe River. Not only the rice fields, but also cows and horses were washed out toward the ocean. Last year, during the ninth year of *Tenbun*[9], once in the spring and once in the autumn, the country was hit by a huge typhoon. Disastrous things continued to happen.

Should I apply for service in the province of Kai[10]? Could things be better there? I am not totally willing to work with Kansuke, but even working with a deformed bastard like him, would be better than being alone in an unknown land.

"But I can't stand him! I hate him!" Daizen stopped suddenly. He detested the idea of working with Kansuke. Other people did not like him, but Kansuke was worse, he thought. When he was a child, he had once ground a caterpillar into the earth with a stone, and now he felt his rage would not dissipate unless he did the same thing to this infamous deformed ronin.

It was early August. There was no wind, but the night air was cold. Fall was rapidly approaching.

Not very far from the Imagawa mansion, the samurai residences were scattered around as if to surround the mansion protectively. Beyond the residential area, the road went down the hill to the castle town. Normally this road was crowded during the day, but after sunset, hardly anybody travelled it. Stores along the road closed their doors tightly when night came.

Daizen stood near the large *enoki*[11] tree for over an hour. He was waiting for Takeda's chief vassal, Itagaki Nobukata. Itagaki was visiting the former daimyo[12] of the Takeda Clan, Nobutora, who had been exiled by his son Harunobu and had found protection under the Imagawa for the past five years.[13] Itagaki was supposed to return to the residence of Shinonome Hanjiro, who had accompanied Nobutora from the Takeda. Daizen was there to attack them on their way to the Shinonome's residence.

He had not seen Kansuke today, but this was certainly the place they had planned to meet, under the enoki tree on the slope. As soon as he saw Itagaki, he was to run out from behind the tree and attempt to kill him. If there were vassals, he was supposed to kill them as well. Kansuke was then supposed to appear. After exchanging a few thrusts and parries of the sword, Daizen was to disappear into the forest nearby.

Daizen looked around in the near darkness. He knew that somewhere nearby the crooked eyes of Kansuke were watching as well.

Daizen could not keep silent for such a long time.

"Hey you, deformed bastard! Kansuke!" he whispered loudly and listened carefully. There was no answer. He clicked his tongue in exasperation and squatted on the ground.

Another hour passed. The darkness around him made him feel aggressive. "I wish that thieves or wild dogs would appear, then I could kill them!" he thought with mounting frustration.

Then, he heard quiet footsteps approaching from the hill. As the footsteps neared, he discovered that there was more than one person. As they advanced, it appeared that there were three people.

"Saeki Mondo!" Daizen called out to the group, which was passing in front of him. Of course, the name he called was not someone in the group. It was nothing more than a fabrication.

The footsteps stopped instantly.

"There is nobody here called Saeki," answered one of them.

"There is no use telling a lie! I came all the way here to take your life!" Daizen shouted with annoyance.

"What is the use of telling a lie!" the man answered, but Daizen suddenly drew his sword. Perceiving the move, the three men jumped back swiftly.

"Wait! We don't appreciate your mistake. I am a vassal of the Takeda Clan; Itagaki is my name."

It was a voice filled with dignity. It was truly Itagaki, Daizen thought.

"I don't really care who you are, I shall take your life, anyway," Daizen yelled out.

"A thief!" Instantly Itagaki whipped out his sword. In no time two white blades were in front of Daizen. Further behind the two swords, he heard the dignified voice again.

"Be careful! Just drive him away!"

When Daizen realized that these two were not Itagaki himself, he leaped forward and slashed one of the samurai's shoulders. The samurai screamed. Daizen jumped away at once, but he immediately lunged forward again and slashed the other samurai's leg. Again, a shriek of pain was heard.

The next moment Itagaki himself struck in silence. As they crossed swords several times, Daizen could hear his opponent's heavy breathing.

"You must have been mistaken. I am a vassal of the Takeda, Itagaki Nobukata." The opponent repeated again. Daizen kept silent. "Are you a thief?"

Daizen was thinking about what he should do with this opponent, whom he was not supposed to kill, as he closed the distance between them. Then, Itagaki stepped forward. He definitely excelled with the sword. It was quite obvious that he was much better than the two previous swordsmen. Daizen advanced close to Itagaki's chest, grabbed his opponent's right arm, and pushed him slowly to the side of the road.

"Who is it?"

Suddenly a lantern shone right into Daizen's face from the side. For the first time Daizen realized that he was pushing his opponent against a clay wall. From the time Daizen heard the chief vassal's voice, he had thought that this person was old, but he was younger than expected. He was a middle-aged samurai.

"I was attacked by a thief and I am having a little trouble dispatching him." Itagaki answered quickly.

"I shall offer you help!"

Clearly it was the voice of Kansuke. Daizen let go of Itagaki's arm and swiftly jumped backward. "Now this is where the plot begins," he thought.

Then a swift blow of the *daito*[14] came down on him from directly in front of him. Instantly he jumped back with a slight "Ah!" sound and stumbled backwards onto a stone.

The second and third attack followed ruthlessly. It was no longer a trick; Daizen felt a thirst for the blood of his opponent well up inside of him. This was not part of the plan! Daizen forced himself to get up, as he tumbled down the slope. He must have been cut between his eyes; he could feel the blood in them. But there was no time to wipe it away.

"Kansuke!" Daizen yelled out and ran into the bushes. According to the plan Kansuke's chase was supposed to stop there.

When he turned around, his opponent's sword was poised near him. And this sword relentlessly followed him everywhere he went.

"Are you mad?!" Daizen yelled out.

"No, I am not mad," the low voice continued, "I shall kill you."

"Try!" Daizen yelled, feeling that the situation had changed. His opponent was determined to kill him. I have to kill him too! His hatred toward this crippled ronin increased ten fold.

But for the first time in his life, Daizen felt something approaching fear. His opponent's sword remained in a surprisingly low position. The small man's sword was almost touching the ground. When the crooked eyes fixed him, Daizen could neither move ahead nor back. The distance between the two closed gradually. Daizen felt as if he was glued to the ground. His opponent's sword flashed in the dim light. Instantly, his shoulder was cut open, then his right wrist and then his legs. Daizen was covered in blood

"Wait! Please wait!" Daizen yelled desperately. But it was as if he were talking to a wall. No matter how much he shouted, his opponent's sword just kept on attacking.

Daizen felt as if Kansuke's body was growing while his own large body was shrinking and becoming ugly. Indeed Daizen's remaining eye was becoming useless, and his leg was crippled.

"Uh!" was the last sound he uttered as he was cut in half from his shoulder to his hip.

Chapter 2

YAMAMOTO KANSUKE JOINS THE TAKEDA CLAN

IT WAS MID-FEBRUARY in the twelfth year of Tenbun when the messenger from the Takeda family of Kai came to Yamamoto Kansuke in Sunpu to request his service. One and a half years had passed since Yamamoto Kansuke had killed the unknown ronin Aoki Daizen and helped the vassal of the Takeda, Itagaki Nobukata. According to the messenger, the Takeda family requested his service and offered a stipend of one hundred *kan*.[15] Kansuke sent back the messenger replying that he would like to think about it for two days.

That day, contrary to his routine, Kansuke left his house. Early cherry blossoms had started to bloom along the banks of the Abe River.

"Capturing castles, capturing castles," Kansuke repeated the same words in his mind for quite a long time. A stipend of a hundred kan! It was not really important how much he received. The point was whether he could participate in planning the strategy for battle formation and whether he could demonstrate his talent for capturing castles and territories. Before accepting this offer of service, he had to extract a condition.

"Capturing castles, capturing castles."

Kansuke walked through the lane of cherry trees without even once looking up at the blossoms. Two women, most likely samurai wives, accompanied by two children, came from the opposite end of the street. When they saw Kansuke, they avoided him with evident fear.

"Capturing castles, capturing castles."

Without glancing at the women, he proceeded, turning up his eyes and staring at nothing. Every time he stepped with his right leg his body leaned heavily to that side.

The laneway entered the center road of Sunpu. The residence of his protector, chief retainer of the Imagawa, was at the entrance to the samurai residential quarter. Since *keyaki*[16] trees surrounded the residence, people in the castle town called his residence "Keyaki Mansion."

Kansuke entered the main entrance of Keyaki Mansion. Without announcing his arrival, he set his foot on the *fumidai*.[17] In the corridor, he met one of his protector's maids.

"Is Iohara-san[18] home?"

"Yes, please wait for a minute while I get him."

Ignoring her comment, Kansuke kept walking. The maid wanted to go ahead of him and tell her master about Kansuke's visit, but she was hesitant to pass him. He had some kind of powerful aura in his short body and figure that humbled everyone before him. Nobody would dare go ahead of him.

"Are you there, Iohara-san?" Kansuke called out in front of the inner part of the room.

"Who is it?" came the response.

"It is Yamamoto Kansuke, I came here to see you."

No answer came from inside. Kansuke could almost sense that Iohara's expression had changed into disgust at the sound of his voice.

"Excuse me," opening the sliding paper door, Kansuke stepped into the room. He was at least polite enough to sit at the edge of the room and bowed slightly.

"I am here today to negotiate."

"What is it?" Iohara asked impatiently.

Iohara was sitting at his desk as if he had been reading. He slowly turned his white head toward Kansuke.

"A messenger came from the Takeda family requesting my service."

A silence hung in the air as Iohara's eyes flicked back and forth. Then he asked, "Well, are you going to offer your service to them?"

"I cannot be a ronin forever."

"How much is the stipend?"

"A hundred kan."

There was a short silence.

"We shall offer you one hundred also, then." Iohara replied. "We have not inconvenienced you until now, have we?"

"I've had enough of being a retainer; I would like to capture a castle."

"Do you really think that you can capture a castle with the art of war which you have learned at a desk?"

"It is possible!" Kansuke growled. Iohara shut his mouth and sat thinking for a moment.

"So you are going to serve them then. I'd better tell my lord."

"It won't make any difference whether you talk to your lord or not. It is obvious that you people don't want to see me go, but at the same time you are too scared to use me in your clan."

"Watch your language!" Iohara said curtly.

Kansuke said, "Isn't it true that you are scared of me? Are you so scared of me that you cannot have my service?" Then he changed his tone, "However, you have been looking after me with food and clothing for nine years. I do have a sense of duty and obligation. So I shall sell only my body to the Takeda, but keep my heart here in the territory of Sunpu."

As Kansuke spoke, a chuckle escaped his mouth.

Iohara turned abruptly towards Kansuke. His eyes, which normally showed indifference, shone with a chill.

"What do you mean by that?"

Iohara observed Kansuke closely to discover his intention.

"I shall receive a stipend from both the Takeda and Imagawa at the same time."

Shocked, Iohara kept silent.

"I have never left here since I believed in the Imagawa's future."

Iohara said nothing.

"The Imagawa family is the strongest family along the east coast, so you can afford to send one of his vassals to the Takeda, can you not?"

After these words, Kansuke stopped speaking with an assured smile on his lips.

The wife of Lord Imagawa was Takeda Nobutora's daughter. Therefore, the two clans were related, but his own son Harunobu[19] had exiled Nobutora when he was twenty-three years old. At present, Nobutora was under the protection of his son-in-law, Imagawa Yoshimoto. On the surface, the Takeda and Imagawa families remained allied, but the feud between Nobutora and Harunobu, father and son, was increasing the gap between the Imagawa and the Takeda.

Therefore, for the Imagawa, it was not such a bad idea to send Kansuke to the Takeda and at the same time to secretly give Kansuke a stipend from the Imagawa.

Kansuke stood up suddenly. But it wasn't until after he had walked out to the hallway that Iohara prevented Kansuke from leaving his residence.

In early March, Kansuke left for Kofuchu[20] along the eastern shore of the Fuji River. He was escorted by the three samurai from the Province of Kai. The slopes of the mountains, which were close to both sides of the rapids of the Fuji River, were adorned with fresh, green leaves.

They stayed two nights at an inn on their way to Kai. Kansuke hated traveling and was in a foul mood. It was rumoured that he had traveled all over Japan to master the art of swordsmanship and there was nowhere he had not left his foot-prints. But the truth was that he knew nowhere but his home province Mikawa and a part of Suruga. It was only a story made up by the public that he had traveled all over Japan. But he did not deny the rumor; it wasn't necessary to do so. Due to his knowledge, he could visualize the castle towns of both the western provinces and eastern provinces very clearly. He had acquired enormous insight through reading about the mountains, rivers, plains, and the climate of each particular province and fiefdom. He could easily visualize each castle and the geographical features around it, with extreme accuracy.

He never missed the opportunity to extract every element of knowledge from travelers from afar. He had an excellent memory and a vivid imagination, which surprised even him. He only had to hear something once and then never forgot any of the details. From a single piece of information, he could extract extensive knowledge.

Itagaki Nobukata came to welcome him at the midpoint of his journey and brought the clothes, horses, spears, bows and arrows, and even the young pages that would serve Kansuke.

Kansuke was very satisfied. Not only had they treated him unexpectedly well, but the Province of Kai was almost exactly the same as the picture he had visualized in his mind. When they entered the castle town of Kofuchu, he thought that even the color of the clouds was exactly as he had imagined.

"How many times have you come to Kofuchu?" Itagaki asked.

"Three times." He answered. That was not a lie, he thought.

That night Kansuke stayed at a wealthy samurai's house which was located north of the Takeda mansion. The next day he accompanied Itagaki to see Harunobu at his mansion. Takeda's mansion did not have the structure of a castle. It was a normal house other than it was surrounded by a moat.

In a spacious room, the twenty-three year old Takeda Harunobu sat and Takeda's ministers and horsemen were sitting opposite each other in rows. Kansuke knelt and prostrated himself at the entrance. Being told to come closer by Lord Harunobu, he stood and proceeded closer to Harunobu, bending his body in a respectful bow.

Beside Itagaki was Obu Toramasa with Amari Torayasu next to Obu. Moving forward, Kansuke glanced at Takeda's three key vassals. When he looked down, Amari's wintry eyes remained in his memory. I don't like him, he thought.

Harunobu did not utter a word, but kept constant watch on Kansuke's grotesque appearance. Suddenly he said, "You are much more sturdily built than I had expected. I am sure you are not satisfied with a stipend of one hundred kan. I shall offer you two hundred."

His voice was not loud but it was resonant. Kansuke lifted his face slightly in astonishment.

Then Harunobu added, "I shall give you one character from my name. From now on you shall name yourself Yamamoto Kansuke Haruyuki."

Kansuke thought, this was an unexpectedly generous young general. He bowed in silence. Itagaki came close by and whispered, "You should show your appreciation by your words."

Kansuke lifted his face, and said in an expressionless voice, "Thank you very much. To reciprocate this honour, I would like to participate in a battle to capture a castle as soon as possible."

"Capturing a castle, you say it so easily, but..." Harunobu started; then Kansuke interrupted.

"Yes, there are secret principles on the capture of castles and the subjugation of territory."

"Have you mastered the secret principles?"

"Yes."

Kansuke's curt answer bore an insolent air to it. Then Kansuke heard Amari's bold, laughing voice.

"How many times you have participated in battles?" Amari asked.

"Not even once."

A burst of laughter erupted from the lower seats.

It did not disturb Kansuke at all. Something was building up within him that made it difficult for him to sit quietly. It was his confidence and bravery, which made him believe that he could capture many castles easily.

After a pause Itagaki said, "You may leave and rest."

Kansuke left Harunobu's mansion.

As soon as he had left, Amari knelt in front of Harunobu and said, "We cannot help thinking of him as a fake who simply wants a stipend, especially when he talks about his ability in military strategy without having participated in a battle even once."

Then, Obu also added, "How about keeping him one year to see what he can actually do. However, since our lord has divine abilities to judge people, you might have some special thought on him.

Then Harunobu simply said, "Ten years ago, when I was thirteen years old, I went to Ushikubo in Mikawa Province and met Kansuke. At that time we exchanged an agreement as lord and vassal, and since then I have let him travel around the country."

Harunobu did not change his expression at all. Everybody knew that his words were false, but it was Lord Harunobu who had spoken and nobody dared to challenge his words. Only Itagaki knew the reason why Harunobu protected Kansuke: Since Harunobu had been ignored by his father and had lived an ill-fated childhood, he had a tendency to show his favor to people who had a strange appearance or were in adversity, simply because they were not trusted by others.

Kansuke spent the second night in Kai under the protection of Itagaki in the samurai residence in front of the Takeda mansion.

The next afternoon, Kansuke climbed up the slope behind the mansion. Right behind the mansion, the base of the gentle hill spread. Even before he was halfway to the top, he could see not only the castle town of Kofuchu, but also part of the plain of the Kai fiefdom.

It looked so easy to attack and destroy the Takeda mansion. It was totally defenseless when viewed from the mountain. The only reason they had kept their fiefdom intact until now must have been that the Takeda family always fought away and never drew the enemy inside their fiefdom. In the eastern coastal region, the castle would never have survived a day in this defenseless situation.

Wind was blowing up from the foothills. It made Kansuke feel good as the wind brushed the perspiration from his skin. Kansuke sat on the bank of a rice field, which was cultivated along the slope, and continued looking down upon the plain. Kai was said to be a mountainous country. Indeed, along the plain he could see the severe line of the mountain ranges.

All of a sudden, Kansuke saw a horseman riding up the slope where he was sitting. When the skillful rider neared Kansuke, he dismounted from his horse and approached him. He asked him politely, "Are you Yamamoto-san? You are summoned to the castle."

"How did you know I was here?"

"Somebody saw you climbing this hill."

Kansuke stood up and said, "I shall be there right way."

The samurai mounted his horse and swiftly disappeared.

Kansuke thought it was the Lord Harunobu who had summoned him. When he entered the castle, red and white striped curtains were hung all around the square, and the sound of drums was heard everywhere. A few samurai ran toward him and said, "Please follow us." He was immediately taken inside a tent.

Amari sat in the center of the tent on a stool and many samurai were sitting on either side of him. Kansuke was immediately taken in front of him.

Amari said to Kansuke, "Yamamoto Kansuke, you are going to show me the way of Gyoryu swordsmanship."

"What an absurd request, I came here thinking that our lord was calling me."

"I have heard that you excel in Gyoryu swordsmanship. Unfortunately we have nobody who has mastered that school, but we have several masters who studied Shintoryu. I would appreciate it if you will have a match with them."

Kansuke had no interest in the game. It was simply a rumor that he was a master of Gyoryu swordsmanship, just as his journeys all over the country were. He had never even held a wooden sword in his hands before this. The only experience he had with a sword was the time he killed Aoki Daizen in Suruga. Even he did not know how he had succeeded that time. He knew that he had to defend himself, so he jumped in and struck at Daizen's forehead, legs, then shoulder, forehead again and, in the end, split his shoulder. He struck him because he thought he had to kill him. But that was enough of the art of swordsmanship! He knew nothing of the Gyoryu, or the Shintoryu. He did not even know the rules of handling a sword.

A few samurai ran toward him and handed him a wooden sword. They then tucked up his sleeves with a sash.

"What a nuisance!" Kansuke uttered. Without giving him time to complete his words, he was taken to the center of the square.

"Nuisance!"

Kansuke tried to escape to the corner, but was taken back to the center again. Then, he saw a middle-aged samurai slowly approaching him with a wooden sword in his hands. Since Kansuke had no intention of fighting, the game started one-sided.

"What a nuisance!" He yelled when his shoulder was struck hard.

"This is absurd!" He yelled again, when the other shoulder was numbed. He could not regain the feeling in either shoulder for a while. Then, his legs were swept from under him and Kansuke fell awkwardly on the ground.

Laughter and cheers spread around the square.

Suddenly the noise dwindled to total silence. One part of the curtain was split open and Harunobu appeared with his pages behind him. Kansuke was summoned.

"I hear you had a match," said Harunobu with his low, but resonating, voice.

"Yes, I won the game," he continued, holding his painful shoulder. "My partner would be no use in real combat. He would be killed with a single blow."

"Why is that?"

"His eyes were dead. Just like the eyes of a dead fish. He could be struck down by a nameless foot soldier."

Harunobu nodded nonchalantly. It was hard to tell whether he believed Kansuke or not. In the square a new game started. Kansuke bowed and left the lord. Both his shoulders and his back were aching. What a nuisance, he thought.

Amari came close to him and said hatefully, "Don't tell an obvious lie when it was so clear that you were beaten."

"Was it your house retainer?"

"I have just hired him recently. He was a ronin from the east, but he has skillful hands."

"But he will be useless in real combat. He will embarrass you." Kansuke then laughed and lifted the curtain and slipped behind it.

That night, Kansuke was invited by Lord Harunobu to visit the castle. Itagaki, Amari, and five or six other generals were with Harunobu.

"Are the samurai and common people different in each fiefdom?" Harunobu asked Kansuke.

"I traveled all over the country and studied family customs. I happened to study Lord Yoshimoto's[21] court and became acquainted with some ronin while I was in Suruga for nine years. I believe that the entire country could be divided into three categories. First, the eastern mentality; second, Shikoku[22] and Chugoku[23]; and then Kyushu[24] would belong to the third category."

"How do they differ?"

"Above Bishu, in other words, in the eastern areas, people are rarely courteous, but are violent and oppressive. When relationships are good, they admire the people who are not worth admiring, but when their relationships turn sour, they speak ill of the people who excel."

Once he started speaking, he was eloquent. No matter what questions were asked, he answered effusively although nobody knew where he had acquired this knowledge. Since Itagaki was Kansuke's patron, he was satisfied with his eloquence, but Amari kept silent with an expression as if he had bitten into a sour grape. For him, everything that Kansuke said was fabricated.

Kansuke answered everything in detail, as he was asked about diverse subjects, such as provincial geography, human feelings, customs, and military structures.

"Are there any ways to cause your enemy to surrender within one or two years of your conquest of their territory?" Harunobu asked.

"Hire the famous or well-liked samurai from the enemy, give them half or all the information you have according to the situation, and arrange marriages with your close retainers. In addition, invite some priests, townsmen, and leaders of the peasantry into your presence and comfort them and ask them about their living conditions. It is not that good an idea to hold a feast. Mori

Motonari, Lord of Aki, who started archery lessons in early child-hood, conquered Chugoku and extended his power to Shikoku and Kyushu. To place those countries under his control, he used this method."

From seven to ten o'clock, he talked with Harunobu. When they heard strong winds outside, they retired from the castle. Kansuke left the castle a little before Itagaki and Amari.

He came out of the eastern gate of the castle and crossed the bridge over the moat. It was pitch black. The branches of the old trees in the castle were creaking in the blowing wind. Kansuke was walking along the moat ready to turn toward the samurai residence.

Suddenly, the naked point of a sword appeared in front of him. It was totally unexpected! Kansuke quickly jumped back. The shimmering point of the sword followed him. He backed up one step at a time all the way to the end of the enclosure, which was at the northeast end of the castle. Still the point of the sword followed him. Then, Kansuke spoke for the first time.

"Who are you?"

"Since you desired a match with a real sword, I came here to offer you the chance."

"Absurd!" said Kansuke.

Kansuke realized that the person who stood in front of him was his opponent from the afternoon match. Kansuke said, "The result was obvious. You are stronger than I am."

"What! I have no intention to listen to you babbling."

In a split second, Kansuke leaped back about a meter and said repeatedly, "Absurd!" Then he continued, "don't lose your mind. I was there simply to answer the lord's invitation...."

Then, Kansuke heard his opponent's laughter.

"Lose my mind? I won't. I shall kill you here and after that simply run away. Is your life so dear to you? Too bad. No matter how much you value your life, unfortunately, I intend to kill you."

"And run away after?"

"Yes, indeed."

"Do you want to kill me that much?"

"Yes, I do."

With this answer, Kansuke made up his mind.

"In that case, *I* shall kill you instead."

Kansuke drew his sword and said, "Come!"

Kansuke shortened the distance between them inch by inch. He stepped forward one step. The tip of his sword cut between his opponent's eyes.

"Uh!" This time his opponent stepped backward. Kansuke continued to close the distance. Again he stepped forward. Since it was his shorter leg that led, his body swayed. Instantly his opponent let out a yell.

"Gyaa!" It resembled the cry of a night bird. The challenger's shoulder was sliced open. Kansuke continued to step forward.

"Wait! Please wait."

Kansuke did not wait. He continued to follow him. Suddenly, another voice came from the dark. The shadow of two or three figures moved. Then, a torch brightened the area. Without knowing, the two of them were fighting in front of the main gate of the castle. Itagaki, Amari, and several others appeared.

"Wait, wait a minute," somebody said loudly. Kansuke ignored the voice completely and continued to step forward.

The cry of the night bird came from his opponent again. Kansuke quietly sheathed his sword and remained standing in the darkness. In the circle of the torch, his larger opponent stood there for a second, and then fell backward. The master of the Shintoryu School was lying with his skull split in half.

Amari glanced at the dead body, then looked at Kansuke. His eyes held an expression as if he had seen something menacing and incomprehensible.

"Are you Yamamoto Kansuke?"

"Yes."

"Is it you who killed him?"

"Yes."

"You are truly the one who killed him?"

"Yes, sir."

Amari abruptly turned his back on Kansuke and disappeared out of the torchlight, leaving alone. Then he turned around and yelled, "Yamamoto Kansuke!"

When there was no response, he continued walking quickly away. To Amari, Kansuke had become in that instant nothing but a monster.

Kansuke proceeded toward the samurai residence with Itagaki. Halfway through the estate, the road descended.

"It is not good to kill a person unless it is in battle."

"Yes," Kansuke said and listened to the horrible sound of the wind. Just like the time he killed Aoki Daizen, he felt slightly tired. He did not find it strange that once he drew his sword and was determined to kill, he could kill his opponent without fail. He felt that he held that kind of power and was that kind of person.

"Starting next month, we will face battles for a long time. I will place twenty-five foot soldiers under you. Serve your master faithfully." Only these words came to Kansuke's ears. He was not listening to what was said before or after.

"A leader of the foot soldiers is…"

Kansuke heard Itagaki's voice again, but was not really interested in anything about his new post.

"Capturing castles, capturing castles," he murmured. He felt as if every time there was a battle he could capture a castle. He felt it was such an enjoyable thing to go into battle with a young lord like Takeda Harunobu and capture castles, one after another. Kansuke felt battle was something which was very quiet. That was because he had never experienced a battle before. He heard nothing of the sound of arms and weapons.

After he left Itagaki, he walked alone toward his residence. Sand blew up from the bottom of the slope. He covered his good eye with his right hand, of which his middle finger was missing. He lifted his face a little, and then he saw the cold, bluish stars which he had never seen on the east coast. They looked so close that he thought he might be able to touch them. Kansuke continued down the slope one step at a time.

IN FEBRUARY OF THE thirteenth year of the Tenbun, Takeda Harunobu set up his battle camp with 20,000 warriors on Mount Misa on the plains of Shinano. Harunobu's intention was to attack the powerful clan of Suwa Yorishige in the Suwa fiefdom.

Since the reign of Harunobu's father, it had been a long-standing plan for the Takeda family to attack the Suwa, the first step in ruling Shinano Province. However, while Nobutora was busy sending warriors to the provinces of Suruga and Sagami, he was reluctant to proclaim war on the Lord of Suwa. Instead, he sent his sixth daughter to the Suwa leader, Yorishige, as his wife and thus placed Suwa under his influence. Nobutora's daughter was called Nene and was noted for her beauty. Unfortunately, two years later, in the twelfth year of Tenbun, she passed away at the age of sixteen.

Harunobu, however, was very different from his father Nobutora. He was determined to put Suwa completely under his rule. He had been searching for a reason to legitimately attack Yorishige for the last several years. Just lately, he happened to learn from the lord of Takato Castle, Takato Yoritsugu, that Yorishige was plotting against the Takeda. Using this as an excuse, Harunobu decided to aggressively attack the Suwa Clan.

Although he had established his army camp at Mount Misa, Harunobu, for some reason, had a heavy heart. When he had chased his father to Suruga because of the differences in their ideologies, he had felt the same way. He felt that this battle was going to leave a bad taste in his mouth. Although his sister Nene had passed away, for Harunobu Yorishige was still his brother-in-law. And using an as yet unproven excuse, he was trying to get rid of a family member.

The battle camp was surrounded by many plum trees. White blossoms were blooming here and there in the clean air of the high plain. The whiteness and purity of the flowers had a strange effect on Harunobu's twenty-four-year-old heart. It made him feel uncomfortable, and he was not inspired to fight at all.

That night when they set up camp on Mount Misa, a messenger from Takato, leader of a middle-sized family clan allied to the Takeda, arrived and reported that his army would break into Uehara Castle²⁵ through Tsuetsuki Sunset Point in two or three days. Uehara Castle was the present residence of the Lord of Suwa. Takato asked Harunobu to send his major army from the east side of the mountain into an attack position.

After Takato's messenger had left, Harunobu summoned his generals and created a new strategy. Harunobu made his brother Samanosuke Nobushige the commander-in-chief and Harunobu himself decided to stay at the Mount Misa camp as a backup, in case he was required.

"It is only a small castle alongside a lake, it won't be worthwhile to send 20,000 warriors," said Harunobu.

It was unlike Harunobu, who loved to fight, to back down like that.

"But I think you ought to at least go to Miyakawa village or near Yasukuni Temple," Itagaki Nobukata insisted, and the other generals agreed with him.

Kansuke, from one of the lower seats, presented a totally different opinion. He lifted his head and said, "As far as I am concerned, since the Takeda and the Suwa are related, although it might sound strange at this stage of the war, I don't think this battle is a good idea. I feel that you have already demonstrated that you are a threat to the Suwa by taking the field. I believe it is better to negotiate for peace rather than shedding blood."

His opinion totally disrupted the atmosphere in the room and provoked a sudden, heart-stopping silence. With a battle imminent, someone had rejected the entire war. Even Itagaki, who normally favored Kansuke's ideas, turned pale.

"Damn you, Kansuke! Watch your mouth!" It was Harunobu's brother Nobushige who finally spoke to break the silence. The young general's anger demonstrated to Kansuke that he would never be forgiven for his statement.

"Leave him be," said Harunobu calmly, finding himself truly relieved by Kansuke's statement. Just like Kansuke had said, he was not really enthusiastic about this battle either. He felt as if he had been saved by Kansuke's words, since Kansuke had said what he would never have dared to say.

"Do you have any ideas on what else we can do?" Harunobu asked Kansuke.

"Yes, I do. You could send me to the Suwa as a messenger. I would explain the situation to them carefully and ask them to swear their allegiance to you. With an army hanging over their heads, they'll never refuse."

There was no way that all the generals would agree with Kansuke's idea, but Harunobu said arbitrarily, "It is not that difficult a task to take Suwa Castle by storm. Even if we do not do it now, we can take it any time we wish. Although I came all the way here, I am not that enthusiastic about proceeding with an attack against Suwa's army. Sending Kansuke as a messenger and letting him meet with Yorishige is a good idea. If he could negotiate peacefully so that both sides can agree, wouldn't it be preferable to attacking the Suwa?"

Since it was Harunobu who had suggested it, nobody dared to disagree with him. Everybody there knew that once Harunobu made up his mind, he always did as he wished. So, it was decided that Kansuke would be his messenger.

"Kansuke, when do you leave?" asked Harunobu.

Kansuke bowed low on his knees and said, "I shall leave immediately."

Kansuke liked this young lord who had hired him two years ago. Harunobu was the only human being Kansuke was fond of. He hated everybody else on earth. He was willing to sacrifice his life for his lord. He did not know why he was so attracted to this man, perhaps because Harunobu treated him differently from others.

There were times that Harunobu called Kansuke "crippled" to his face. But it did not make him angry at all. There was never any disgust in Harunobu's voice when he spoke to Kansuke. Kansuke, who was brought up as an outcast because of his deformities, learned for the first time that there was one person who accepted him as a normal human being.

Kansuke had felt Harunobu's passive resistance against this coming battle. He had a peculiar feeling that Harunobu was not acting normally and was reluctant and uneasy about the war. Sitting in his lower seat watching Harunobu, Kansuke was worried, and his heart pounded in his throat. When he lifted up his face, his eyes met Harunobu's, and somehow the words had just jumped out of his mouth as if he was possessed by something.

It was not an appropriate suggestion at a time like this. It was a suggestion that might have jeopardized his life, but he was not quite sure if he had uttered his own idea or if Harunobu had entered his mind and allowed Kansuke to say his own words. The only thing he knew was that he had to say it.

And when Harunobu agreed with him, he was more satisfied with himself rather than proud, simply because of the idea that only he could read Harunobu's inner thoughts.

Kansuke looked up in admiration at the young military commander, who had a wide forehead and piercing dark eyes, and said, "It is not the way of a lord to hasten an army in vain. I, Yamamoto Kansuke, will leave right now as a messenger and do my best to secure Suwa in our hands without losing a single warrior."

His words sounded insolent and offensive to everyone in the room except Harunobu, who smiled with pleasure.

Kansuke asked Harunobu to send a messenger to Takato, Harunobu's ally in the war, saying that the Takeda had decided not to attack the Suwa and that he had left the camp of Mount Misa that night with his three horsemen.

The next morning Kansuke's party descended into the Suwa Valley, carefully avoiding the areas where the enemy's armies were located. They arrived at dusk near Uehara Castle where the lord of Suwa lived.

When they approached Suwa's first fortification, they galloped side by side on their horses as fast as they could until they reached the front gate.

"We have brought an urgent message, we must see the Lord Suwa immediately," yelled Kansuke in all directions as he circled his horse in front the castle. His three fellow horsemen yelled out the same message. They were instantly pulled down from their horses and surrounded by scores of samurai. They were held in custody for more than an hour before they were finally taken to Yorishige.

Torches were burning brightly in the room as they were pulled unceremoniously into Yorishige's presence. Yorishige was slightly older than Harunobu. He didn't appear to have any outstanding qualities other than the fact that he could pass as a woman because of his beauty.

When Kansuke recited Harunobu's message, Yorishige suddenly burst out laughing; it was a hysterical laughter devoid of humor. He then stopped laughing and said, "Please tell your lord that I will comply with all his wishes."

It was as if the death sentence, which Yorishige had expected to be announced today or tomorrow, had suddenly been lifted from his shoulder.

Kansuke proceeded saying, "We would like to determine the boundaries of your territory now, so that we will not have any difficulties later."

"We will make a boundary at the line of the ivy bush. We will not touch a single grain of rice east of it," a pale Yorishige said in a business-like fashion.

"Fine, my lord. We would like you to reconcile now with your brother-in-law."

"I agree. I must soon go and visit Kofuchu and meet your lord, as his brother-in-law."

It was clear that Yorishige did not favor this battle either. Negotiations on the smallest points were concluded without any problems.

After the sake²⁶ and a feast, Kansuke retired from Yorishige's presence and returned to his guest quarters.

Contrary to when Kansuke had arrived, his party was ushered out more courteously. Yorishige himself escorted the four of them to the main gate of the castle. Along with Yorishige stood his fourteen-year-old daughter attended by her ladies and maids. Much like her father, she was extremely beautiful.

"Is she a princess?" Kansuke asked Yorishige and learned that she was his daughter. Of course, she was not a daughter by his consort, Nene, who had died two years earlier, she was his daughter by his concubine Omiji.

Out of all the people present, only this young princess looked at Kansuke with a clear expression of hostility. Every samurai under Yorishige's rule appreciated the peaceful negotiation, but Kansuke felt that only this girl gave him her honest feeling that she did not agree with this settlement, and that gave him a refreshing sensation.

It was noon of the next day when Kansuke returned to the camp of Mount Misa and brought Yorishige's response to Harunobu.

Harunobu was satisfied with the Suwa's decision and met with their messengers who came along with Kansuke. That night sake was served to every warrior, and three days later he returned with the army to Kofuchu.

At the end of March, Yorishige came to Kofuchu and met Harunobu to reconsolidate the old relationship. Harunobu welcomed Yorishige and entertained him warmly while he stayed in Kofuchu.

Yorishige visited Harunobu for the second time in April. This time, again, Harunobu treated him well and held a large banquet in his honor. He hired Noh²⁷ actors for Yorishige and allowed all the major samurai to watch the play.

After Yorishige had left, Harunobu asked all the generals what they thought about Yorishige. Every one of Harunobu's generals had a good impression of him. They found him refined, warm, and tactful.

"He seems to be extremely brave and audacious to come to Kofuchu with only a few retainers. Even though you are his relative, it is still a warring era." Harunobu's brother Nobushige said admiringly.

"He is a rare type of young lord." Amari said, also holding a high opinion of him.

"What do you think of him, Nobukata?"

Asked by Harunobu, Nobukata answered, "I believe that in the future he could be your ideal ally."

"Now, Kansuke, what do you think?" Kansuke was asked last.

"I will not be able to give you my thoughts unless you make everybody leave this room."

Harunobu did not clear the room. Instead he said, "Kansuke, let us go out to the garden. We will discuss it there." He stood up and started to descend the stone steps to the garden. Kansuke got up from his knees and quickly followed in his lord's wake.

All around the mansion sweet chestnut trees were planted. Reaching the line of trees, Harunobu broke the silence and said, "The cicadas are singing all over." It was a rather hot day, but under the shade of the trees, it was cool. After taking the field at Mount Misa, there weren't any battles for a change, and summer was just around the corner.

"Will you kill him?" said Kansuke suddenly.

"Whom?"

Shocked by the words, Harunobu turned around and looked at Kansuke.

"The Lord of Suwa."

"Would you like to kill him?"

"It is better…" Kansuke said.

"But it was you who recommended the peaceful negotiations with him. If we kill him now…"

"We cannot help what people may say. But if we do not kill him now…"

"I guess there is no other way," said Harunobu and added "Kill him!"

"My Lord, please leave everything to me," Kansuke replied without changing his expression at all.

Harunobu did not understand how Kansuke had the exact thought as he himself did. Since the first time he was visited by Yorishige, he had been anxious to kill him. He somehow had a premonition that if he kept Yorishige alive, this man would cause some adversity later on.

Similar to his intervention at Mount Misa, Kansuke felt some uneasiness in Harunobu's expression when he was asking for evaluations of Yorishige's personality. Because of it, Kansuke himself also felt uneasy.

What could this be? At that time, when Harunobu called his name, he looked up at his Lord, and then totally unconsciously, the words "make everyone leave this room" came out. Then the idea of killing Yorishige, which had been concealed in the inner part of his mind, suddenly surfaced.

In mid-June, Yorishige visited Kofuchu for the third time. Again, a Noh play was held at the castle to entertain him. Halfway through the Noh play, a mid-ranking samurai Ogiwara Yaemonnojo walked calmly to Yorishige's seat and said very quietly to Yorishige, "By the order of our lord, I shall take your life." His words were polite, but a split second later, his sword was drawn and plunged directly into Lord Suwa's heart. Yorishige tried to draw his *wakizashi*,[28] but he was instantly killed by the second stroke aimed at his neck.

Everybody who was watching the Noh play stood up at this unexpected happening. Nobody knew whether Harunobu ordered this act by Ogiwara or not.

Kansuke, who was at the corner of the room, pushed his way through the people crowding around and reached the corpse. He stared at the corpse for a while, a slight smile on his face. Then he told Ogiwara, "Stab him in his neck once more." Ogiwara did not realize that Kansuke's eyes were focused on him; he stood there distractedly for a moment. Kansuke yelled at him again, "Stab his neck once more!" With that Ogiwara bent over and charged Yorishige's corpse.

About an hour later, Kansuke appeared in front of Harunobu.

"What made you think of killing Yorishige?" Harunobu asked Kansuke.

"Although peaceful negotiations were completed, he had to have definite reasons to visit us here twice in March and April. He had to have some plot to put us off guard. As common courtesy dictates, you would have had to make a visit to Suwa at least once. I felt that danger awaited you there."

Suddenly Harunobu burst into laughter. "It is a challenging charade to attempt to save his life on the one hand and to kill him on the other."

"Yes, it seems that intense activity must commence and continue for a while, since at this point it is absolutely necessary to take Suwa by force."

"Shall we pitch our camp at Mount Misa tonight?"

"I think it is too early. It is better to see how our enemy reacts. If we send the army to Suwa right after killing Yorishige, it will surely give them the impression of foul play. How about waiting until they come and attack us? We can leave it until then."

Harunobu thought for a while and then said, "All right, call Nobukata. He may be getting ready for war right now."

As Harunobu predicted, Itagaki Nobukata came to see him fully armed and ready for battle.

"Why are you prepared for battle?"

"Since you have killed the Lord of Suwa, we have no other choice but to attack."

"Why don't we wait until they attack us?"

Itagaki thought about Harunobu's idea briefly, displaying a slight frown, and then glanced at Kansuke. Itagaki said coldly, "We should have attacked Suwa at Mount Misa last time. We are prolonging things for nothing." Itagaki had always favored Kansuke, but now he looked at Kansuke accusingly.

Kansuke's small frame stiffened slightly and he sat up straighter under the reproachful glare of his superior general, but as usual, nobody knew where his cold and hard eyes were gazing. He was secluding himself in his mind and already drawing up the formation of Uehara Castle, which he had recently visited to negotiate with the Lord of Suwa. Completely ignoring Itagaki's accusation, he was thinking of the best way to capture Uehara Castle. He thought it could be taken within three days. Once Uehara Castle fell, Takashima Castle, which was about two miles away from there, would be very easily captured within a day. No matter what, the attack ought to be in winter when Lake Suwa was frozen.

"The battle should be held in winter," Kansuke blurted out to no one in particular. His surprisingly loud voice seemed to echo around the gardens.

In the fourteenth year of Tenbun, on the nineteenth day of the new year, Harunobu sent his army out for the second time to conquer Suwa.

His brother Nobushige directed the entire army as commander-in-chief, Itagaki led the first line, and Hyuga Masaharu was responsible for the rear. It was an army comprised of 37,000 warriors. The Suwa army did not stay at Uehara Castle, but instead placed their camp at Fumonji Temple.

The Takeda army was so overwhelmingly dominant that they broke through the line of Fumonji Temple in only one day's battle and captured Uehara Castle as well. Soon after, they quickly besieged the residence of the Lord of Suwa, Takashima Castle, beside Lake Suwa. The warriors led by Itagaki captured over 300 warriors under the Suwa rule. Thus the great family of Suwa fell under the Takeda.

In this, his first battle, Kansuke was the strategist behind Itagaki.

On the night they entered the enemy's castle, Kansuke was the first one to break into the castle, using a huge spear which looked unusually large beside his small body. All the guards had already fled in fear, and not a single enemy remained in the castle. Kansuke climbed up onto a castle turret and stared down at the lake below. It was a very quaint scene, dreamlike even, since so many bonfires were set along the lake and their light was reflecting everywhere on the surface of the water. All the warriors were still excited over the victory of the day, and their continuous shouts of joy pierced the cold night air.

Kansuke descended from the turret, passed through the spacious rooms in the castle tower, and stepped into the waiting room next to it. Kansuke stopped suddenly in shock. In one corner of the room a properly dressed young woman was sitting with two ladies in waiting. One was old and wrinkled, and the other was young.

When Kansuke approached, the young maid said, "Do not come near her." Kansuke, strangely overwhelmed by her voice, could not go any closer. The young maid yelled again, "Please leave." It sounded to him as if his existence offended them.

"Is this Lord Suwa's daughter?" Kansuke asked with a rather hoarse voice.

"Yes, so don't come any closer."

"If you tell me not to come any closer, I will not, but what is the problem?"

This time the old maid answered him, "Please don't let anybody come in until we commit *seppuku*.²⁹"

Kansuke focused his eyes on Yorishige's daughter, the same one he had seen last year. When he had seen her at the gates of Uehara Castle upon his first departure, her eyes were burning with hostility, but this time she was a very different and quiet person.

"If you were going to commit seppuku, why did you not do it before. You must have had enough time to do so."

One of the maids answered, "We were trying to stop her from killing herself, because we pitied her so much. But now..."

Then, Yorishige's daughter staggered to her feet, laughed bitterly, which startled Kansuke, and said just as coldly, "The truth was that I was running away because I did not want to end my life here. I don't want to commit seppuku!"

"Princess, please control yourself." The two maids followed the princess as she started to walk out the door.

"No, no, I don't want to commit seppuku!" The princess staggered around aimlessly.

Then, they heard a loud noise; many samurai were entering the large room. Kansuke who was staring at the princess in admiration, suddenly stood up and grabbed her in his arms and asked, "Why don't you want to commit seppuku?" Trying to shake him off, Yorishige's daughter looked up at Kansuke's face, once again with her eyes full of hostility.

"Everybody is dying here. And yet I am the only one who

would like to live," she said. These honest words had a strange beauty in them, which Kansuke had never heard before. Any samurai's daughter would never utter such blasphemous words,[30] but her honesty touched Kansuke's heart.

"What happens if I die? I would rather live and see with my own eyes what happens to this castle and the lake. I don't want to die. No matter how hard it will be, I would rather live. No, I don't want to kill myself!" She talked as if she were possessed.

"Let me go!" She struggled to free herself from Kansuke's arms. Kansuke let go of the princess, and she fell to the floor with a thud. An image of a broken and scattered string of crystal beads appeared in his mind as the princess cried out in pain. The beautiful girl suddenly lost consciousness.

"Bring her!" Kansuke ordered her waiting maids. The two women, who seemed as if they too had lost interest in committing seppuku, carried her from the room following Kansuke's orders.

Kansuke started to walk ahead of them. The large room was filled with samurai whose facial expressions were all frenzied like the King of *Asura*.[31] They were all looking for something valuable that they could plunder. Kansuke guided the women through the growing mass of lustful warriors. There was something about his small monstrous appearance and the long spear in his hand that created a certain kind of fear in the samurai. Even the most violent and crazed samurai walked carefully around Kansuke's party.

Yorishige's daughter, Princess Yuu, was taken at once to Kofuchu, but she was returned to Suwa not long after and was temporarily kept in the Suwa Shrine.

One month after the battle of Suwa, Kansuke was invited to Itagaki's residence. He was consulting with Kansuke on something rather unexpected.

"Our lord would like to have Princess Yuu as a concubine. Is it possible for you to prevent this?" said Itagaki. It was not surprising for Itagaki to have asked Kansuke. Kansuke had a lot of influence with many people, most importantly Harunobu. Major and senior vassals were against Harunobu's wish on this matter, but he would not listen to any of them. Kansuke was called upon to persuade Harunobu, since Harunobu trusted Kansuke, and if Kansuke talked to Harunobu, he might just listen to him.

"If the lord is so enthusiastic about her, I don't see any reason why he should not have her as his concubine." Kansuke replied quickly. Kansuke suddenly had a strange feeling that he needed to tie these two high-ranking personages together. He thought of the words of Princess Yuu about how everyone was dying but she simply wanted to live.

If a male child were born to Princess Yuu and Harunobu, the line of Suwa would continue. If this child of Suwa blood inherited the Takeda Clan, the people of Suwa would forget their grudge against the Takeda and might return to his allegiance. Maybe Harunobu was thinking the same thing. Thus, Kansuke gave Itagaki his opinion.

"But if they don't produce any children," Itagaki said, "people will say that the Takeda killed Yorishige, conquered his fiefdom, and forced his daughter to be his concubine. This does not sound good to the ears of lords of other provinces, and the people of Suwa will never let go of their hostility."

"Yes, but if we do nothing, they will never let go of their hostility anyway. If Harunobu does take Princess Yuu as a concubine, at least we will have some hope of correcting this grievance."

"Well, should we have a special prayer for a male child then?"

It sounded as if Itagaki was becoming convinced by Kansuke's words and ready to have Princess Yuu taken to the Takeda.

"Our only problem is whether or not the princess will accept it."

"Well," said Kansuke, "fate made me save her life. I shall take on the role of convincing her."

A month later Kansuke went to Suwa. Since he learned that Princess Yuu had moved to Kan-non-in Temple, the temple on the north side of the lake, he rode his horse along the lake from Takashima Castle to the north.

From the top of a hill where the Kan-non-in Temple stood, he could see Takashima Castle far away on the other side of the lake. The ice on the lake had already thawed, and spring was imminent.

Kansuke saw the princess for the third time.

"I came to take you with me," said Kansuke. Princess Yuu simply nodded calmly.

The next day, Itagaki, who was at Takashima Castle, sent three palanquins for Princess Yuu and her two maids, and for protection Kansuke and ten other riders followed as they headed to Kofuchu. The villages they passed were filled with peach blossoms in full bloom.

"Please stop, I am so tired." Every hour or so they needed to rest because of the demands of Princess Yuu. Whenever they reached the top of a hill without fail and also at the bottom of the hills, she wanted to rest. Princess Yuu was an extremely moody person. When she got out of the palanquin at the top of the hill, she asked, "How soon can I go back to Suwa?"

"After you give birth to a Prince I shall escort you home again," said Kansuke. As soon as Princess Yuu heard that, her face paled, and she entered her litter and never lifted the bamboo blind again. From then on the procession advanced without stoping through the range of small hills.

Kansuke was constantly dreaming of the baby who might be born to Harunobu and Princess Yuu. For Kansuke, who had never been loved nor loved anybody all his life, it was as if he found a couple that he could truly serve from the bottom of his heart.

"This is going to be fine!"

For now Kansuke dismissed all of his thoughts of Princess Yuu and decided to suggest to Harunobu that he should capture Shinano using Suwa as a launching point.

Chapter 4
KANSUKE CONVINCES PRINCESS YUU

PRINCESS YUU WAS TRANSFERRED to Kofuchu and taken to the residence of Itagaki Nobukata. His mansion was located in one corner of the samurai residential district. Although it was Kansuke's duty to convince Princess Yuu to be Harunobu's concubine, Kansuke, nonetheless, found it a very difficult task. Since the princess had come to Kofuchu, Kansuke had visited her several times, and each time he tried, unsuccessfully, to convince her to change her mind.

Princess Yuu was sitting on the veranda and absent-mindedly looking at the inner garden, which was surrounded by large trees. When she saw Kansuke, she was combing back her black hair that was cut straight at shoulder length.

Before Kansuke could say a thing, the princess said, "If you are here to convince me about the matter which you mentioned last time, my mind has not changed since then, and I have nothing new to tell you."

"I have no intention to force you, if you have no interest." Kansuke answered her as he knelt down in the garden just in front of her.

The princess continued, "Lord Harunobu killed my father, therefore he is my enemy. As you said, yes, we do live in a time when either you kill or you are killed. If Lord Harunobu did not kill my father, my father would have killed him. It was simply my father's misfortune, and I do not hate the lord for that. But to be his mistress—I cannot surrender myself to that kind of torture."

Listening to her Kansuke felt that she was quite mature for a fifteen-year-old girl.

"But since you have survived without killing yourself by the sword…"

"I have to expect that kind of humiliation, I know that."

Her beautiful eyes flamed with anger, and she continued, "Since I have survived without killing myself according to the common practice, I would like to live my life the way I want to all the more. If I had known I was to be the concubine of my father's enemy, I would have preferred death."

"I see," Kansuke was elated to converse with this bright girl.

"Please excuse me for saying this, but after all, you are only a woman, therefore no matter how adventurous your life would be, there is a limit to the things you could achieve in this society. But if you bear a male child, your son will have both Takeda and Suwa blood. If it is your child, I am sure the child would be a bright one, and it is up to you what kind of spirit you will instill in him. Please think about it very carefully."

Kansuke looked up at the princess. The Princess's eyes shone suddenly, but she was not looking at Kansuke.

"I shall visit you again, Princess, a few days from now."

That was all he said that day, and he left her residence.

The next day Harunobu asked Kansuke, "How is the matter of the princess proceeding?"

"She seems to be very happy about becoming your concubine," answered Kansuke, but added right after, "But please leave it to me for a while, since you have to take your wife's feelings into consideration."

Harunobu had a wife who was twenty-six years old and about a decade older than Princess Yuu. She was called Sanjo-no-Uji. Harunobu had two sons from this wife; one was Yoshinobu, nine years old, and the other was Ryuho, six years old. Because of this, Harunobu could not openly talk about Princess Yuu.

Kansuke didn't like Harunobu's wife or her children. Harunobu's legitimate son, Yoshinobu, was pale and nervous looking. He did not demonstrate any potential to be a future great leader like his father. Once, when Yoshinobu saw Kansuke in the castle corridors, he followed him everywhere imitating the way he walked. Kansuke hated the child because of his arrogant behavior.

His younger brother, Ryuho, seemed to have a better personality, but he was born blind.

Kansuke felt that it was important for the Takeda family that the relationship between Harunobu and Princess Yuu be consummated. A child born to the brilliant princess had to be an ideal heir for the Takeda family. The problem was whether he could convince the princess or not, but Kansuke felt confident that, in the end, he could change her mind.

A few days later Kansuke visited Princess Yuu again.

"Have you made up your mind yet, Princess?" asked Kansuke. Then the princess responded sharply with a question, "Are you on the Takeda's side or the Suwa's? Which side are you on?" She looked at him sternly and added coldly, "Since I do not feel well today, I would like you to leave me," and entered her room leaving Kansuke outside. Kansuke felt that it might not be an easy task to convince her.

When Kansuke came out of the gates of Itagaki's residence, he saw Harunobu's wife Sanjo-no-Uji. Kansuke was alarmed, because it was quite evident why she was there. Kansuke stopped at the gate and bowed to her.

"Kansuke, I met you at the right place. I heard that you brought a woman with Suwa blood into the city and you were hiding her here. Is it true?"

"Yes, it is true," Kansuke answered vaguely.

"If she is a hostage, you should treat her as a hostage. I shall not allow you to treat her as anything more."

Kansuke saw the flame of jealousy in her eyes and said, "If you mean whether she is a hostage from Suwa, yes, she is. I am looking after her."

"Will you let me see her?"

Kansuke felt that he should not allow her to do so and said quickly, "Since the yard was not cleaned this morning, could you wait a while?"

Kansuke bowed to her and went back to the residence where Princess Yuu was hidden and asked her hastily.

"Princess Yuu, would you please hide yourself somewhere?"

"Why do I have to hide myself?" she asked quietly.

"The consort of the lord is here."

"I shall meet her then."

"It is better if you do not see her, Princess."

"Why not? Isn't it she who should feel guilty meeting me? Since I am the one whose father was killed by her husband."

Kansuke knew that he could not change her mind. Though her family was destroyed, her strong bloodlines still motivated her. Her eyes were clear and her cheeks were filled with excitement. Kansuke observed her with admiration. He suddenly realized what propelled her strength; it was her competitiveness toward Harunobu's wife.

"Fine, I shall bring the lord's consort here," Kansuke said without changing his expression.

Kansuke left and soon returned accompanying Sanjo-no-Uji and her maids. Sanjo-no-Uji came close to the veranda.

"Is she the daughter of the Suwa?" she said haughtily and looked down at Princess Yuu who sat there bowing slightly. "So, she came all the way from Suwa wishing to be the concubine of the man who killed her father! Well, I am glad that it was not *our* family who was destroyed!" saying this Sanjo-no-Uji turned and left.

Princess Yuu remained in the same stance for a while, even after the Sanjo's group had left; then she lifted her face and said to Kansuke, "Yes, she is lucky that it was not her family who was destroyed." After a while she continued determinedly, "Kansuke, as you suggested, I should intermingle the blood of the Suwa in the family of Takeda. I don't have the slightest idea what that will do, but after all, this could be the reason that I survived." Suddenly tears filled her eyes and ran down her cheeks. Kansuke watched her in silent amazement.

After Harunobu destroyed the Suwa family, he started to attack the neighboring areas using Suwa as his base. By the third month of the fifteenth year of Tenbun, he had started a campaign to attack Toishi Castle in Shinano Province and faced the army of Murakami Yoshikiyo. Murakami was the leader of a powerful family of northern Shinano and resided in Katsurao Castle. Toishi Castle also belonged to him.

When Harunobu left the castle town of Kofuchu, it was the eighth day of the third month, the hour of the sea horse.[32] Cherry blossoms had already fallen, and the spring sunshine made the Takeda's warriors feel quite hot.

It was the Takeda's tradition to carry two banners when entering a large battle. Both of them were treasures of the house; they were called *Suwa Hossho*[33] and *Sonshi Niryu*.[34]

The two banners were fluttering in the spring breeze. One banner, Suwa Hossho, was red and said in gold writing "Suwa, descendant of the Great *Kami*.[35]" The other banner, Sonshi Niryu,[36] also had gold writing, but on a background of dark blue: "Be as swift as the wind, be as thoughtful as the forest, attack as fiercely as fire, and be as composed as the mountain" (*Fu-Rin-Ka-Zan*[37]). Both vertical banners were about four meters in length. On both sides of these banners, warriors carried small replicas of the banners attached to their backs. The army marched day and night, passing Lake Suwa and then proceeding north. Two days later they were at Komuro.

In preparation for the attack on Toishi Castle, Harunobu divided his armies into four groups and placed them in strategic areas to prevent any incursions by the four neighboring enemies. Harunobu himself, along with the remaining 4,000 samurai, marched to attack the castle.

Toishi Castle was small, set on a mountainside, and quite easy to destroy, but Murakami's army would be coming to assist the army defending the castle. Because of this, Harunobu would have to divide his army into two groups, one, which would attack the castle, and the other, which would stop the reinforcing army.

Just before the attack on the castle, Harunobu's army heard news of the arrival of 76,000 samurai under the leadership of Murakami. Each of the groups led by the Takeda's leaders Amari, Oyamada, and Yokota fought to stop Murakami's army on the northern side of the castle. Having no time to consider his actions, Harunobu had to start the attack by leading the main group from the west side of the castle.

Yamamoto Kansuke was placed in Harunobu's main group with twenty-five samurai to hold the area.

As soon as the battle began, Kansuke felt that the outlook was not in their favor. It was an unreasonable war to start with, and furthermore, their small army was divided into two.

If General Itagaki, who was closest to the Takeda, were there, he would have asked Itagaki to suggest to Harunobu that falling back was probably the best course of action. But Itagaki was leading a troop to protect Suwa. If Harunobu had asked Kansuke's opinion, he would have suggested retreat. But Harunobu did not ask him, so the battle continued unabated.

The armies of Amari, Yokota, and Oyamada were all on the defensive from the beginning, being outnumbered two to one.

One samurai who stood out among the enemy was Kojima Gorozaemon who was well known even in Takeda's Province of Kai as a bold and fierce warrior. He was riding an exceptionally large horse and wielded a huge spear with ease.

Even though he was the enemy, the Takeda's warriors admitted that his performance was outstanding. Aiming at this fierce warrior, a young samurai from the Takeda army spurred his horse on. Compared to Kojima, he looked terribly small. He was a young samurai who was the twenty-three-year-old adopted son of Yokota Bichu-no-kami Hikojiro. They exchanged blows several times and becoming interlocked, they both fell from their horses. After a short but fierce battle one blood-covered samurai stood up. Upon closer view it appeared that it was young Hikojiro. It was an extraordinary fight and nobody expected Hikojiro to prevail.

His great achievement was reported to headquarters at once.

"He killed Kojima Gorozaemon!"

This news seemed to impress Harunobu, and he took this as a good omen.

"What does that do for us killing just Kojima Gorozaemon?" Kansuke asked him. As for Kansuke, it seemed to be stupid for them to praise man-to-man combat. Even a widely reputed great samurai could die all too quickly in a battle like this. How could anyone rely on individual skills of swordsmanship? Kansuke felt that everybody was missing the point at the most important time of the battle.

Kansuke's words sounded conceited to Harunobu.

"Killing Kojima Gorozaemon is like killing one hundred warriors," Harunobu said.

"It is dangerous," Kansuke uttered. Nobody around him understood the meaning of his words.

"What is dangerous?" inquired Harunobu.

"Both Generals Amari and Yokota are facing danger."

"How can you see their formations from here?"

"I can see both of their formations from here."

When Kansuke said this to his lord, his repulsiveness disappeared and he showed brilliance with an aura of divinity over him.

It was about one hour later that they heard the news of the deaths of both Amari and Yokota. Almost at the same time, both of their respective formations suddenly fell apart. The offensive team at Koseki Castle was gravely influenced by the news and began to waver. Harunobu tried to re-form the troops, but it was almost useless. Imminent defeat seemed inevitable. Harunobu suggested the idea that he would send messages to both Oyamada's and Morozumi's formations and have the entire army attack the Murakami army together in a full frontal charge tactic. Harunobu was overly desperate at this point and was willing to lead the entire army himself.

"Do you think it is right for the commander-in-chief himself to lead our army?" Kansuke demanded of Harunobu.

"Is there any other way at this point?"

"You are prepared to die on the field of battle then?"

Harunobu did not reply to this. To Kansuke, Harunobu looked extremely young in his moment of indecision. Kansuke said very calmly, "Yes, it is vital to have a final victory by risking your life. However, you are upset now since large numbers of your warriors have lost their lives. When people are angry, they often act impetuously."

Harunobu looked down at the small figure of Kansuke from his position astride his horse. It was hard to tell whether Kansuke was stupid or brilliant, and he looked so unbelievably ugly and yet so unbelievably calm. In spite of that, Harunobu felt he could trust Kansuke more than anybody else.

"Do you have other ideas for a counterattack?"

"Yes, I have!"

"Is it possible to get through this mess?"

"There is only one strategy that can lead us to victory. Please give me fifty horsemen." Kansuke said.

As soon as he had gathered them, he made a U-turn and dashed at full speed about two miles and came out behind the Murakami army. There he yelled out his orders to the horsemen, "I would like all of you to gallop at full speed through the Murakami army at the risk of your lives. All you have to do is gallop at full speed. There is no need to kill anybody. I shall take the lead."

The horsemen all galloped straight through Murakami's army from the rear, dividing it into two. They galloped with great speed, not once losing their straight line through the formations.

Kansuke believed all he had to do was to destroy the war formation of the enemy. If he could succeed in doing that, the bright young Harunobu would be able to reform his own partially broken formation.

Leading his fifty warriors, Kansuke was galloping at full speed. His body was bent in half, and he was waving his sword back and forth. His strategy was to harass the enemy to induce them to break formation. Harunobu would not miss his chance to regain the offensive by taking advantage of the disorder that Kansuke would cause.

He looked back as he hit the midpoint of the enemy formation. Fifty horsemen followed him just like a black stream.

Suddenly, Kansuke heard a war cry. He realized that the formation he was galloping through was in disarray, much like a hornet's nest knocked from its perch. Further away on the hilltop, the huge blue flag over the Takeda's headquarters was billowing and floating in the wind. He did not know what time it was, but the gold characters of the flags were glittering under the setting sun.

The war cry came from the Takeda army. Kansuke galloped through the entire formation of the enemy and made another U-turn and galloped back into the fray at full speed. It was not necessary to attack any of the enemy; all he had to do was just cut down any samurai who were in his way. War cries and the sound of conch shells and drums were heard from every direction. The boom of the guns were heard above all the noise.

Suddenly, Kansuke was thrown from his horse. It had apparently hit a big root sticking out of a pine tree. Blood coursed from his forehead and ran down his eyes. He tried to raise his right arm, but it would not move. Although he had no idea when he had received them, his body was covered with wounds.

Taking advantage of Kansuke's strategy, the Takeda's forces had shifted from defense to offense. The Takeda's cavalry squadron attacked and harassed the scattered Murakami enemy force, and finally the enemy began to retreat. During this battle, the Takeda force lost 720 warriors. The enemy's head count was 193 losses. Although the Takeda's losses were far greater, the shouts of victory now rose from the Takeda's headquarters.

Kansuke was awarded 800 kan[38] and he was promoted to the rank, leading seventy-five foot soldiers.

A month and a half after the battle of Toishi Castle, Princess Yuu gave birth to a male child. In those days she had her own residence halfway down the mountain behind the castle. Kansuke visited her residence as soon as he heard the news. Nobody but Kansuke had paid her a visit yet.

He was taken to her bedroom. Princess Yuu was lying quietly on her back. Without giving him any chance to congratulate her, the princess said, "Following your orders, a male child was born who holds both the blood of the Takeda and the Suwa. Who knows what kind of destiny he has in store for him, but he is sleeping peacefully here now."

Kansuke uttered a short laugh and said, "Now the Lord of Suwa has been born. This is a very happy occasion. Congratulations."

But the princess responded accusingly, "It was you who planned the surprise attack against my father. And yet, you are happy about this birth?"

"Yes," Kansuke had difficulty in continuing his sentence. She was absolutely right. He had no idea until now that Princess Yuu had known that it was he who planned to kill her father. Kansuke was thrown off guard.

The princess continued, "I simply mentioned it; I bear no grudge against you. You do not have to worry about that. What I really wanted to ask you is would you please take care of this child?" Princess Yuu turned her face to Kansuke.

"Yes," Kansuke answered.

"Do you understand what I mean?"

"I beg your pardon?" With the weight of this responsibility, Kansuke felt his body trembling. His knees were visibly shaking, and he could see that his hands on his knees were also trembling.

"In the future I would like this child to be the heir of the Takeda Clan," Princess Yuu stated her desire fearlessly. Kansuke was startled by her openness and looked around him with alarm.

"I let my life be under your control. You told me to live; therefore I lived. You told me to come to Kai; so I did. You told me to be his concubine; so I did. You told me to have his child; so I did." Briefly she stopped talking. Then she continued: "Please look after this child."

After Kansuke left the residence of Princess Yuu, he descended the slope of the hill and came out on the east side of the castle. The opposite side of the rice field was filled with azalea blossoms. It looked as if the entire mountain was covered with beautiful flames. A warm wind was blowing from the west to the east. This rare battle-less month was just about approaching its end.

That day, Kansuke visited Harunobu to congratulate him on the birth of his son. He said to Harunobu, "The birth of your son will soften the hatred of people of Suwa. The best thing for you to do is to make this child the lord of the extensive territory of Ina and Suwa Provinces as soon as possible."

Kansuke felt that it was vital for the Takeda to place Princess Yuu's child in the Ina and Suwa area for the safety of the child as well as to settle the uneasiness and hostility of the people of the area.

Princess Yuu's son was named Shiro.[39] Harunobu had two sons from his consort. Since Princess Yuu's child was Harunobu's third child he was expected to be called Saburo[40]; however, he was named Shiro instead.

When Itagaki Nobukata came from Suwa, he asked Harunobu the reason for this. Harunobu laughed meaningfully at that, but gave him no reason; after a while he said, "Kansuke would be a better person to ask if you really want to know the answer."

Itagaki invited Kansuke to his residence in Kofuchu and asked: "Why did you recommend the name Shiro to the lord?"

"Because I felt that it is necessary for the lord to have a third son," Kansuke answered.

"A third son?"

"Yes, sooner or later the Takeda will be forced to strategically adopt a son."

"Adopt a son? From where?"

"I have no idea. Maybe somewhere like the Hojo or the Uesugi Clan. In that case it will make a big difference to place the adopted son above his concubine's son, regardless of his age. We always have to think ahead in this warring era."

Kansuke was obviously thinking to adopt this child for political purposes.

"Could it be from the Hojo Clan?" Itagaki asked.

"Well…"

"Then from the Uesugi Clan?"

"Well…"

"Well, where will Takeda Saburo come from?"

"Either of them will be fine, I suppose," Kansuke answered without changing his sitting position. This time it was Itagaki who felt a chill and a disturbing sensation in his spine, sensing Kansuke's bold strategy.

A month later, Kansuke went to see Iohara in the castle town of Imagawa where he used to live. In the midst of a heat wave, Kansuke had asked for a holiday, using the excuse that he would like to pay his respects to his past master. He left for the province of Suruga, but he had a secret reason for this visit.

Chapter 5
LOVE AND HATE

IT HAD BEEN THREE YEARS since Yamamoto Kansuke had last entered the castle town of Sunpu. Kansuke visited the Keyaki residence of Iohara Tadatane. The way Iohara treated Kansuke was slightly politer than he was used to.

"We have heard of your success in Kai even in our province. You are lucky to work for a good lord," Iohara said and added, "What do you think of Harunobu's abilities?"

Iohara still treated Kansuke as if he was one of his subjects who were sent out to Kai; however, Kansuke had changed completely. He could not believe that he had actually thought about earning stipends from both the Takeda and the Imagawa.

"The Lord Harunobu is a brilliant and honest general. The great general does not pay heed to flattery, nor does he care how his employees look. He judges his samurai on their bravery and resources. I was promoted to a position with a stipend of 800 kan within three years. Doesn't this prove what I have just explained about him?"

It was quite obvious that Kansuke never appreciated that the Imagawa Clan had failed to hire him, after serving them for nine years. Someday, in the future, Kansuke would conquer the Imagawa with the power of the Takeda. But until that time, the Takeda had to have a good relationship with the Imagawa.

"The reason why I am here is not to brag about my lord though. The Lord Harunobu has two sons, Yoshinobu and Ryuho. To be blunt, Yoshinobu does not have leadership qualities and Ryuho is blind. He needs to adopt a child as his true heir."

"You mean to say that he wants a child from the Imagawa Clan?"

"It does not matter how old he is. We would like to raise the child as a third son."

"Unfortunately, the Imagawa Clan has no children," said Iohara.

"None even from his concubines?"

"No, there are none."

Kansuke was well aware that there was no suitable child to be adopted from the Imagawa family. But it did not matter even if the child was from a concubine. He thought there might be one and maybe Iohara might know about it.

"Is that the only reason you are here?" Iohara asked and laughed. Kansuke did not answer this taunt.

Kansuke left the residence of Iohara and stayed that night at the temple near the Abe River where he had lived for nine years.

A young samurai, who was also seeking the employment of the Imagawa when Kansuke was there, quietly visited him, knowing that Kansuke had returned. When he entered Kansuke's room, he was taken aback at seeing Kansuke sitting in the middle of the room meditating.

"Master, what are you thinking right now?" the young samurai asked directly.

Kansuke said without hesitation, "Within the next ten years or so, the Hojo, the Imagawa, and the Takeda have to become allied. How can it be done?"

"Well…" The samurai was troubled by the question for a while, then asked, "Why ten years?"

"Don't you understand? The Takeda have to fight with the Uesugi. The Imagawa will rush to attack the western provinces, and the Hojo have been fighting in the Kanto⁴¹ area."

"And ten years from now?"

"Then, the three of us will have to fight each other. Until that time, how can we keep peace among the three for ten years?"

"I don't know."

"It's simple. The Takeda, the Imagawa, and the Hojo, all of them have male and female children. The three families have to intermarry."

"Could it be possible?"

"The Takeda's Yoshinobu, the Hojo's Ujimasa, and the Imagawa's Ujizane are all nine or ten years old. For Yoshinobu, the daughter of Imagawa, for Ujimasa the Takeda's daughter, and for Ujizane Hojo's daughter..." Kansuke said with a straight face, and then suddenly he thought of the open space for the third son who had to be adopted from the Hojo Clan. If the Takeda sent their daughter to Hojo, then the son had to be adopted from the Hojo as a hostage.

"Within a few years, this could be arranged," Kansuke said. The quicker, the better. The Takeda must have an alliance with the Imagawa and the Hojo, and meanwhile the Takeda have to defeat the Uesugi. War with the Imagawa and the Hojo would come after. Princess Yuu's child would achieve that.

The young samurai left Kansuke's side a short time later. Since Kansuke was immersing himself in his own thoughts, there was no use him to remain. In the eyes of the young samurai, Kansuke looked totally different from the person he had been three years before. At fifty-four years of age, Kansuke had become more reticent and withdrawn.

But Kansuke felt that he had more freedom. He had no regrets, even if he died in battle. Fear of death was nonexistent in his mind. He loved Lord Harunobu. He also loved Harunobu's concubine Princess Yuu and her newborn son Katsuyori. His dream was to ride over the fields and mountains of Kai and Shinano—a dream only Kansuke, who was born deformed, knew about.

That night Kansuke slept on his dream. The dream of the body of the little child, Katsuyori, remained tucked firmly in his arms.

Since the battle of Koseki Castle in March, when the Takeda had defeated the army of Murakami Yoshikiyo, they had enjoyed unusually peaceful days in the castle town of Kofuchu. The days and nights had passed quietly from spring to summer and summer to autumn without the turmoil and noise of battle. Peace reigned not only in the castle town, but also in the villages, mountains, and valleys around it.

However, instead of battle, there were many natural disasters. Heavy rain, which started early on the morning of the fifth of July, did not stop for three days and caused enormous floods all over the province of Kai. Many rice fields were washed away. In Kofuchu on the hill behind Harunobu's mansion, there was a massive landslide.

On the fifteenth of the same month, a strong wind blew at night, and the rice plants were badly damaged in many places. The next morning there were many peasants who were struck dumb with shock when they went into their fields.

The impact of these two natural disasters started to materialize in the autumn, and many people died from starvation and malnutrition. The cost of everything went up drastically. Although there were no battles, people in the Province of Kai were suffering.

On September the ninth, the day of the Chrysanthemum Festival, the Takeda troops gathered at the Kofuchu mansion. On the floor of the grand hall, chrysanthemums were arranged beautifully, and the samurai, who sat in rows on both sides of the flower arrangements, were treated with sake and a bowl of chestnut rice. Just as on New Year's Day, the generals of the Takeda sat at the head table facing the warriors. But this time, after the battle of Koseki Castle, two generals, Amari Toyayasu and Yokota Takatoshi, who had been killed in the battle, were missing. There were only three generals, Obu Toramasa, Oyamada Masatatsu, and Itagaki Nobukata. This filled all with sorrow.

Since the battle of Koseki Castle, two generals, Obu and Oyamada, had been stationed in the north of Shinano as defense against the Murakami army. But these two came to Kofuchu for this occasion. Itagaki also came all the way from his station with the Suwa. Other members of the Takeda Clan who attended that day were Samanosuke Nobushige, Sonroku Nobutsura, Emontayu Nobutatsu, and Anayama Nobuyoshi. Some new faces were Baba Nobuharu, Yamagata Masagake, Naitou Shuri, and

Akiyama Nobutomo who were promoted to middle rank generals. Each was the young heir of the renowned families who had worked for the Takeda for generations.

Both Generals Obu and Oyamada briefed Harunobu about the movements of their present enemy, Murakami Yoshikiyo.

Murakami had kept silent since he was defeated at the battle of Toishi Castle, but it was known that he was not the type of person who would withdraw for good. It was quite obvious that he would move his army in the near future—most likely in the next spring when the snow started melting. Both Obu and Oyamada agreed on this point.

"I don't think there will be any battles until next spring. By that time, we should be prepared, and this time we must capture his head and prevent any future problem," Obu said. Nobody perceived any error in his opinion, and they continued to discuss how they were going to prepare their armies.

Kansuke was sitting in the middle of the right-hand side facing Harunobu. Suddenly he bent his body and said, "I would like to say something. I believe that the battle will be held this year, or even tomorrow."

Everybody's attention was focused on his small body.

"When it comes to the movement of the Murakami army, there is nobody who knows more than Obu and myself," Oyamada said to Kansuke accusingly.

"I am not talking about the Murakami army."

"I can't think of anybody strong enough to be worth worrying about in our four neighboring provinces but Murakami."

"I, Kansuke, also know no one who would make such a move. But I know that there has to be somebody who believes that this is the ideal opportunity to attack the Takeda. Yes, we did defeat the Murakami this spring, but both generals Amari and Yokota died at the battle and everybody in the entire country must have heard by now that we have lost over 3,000 warriors. It is unnecessary to state that the bravery of both Generals Obu and Oyamada is well known; however, they cannot move from the northern end of Shinano Province to defend against the

Murakami army. It is too far. Besides, please excuse me for saying this, but the rest of the samurai are all rather low ranking and none of them have more than one hundred horsemen. On top of that fact, we have been suffering from natural disasters lately. If somebody attacks us, the province of Kai, with their large military power..." Kansuke lifted his face and looked at Harunobu without finishing his words, his point being quite obvious. Kansuke was talking to Harunobu. He had no interest in listening to any of the other samurai's opinions.

Harunobu laughed and finished Kansuke's sentence saying, "We have absolutely no hope?"

"No, my lord."

"Will the Takeda be destroyed?"

"There are enemies who would like to think so; therefore, they are dying to attack us."

"Who would attack us in that case?"

"I don't know. I don't even know that somebody might consider all these facts. If there are some and if they were hoping to destroy the Takeda..."

Suddenly somebody yelled out, "Who would think of such a thing!" It was Anayama. "Both the Imagawa and the Hojo share boundaries with us, but it is impossible for them to think that they could attack us."

But Harunobu stood up suddenly and started saying, "If it is possible to think..." Then he stopped and walked away to the inner room. He did not look upset. Kansuke thought Harunobu must have been trying to figure out who could be willing to attack him?

After Harunobu had left, nobody was willing to speak.

At the battle of Toishi Castle, it was Kansuke who had turned a dead end battle into a victory by his strategy. Everybody gave him credit, but nobody appreciated his outrageous ideas. To their ears, it simply sounded like he held a conceited opinion.

As usual, Itagaki tried to mediate.

"Maybe you have had a little too much to drink to suggest such an idea, Kansuke. Mind you, it is an interesting opinion. If there is a war within this year, I shall let you have one of my strong retainers, of your own choosing. But if you lose, then what will you give me?"

Itagaki was trying to change Kansuke's words into less serious ones. However, Kansuke gave his answer instantly without any hesitation, "I shall give you my life!" This was no joke. He had no smile on his face. He did not say this to Itagaki alone. He intended it to be heard by every samurai.

"You stupid idiot, your mind is befuddled by sake!" Itagaki forced a smile.

But it was not a joke to Kansuke's ears; he could hear the sound of swords clashing together. He could hear the sound of the conch shell, the beat of the drums, and many hundreds of horsemen continuously galloping over the hill.

Kansuke was thinking that someone who had the intention of overthrowing the Takeda would never miss such an excellent opportunity. There was no better chance. There had to be somebody who thought the same as he did, in this time of constant civil war, in this era of life and death, and in this time when territory was repeatedly lost and won.

There has to be another battle in the near future. But Kansuke himself had difficulty in figuring out who could be their enemy. He would not be surprised though, if any one of the Imagawa, the Hojo, Nagao Kagetora, or Murakami Yoshikiyo attacked them.

A month had not passed since the day that Kansuke had predicted the coming of war, when 23,000 warriors allied under Uesugi Norimasa swarmed down from the Fuefuki Sunset Point.

First word of the attack arrived from Sanada Yukitaka in Shinano Province. Riders brought the news that one of the Uesugi armies had left Joshu Province in the autumn rain. The first rider was carried in by several of the Takeda samurai as soon as he dismounted from his horse, but the second horse arrived without a rider. The riderless horse, with an arrow stuck in its back, galloped by frantically in the direction of the Takeda's mansion. The severity of the state of emergency was immediately felt.

In less than an hour, the beating of drums was heard at every checkpoint in the city, calling retainers to arms.

Bonfires were lit on all the street corners, and horsemen started arriving at the castle one by one. The riders were from the citadels in various areas such as Aiki, Shibata, and Unno.

It was truly an emergency situation. No time was wasted. The attack by the Uesugi was totally unexpected by both Harunobu and Kansuke. The Uesugi family had been fighting with the Hojo family for a long time in the central Kanto district, often losing to them. They must have changed directions suddenly to attack the Takeda family in order to attempt a comeback.

Unfortunately, Harunobu was suffering from a high fever and the meeting of the generals was held at Harunobu's bedside.

"Who will be in charge of this battle against the Uesugi?" Harunobu asked. Both Nobushige and Anayama accepted the role immediately. It was quite an obvious decision in everybody's mind since the three highest generals, Obu, Oyamada, and Itagaki could not move from their own positions and there was nobody else besides these two who could direct the army.

Harunobu looked at Kansuke.

Kansuke answered without any hesitation, "How about placing General Itagaki in charge of this battle and using Anayama and Samanosuke to defend Suwa Province?"

"Is there any reason why I should do that?"

"The General Itagaki has been stationed in Suwa for the last three years, therefore he knows more about the people's minds and behavior in Shinano, and besides he must have many retainers who have good knowledge of the geography of the area.

With Kansuke's suggestion, Harunobu instantly made up his mind and said, "All right, I shall order Itagaki to take charge."

The voice of authority in cases like this, Harunobu always made quick decisions, and it was almost refreshing to see his resolve.

Itagaki Nobukata was appointed commander-in-chief to fight against the attacking army of the Uesugi, and to fill his position in Suwa, Anayama and Nobushige were sent along with four groups of foot solders.

Kansuke thought that in this crisis of the Takeda, the best fighter, General Itagaki, should be dispatched. Of course, Harunobu would be a better choice as the leader, but as he was sick, nobody but Itagaki could take his position. Both Anayama and Nobushige had weaknesses that could be detrimental to the war effort.

Kansuke asked Harunobu if Kansuke himself could be on Itagaki's team, and he received permission. He predicted this battle would be a desperate one, and he was well aware of Itagaki's weaknesses when it came to desperate battles. Before taking the field, Kansuke wanted to see Itagaki to give him some advice.

That night Kansuke left the castle town of Kofuchu along with several post horses for the Suwa Province. The samurai on the post horses were all young, skillful riders, but fifty-four-year-old Kansuke was not inferior to any of them. He had a rather strange way of riding his horse: his small body sat on the back of the large horse and he bent so close to its neck, that it looked almost as if he was chewing on the horse's mane.

The group of horsemen galloped like the wind and by the next morning they were entering the castle town of Suwa. When they dismounted inside the boundaries of the castle, Kansuke sat on the ground and could not stand up. All the young riders could hardly believe that Kansuke had actually been capable of following them all the way to Suwa, especially in the untrained way that he rode.

Kansuke said, "I want you to carry me inside the castle." He entered into the castle on a stretcher and was brought in front of Itagaki.

Itagaki was already dressed and armed, ready to take to the field.

"Before they climb over Fuefuki Sunset Point…" Kansuke mumbled these seven words, and then he smiled and said, "I am tired."

"That's what you wanted to tell me?" asked Itagaki.

"Yes, this is what I wanted to tell you."

"Is this your way of repaying the favor of my recommendation of you to the Takeda?"

"Yes, sir."

"You didn't have to come all the way for that. I know that much myself."

"I realize that, but you don't know as much as I do. You lack tenacity and perseverance when it comes to fighting a losing battle."

"Don't be silly!"

"You were always like that in previous battles."

"Don't be silly," Itagaki repeated, and he looked offended. Although Itagaki always showed some consideration toward the rather monstrous-looking Kansuke, more than anybody else anyway, it was partially because he was the one who had recommended Kansuke to be employed by the Takeda. It was not because he truly cared for him; to the contrary, he often felt hatred toward him.

At this moment, however, he was given a feeling of assurance by Kansuke's honesty and his confident and positive way of thinking.

"Will you accompany me to the field?"

"If you attack them before they reach the summit, it is not necessary for me to accompany you at all, sir."

"Don't worry, I know! Then you stay here and rest for a while," Itagaki said with a pale face.

That night, a part of Itagaki Nobukata's troops left Suwa as the forerunner to the army. Kansuke returned immediately to Kofuchu.

Itagaki himself had left on October the fourth with his own army to join the main troops from Kofuchu.

On the fifth, Lord Harunobu felt a little better and left Kofuchu at about eleven o'clock with his entire reserve of 4,500 troops to join the main army.

Information was dispatched constantly from Itagaki to Harunobu on horseback. On the sixth, at eleven o'clock, he received news that they had passed Oiwake in Komoro. After that, contact was cut off for a while. The next messenger that came said that Itagaki's troops had fought with the Uesugi army on Fuefuki Sunset Point and had won a great victory. They had captured 1,219 major soldiers and raised a shout of victory at two o'clock in the afternoon. The next morning, as soon as Harunobu arrived at the new battlefield, he made Itagaki's troops retreat to the rear guard, placed his own reserved troops on the front line, and fought against the 16,000 enemy soldiers who formed the second formation at Fuefuki Sunset Point. The previous day's victory by Itagaki's troops brought momentum and spirit to Harunobu's reserve troops; they captured 4,306 soldiers, and the Takeda won a second victory.

That night at headquarters, they recorded the names of the samurai who had died and held a ritual celebration of their victory. It was a windy night. A bonfire was burning high and fiery sparks were blown toward the samurai who were sitting in a row.

Harunobu was in command and sitting on a stool. Obu was his sword bearer. On Harunobu's right side was Itagaki, with the role of carrying a fan. On the left was Hara Mino-no-kami who sat with a bow and arrow made out of crow feathers. Kansuke had the role of carrying a huge conch shell. In Kansuke's eyes his lord, Harunobu, who sat there with his back rigid and straight, looked extremely handsome, masculine, and brave.

The sound of a huge drum, which was beaten by Obata Oribenosho, traveled through the night air of the new battlefield. An "Oh" issued forth from the mouths of all the samurai; a strong shout of victory was raised.

The samurai were all young. Only Kansuke looked particularly old. Kansuke sniffed and thought that his beloved young lord would defeat Murakami Yoshikiyo and then Nagao Kagetora (later known as Uesugi Kenshin) who lived on the other side of Murakami. But before that, they would face many small battles similar to the one just fought, Kansuke was thinking as he held the conch shell. To everybody's eyes, Kansuke's face looked like a ball of fire, anger emanating from it, a guardian god of the temple gate in the flying sparks of the bonfire.

Princess Yuu went back to Suwa at the end of November in the fifteenth year of Tenbun. Since the time of peach blossoms (March) of the fourteenth of Tenbun when she had come to Kai, close to two years had passed. In the meantime, Princess Yuu had borne a child, Katsuyori, in whose veins the blood of both the Takeda and the Suwa flowed.

People talked about Princess Yuu's journey home quite often. Some said that it was a plot by Harunobu's consort Sanjo-no-Uji, and others said that it was a political plot to ease the hatred of the people of Suwa toward the Takeda.

Whatever the truth was, Princess Yuu had no idea why she was going back. She simply followed Kansuke's suggestion when he visited her one day and told her that it was about time that she should show her son Lake Suwa before it became too cold.

Itagaki Nobukata had been governing the Suwa area since the Suwa family had fallen. Not long after Kansuke received Itagaki's message that the preparations had been made to receive Princess Yuu, she and Katsuyori left Kofuchu.

A long procession of several hundred servants and eight palanquins, which carried Princess Yuu, Katsuyori, and their maids, headed toward Shinano Province from Kai over the mountains and fields which were starting to show some signs of the coming of winter.

Princess Yuu was in the second palanquin, and in the third palanquin, Katsuyori's nurse held the child in her arms. Several strong and powerful samurai formed a circle around these two palanquins to guard them. One distinguished horseman was riding his horse close to Katsuyori's palanquin. It was Yamamoto Kansuke.

The last time Princess Yuu came from Shinano to Kai, she was quite capricious and stopped the procession often, but this time she was different. Not even once did she lift the blind, and she sat quietly in the swinging palanquin. Within less than two years, she had lost her girlishness and had grown into a mature young woman. Her natural beauty was supplemented with radiance acquired with age, and she had acquired a new, refined composure. A creamy white complexion, full pink cheeks, lovely black eyes, and a high and well-chiselled nose were the legacies of generations of lords of the distinguished Suwa family, which had now perished.

On the second day, the procession was journeying beside the fast flowing Kamuna River. Around noon, they rested for a while on the riverbank near Nirasaki. It was then that Kansuke, kneeling down beside her palanquin, asked her quietly, "Would you like to come out?"

"No, I shall rest in the palanquin," she answered in a clear voice.

"Are you tired?"

"No, not really, I am fine."

"Why don't you open the blind a little? This is probably the most beautiful scenery in the entire country of Kai, and besides this is an area of strategic importance. Someday when your son builds his castle, this would be the ideal place."

Princess Yuu must have been touched by his words, because she lifted her blind quietly. Kansuke stared at her slim pale wrist in admiration.

"Where will you build the castle?"

"It will be on that plateau."

The area where Kansuke pointed was a plateau that looked like an island in the far away vast green plain, which local residents called Seven Mile Rock.

"The Kamuna River and the Shio River surround that plateau. Three steep mountain peaks, Yakushi, Kannon, and Jizo, surround and close in on the plateau. One side faces mountains and the other three sides look toward plains. Standing on that plateau, one can see everywhere on the plains. By the time your son reaches adulthood, samurai will be fighting with guns. It is not necessary to have a castle located in an inaccessible place. That is an ideal location for his castle. And yet, a plateau like that, bordered with cliffs on four sides, will be very difficult for anyone to scale."

Kansuke felt that was an ideal place to build a castle. He had ridden his horse through this plain many times, and each time he passed it the idea of building a castle on the plateau arose. Ten to twenty years from now, this would be the center of the country of Kai, and whether they liked it or not, the Takeda would transfer their headquarters here. The person who would build the castle would most likely be Katsuyori. Yes, it had to be him.

Princess Yuu was looking around at the endless view.

"The leaves are colored beautifully," she said. Indeed, the plateau that Kansuke had pointed out was covered with the flaming crimson leaves of departing autumn.

"Are those colored trees *haze* trees?[42]"

"Ah..."

Kansuke had no knowledge when it came to trees and flowers. For Kansuke it was strange and amazing that women were actually interested in the names of trees.

"There are no haze trees in Kofuchu, but there are a lot of them in Suwa," Princess Yuu said quietly.

"Are you fond of haze trees?"

"Since I was very little, I was brought up looking at them. In the autumn I always want to see the red haze leaves."

"You will be able to see them all the time from now on, Princess," Kansuke said.

"What?" Princess Yuu gasped in surprise; then she lifted the blind and came out of the palanquin and stood up straight.

"Kansuke, what did you say? Are you telling me that I will live in Suwa from now on?" she asked sharply. "Are you telling me that I should live in Suwa far away from my lord? Is this some sort of plot?"

Her expression was calm, but the words were piercing and they transfixed Kansuke's heart like a spear.

"Ah...mm" Kansuke did not answer; rather, he was incapable of answering.

"Kansuke!"

"Yes, Princess."

"Surely you are not leaving me with Itagaki in Suwa, are you?"

"No, never!"

"In that case, it is all right."

Kansuke was bowing on his knees, his right hand touching the ground without lifting his head, shocked by how quickly she had caught on to the plan.

Princess Yuu's journey to Suwa had been decided upon between Harunobu, Itagaki, and Kansuke. Itagaki was going to keep Princess Yuu, and her baby Katsuyori, as her guardian in Suwa.

The main purpose was to get Katsuyori used to the people of Suwa and to try to get rid of their resentment for the Takeda. Kansuke also felt that by doing this, the life of Katsuyori would be protected. He was very much aware of the fact that since this baby had Suwa blood, people of the Takeda were watching him closely. As long as Katsuyori lived in Kofuchu, this newborn baby's life was placed in a delicate situation.

When the procession of Princess Yuu entered the boundaries of Suwa, who knows how they learned about it, but the farmers of Suwa all welcomed the procession on their knees, shoulder to shoulder, on the side of the road along the bleak early-winter rice fields, their heads touching the ground.

Princess Yuu lifted her blind when she heard Kansuke's voice saying, "Princess, we can see the lake."

The procession stopped. The dark blue surface of the lake with its sharp, choppy waves entered Princess Yuu's view.

"Isn't it beautiful, Princess?"

"Indeed, it is beautiful!"

Princess Yuu sat looking at the lake for a while and then trembled, saying, "Oh, it is cold!" and closed her blind.

The procession advanced, without resting, along the lake, with waterbirds flying away occasionally and headed for Takashima Castle.

Itagaki had decided that Princess Yuu would make Kan-non-in Temple her residence rather than Takashima Castle where she had once resided. It was Itagaki's idea that she would not suffer then from the memories of her life in Takashima Castle, as princess of the Suwa.

Kan-non-in Temple was in the village of Kosaka about a mile from Takashima Castle. The residential area of the temple had been beautifully renovated recently so that they did not recognize it. In the small village of Kosaka, where people lived on fishing and farming, many new houses and offices were built for the samurai who would live there to guard and protect the princess and her child. Princess Yuu would stay three nights at the castle and then move on to the temple.

Early in the morning, the first snow fell in the area of Suwa. The Yatsugatake Mountain Range was totally white, and the lakeshore and the fields around it were also lightly dusted with snow. Around noon, the palanquins of Princess Yuu and her baby Katsuyori left Takashima Castle and moved along the east side of the lake. Kansuke, who had already been at the village of Kosaka since the previous night, was waiting with several samurai for the two palanquins at the foot of Kan-non-in Temple.

The palanquins were visible from afar, but it took a long time for them to arrive. Since the road was muddy, it would have been difficult to walk. Finally, the palanquins entered the village and stopped right in front of Kansuke and his group.

"Her room is warmed up, I hope," Kansuke made sure several times and then said to the princess, "It must have been a hard trip in the cold weather."

There was no answer from inside.

"Princess, you are here. Please come out of the palanquin."

Kansuke repeated his request, but again there was no answer. From the second palanquin, the baby Katsuyori came out, held by his maid who stood on the snow. Kansuke felt a stab of worry. He lifted the blind of the palanquin a little.

Suddenly, Kansuke turned pale. There was no Princess Yuu. In the palanquin there was one of the maids with whom Princess Yuu had been saved from Takashima Castle on the night of the fall of the Suwa. This young maid was lying down, her face covered with blood. Both her hands grasped a dagger, which had been thrust into her throat.

Kansuke quietly closed the blind, inserted his hand into the palanquin, and placed it over the woman's forehead. It was still slightly warm. Kansuke ordered the samurai to carry the palanquin into the residence of the Kan-non-in Temple. Kansuke brought

Katsuyori inside and ordered everybody to leave at once. When he made sure that nobody was around, he lifted the blind again.

"What happened to the princess?"

He inserted the upper half of his body into the palanquin and lifted the woman's body and shook her with all his might saying, "Where is the princess, where is she?"

But the woman never opened her eyes. There was no sign of life. Kansuke gave up and stood at the entrance. Very fine snow started to fall again.

Kansuke felt that nobody should know of Princess Yuu's disappearance.

He decided to take the palanquin out of the Kosaka Kan-non-in Temple, saying that something urgent had happened that night and Princess Yuu had to go back to Takashima Castle. Snow was still falling continuously. This time only two servants carried the palanquin, escorted by Kansuke himself on his horse.

Kansuke went down the slope from the Kan-non-in Temple onto the road along the lake. To go to Takashima Castle, Kansuke took the opposite road from that which they had taken that afternoon. One of the carriers commented that it was the long way back; Kansuke ignored the comment and ordered him, "Proceed!"

When they had proceeded half a mile, he stopped the palanquin and told them, "Princess Yuu is cold, so you go back to Kan-non-in and get a foot warmer."

After they disappeared from sight, he watched in their direction for a while. Then he made sure that nobody was around and dismounted from the horse and quickly went to work.

He was at the exit from the lake of the Tenryu River. The great Tenryu River started from Lake Suwa and ran through the Ina Valley all the way down to Totomi.

Kansuke lifted the blind of the palanquin, dragged out the woman's cold dead body, and carried it to the lakeshore through deep snow over his knees. The surface of the lake was quiet except for the egress of the Tenryu River. Kansuke stood there watching the roaring current at the mouth of the river for a while with the dead body in his arms, and then he threw the body into the current. As the body left his arms and was swallowed by the water, he fell backwards. Soft snow buried his body up to his waist. He grabbed the bamboo leaves that were sticking out of the snow and lifted himself up. A few meters away from where he was, several waterfowl flew away. The sound of flapping wings mingled with the roaring of the water. Suddenly, he felt oppressively lonely.

Kansuke had thought that he should get rid of the servant's body. Nobody knew but he that she had committed seppuku. "But where is Princess Yuu?" He had to find her before anybody noticed she was gone. He did not want Harunobu or Itagaki Nobukata to learn about this.

It was not that he did not want them to know of his oversight, actually he did not even think of that at all. This had nothing to do with Harunobu or Itagaki. What could they do if they learned about it? Kansuke felt it was only he who could understand and talk about her agony with her as if it were his own problem. He had to look for her on his own. Kansuke was thinking of her just like a father would worry about his runaway daughter.

When the two carriers returned, he inserted the foot warmer in the palanquin in which he had placed several heavy stones beforehand. The palanquin started to move. From this point, Kansuke took the usual way to Takashima Castle.

Kansuke was thinking that if the carriers noticed that the palanquin was empty he would be ready to kill them. As they proceeded, the snow piled up on Kansuke's head and shoulders.

Princess Yuu must have tried to go back to Kai, afraid of being sent away from Harunobu. Although the maid had followed the princess's orders, she must have realized the serious responsibility she had assumed; she must have decided to commit seppuku. This was all that he could think of.

It was the second hour of the Boar when the palanquin entered Takashima Castle. As soon as they entered the gate, he let the carriers go back to Kosaka Kan-non-in Temple, removed the stones by himself, and ordered the samurai in the castle to take the palanquin away.

The first part of his job was done. At the entrance office, Kansuke wrote a letter to Itagaki at once. The letter contained the short message that Princess Yuu had caught a cold and was resting and since Kansuke would look after her, nobody was allowed to visit her.

"Please take this letter to General Itagaki tomorrow morning without any delay and make sure it gets there." With his orders being followed, he climbed onto his horse and left Takashima Castle.

It was still snowing. "Where is the Princess in this snow and what is she doing?" He did not know what time and from which place she had run away. When he came out of the gate of the castle, he stopped for a while on the back of the horse. He was not sure which way he should be heading. Normally Kansuke could think things through. But this time, his mind seemed to be stuck in a deep fog. He had absolutely no idea where Princess Yuu was. Kansuke spurred his horse and galloped along the way to Kai. This was the road that he and Princess Yuu had travelled only four days ago. Now everything looked different. With the first snowfall, even the scenery was unrecognizable.

Leaving Takashima Castle behind, he arrived at the first village called Miyakawa. He knocked at every door on the street.

"Did you see the princess? Did she come to look for a place to stay? If you don't tell me the truth your whole family will be crucified." Kansuke shouted at every door.

At every house, whoever opened the door cowered in fear. In front of their eyes stood a monster riding a horse with his spear in his hand. Even at his best, he had a frightening face. But tonight his face had an inexplicable expression. It was as if he were possessed by a devil.

While he was searching the village, day broke. The snow stopped falling at dawn. Riding in about two feet of snow, he moved southeast across the plain. Every time he came across a village, he knocked at every door. As time passed, he began to feel desperate.

"Princess, Princess!" repeating her name in his heart, he directed his horse hopelessly. At about noon, he stopped for the first time. When the horse stopped, he fell head first into a snow-covered bamboo bush due to both fatigue and despair.

Neither capturing castles nor territorial wars meant anything to him now. No more dreams of eating up the neighboring land like a silkworm eating mulberry leaves. Since the beautiful princess had disappeared from his world, he had no further desire to live. For the first time, he realized how strongly he was attached to her.

"Princess, Princess!"

For Kansuke, the princess was his dream, just as Harunobu was his dream. For Kansuke, both of them were his greatest and only dream in the world. Harunobu was his reason for life, and Princess Yuu was just as vital to him. His great dream would never come true if he was missing one of them.

It was almost seven o'clock in the evening. He had gone through several villages in the mountains and returned to the village of Miyakawa, where he had gone the previous night. More than one day had passed since she had disappeared.

At night, the snow on the road was frozen and had become icy. Since his horse was having difficulty walking, he decided to return to the castle at once and tell Itagaki everything. There seemed to be no other way than to search every house using Itagaki's troops.

When he reached the midpoint between Miyakawa Village and Takashima Castle, he stared at a thicket of assorted trees and felt he saw a light. He stopped his horse and looked through the trees. The light had disappeared. He kept riding again, passing the forest, but intuition prevented him from continuing. He turned his horse around and went back to the point where he thought he had seen the light.

This time he could see a stream of light in a thicket of assorted trees. He steered his horse into the forest. Soon, he came to a narrow path and followed it to a small shrine. The light came from there.

The shrine was old and decayed and was so small that it could hold only two or three people. If looked at during the day, it would be a dilapidated building, but snow was covering it and at least it had the form of a shrine.

He yelled from the back of his horse, "Is anybody there?"

Suddenly the light blinked off.

"Is there anybody there?" he shouted again. There was no response from inside. From his horse he knocked on the door of the shrine with the handle of his spear. Then, a beautiful clear voice answered, "Who is it?"

"Is it the princess?" he cried out; then a few seconds later he heard a very calm voice.

Princess Yuu's clear voice answered, "Kansuke!?"

He dismounted, ran up the stone staircase of the shrine, knelt down in front of the door, and asked, "Are you all right, Princess?"

Without answering his question, she asked him in a rather accusing tone of voice, "Why did you come here? I am telling you, Kansuke, no matter what you say: I am going back to Lord Harunobu. I am not going to live in Suwa."

"Yes, Princess."

"Do you acknowledge that Kansuke?"

"Yes, Princess," he was so anxious to get into the shrine and see the Princess with his own eyes. "I promise to do anything you say, Princess."

"In that case, you may open the door."

Kansuke opened the door. He cowered in the dark and took out some flint. He lit the dish on the floor that was filled with oil.

Princess Yuu was sitting neatly on the wet floor. Her long hair was hanging over her back, and her long overgarment was spread on the floor. Even in this snow-covered old shrine, her beauty and dignity shone through.

"Princess, for heaven's sake, I would like you to go back to Suwa. There I will listen to any of your proposals," Kansuke said.

"I cannot walk any longer," Princess Yuu answered.

"Are you sure you cannot walk?"

"My feet are so cold, I cannot move even one more step."

"I understand, but that means that you cannot walk even to Kai where the lord is?"

Princess Yuu said nothing.

"Did you eat anything, Princess?"

"I have not had anything to eat since yesterday morning."

Kansuke realized that the last time he had eaten was with the princess. He felt no hunger; yet he could feel how hungry Princess Yuu could be, and he could barely stand the idea of her going hungry.

"Let's go back to Suwa as soon as possible and have something warm to eat, Princess."

Then, Princess Yuu said in an extraordinarily quiet voice, "Cold feet or hunger has nothing to do with human suffering. Kansuke, you do not understand anything at all."

"Of course I do. I understand all the suffering you are experiencing."

"No, you do not," Princess Yuu breathed fiercely.

"You are talking about the agony of being away from Lord Harunobu, are you not?"

"It is one of them, but it is not all," Princess Yuu added, saying, "Do you understand why I escaped from the palanquin and ran away to this place? Do you really understand why I would like to go back to my lord so much?"

He felt a little worried about Princess Yuu's tone and hesitated to respond. Then she continued, "It is because I wanted to kill him."

"What?" He could not believe what he had just heard. He had never been as shocked as this in his entire life.

"What did you say, Princess?"

"I shall repeat it as many times as you wish. I wanted to kill him."

Kansuke instantly imagined this beautiful princess chopping Harunobu's head off and felt a chill run down his spine.

"Do not worry, Kansuke. Now, I simply want to see him, that's all."

Kansuke sighed in relief. However, his relief did not last long.

"But tomorrow, I might want to kill him again."

"Princess!"

"But the day after tomorrow, I might feel that I just want to see him."

"Princess!"

He could not say anything else; he was so stunned by her words. He could no longer handle this chaotic situation. He felt that if he did not repeat that one word, princess, he would have fallen apart.

"I shall always be torn between these feelings as long as I live. I hate my lord because he killed my father and made me his possession and then he tried to let me go again. And yet, he was the one who produced Katsuyori from me and told me time and time again that he loved me."

She wept quietly, her shoulders trembling. Kansuke was totally at a loss watching Princess Yuu's small frame trembling as she lay on the cold wet floor.

Kansuke learned for the first time that both love and hate could coexist at the same time and appear alternately without any logic. This discovery was beyond his understanding, and he had no idea how to cope with it.

If he kept her in Suwa, this hatred toward Harunobu could increase. That he had to avoid. And yet, if he brought her back to Kai and left her beside Harunobu, one never knew what treachery would occur to her. Harunobu's legitimate wife Sanjo-no-Uji and the Takeda's close relatives would watch her very carefully with jealous eyes. This could endanger her safety. Probably the best thing to do was to keep her in Suwa for her safety and somehow maintain Harunobu's love toward her.

The day after Kansuke had brought her to Kan-non-in Temple, he went to see her. She was lying in her bed, saying that she had a headache.

"How are your feet, no longer painful?"

"Yes, they are still painful."

"That is too bad. You should not have done such a naughty thing. How is the rest of your body?"

"I am just hungry."

"You say you are hungry, but I heard that you ate nothing."

"No."

"That is not good at all, Princess," Kansuke said accusingly.

"Do you not remember that I promised you that I was not going to eat anything until I was in a palanquin going back to Kai?"

"Yes, you did, but…"

"I always keep my promises."

It seemed that nothing could deter her.

"Princess, can I ask you a question? Once you go back to Kai, you'll realize that you have to live separately from Master Katsuyori. You understand this, do you not?"

"Yes, I do understand."

"Will you not miss him?"

"There is no mother who would not love and miss her child."

"Then you should live here with Master Katsuyori. The Lord Harunobu can visit you anytime."

"I cannot rely on him. He would not leave Kofuchu unless there is a war."

"But if you go back to Kai, you have to leave Master Katsuyori here."

"I shall take Katsuyori with me."

"No, Princess, there is absolutely no way you can do that!" Kansuke said. He felt this was the time that he had to tell her everything openly and honestly. "Master Katsuyori will not live in Kofuchu for a long while. You never know what kind of danger he might be exposed to. Do you not understand? Master Katsuyori has Suwa blood in him. Some of the Takeda family believe that the blood of the Suwa is a curse to the Takeda. Therefore something could happen to your baby…"

"Is there such a plot?"

"Oh, no, not now. We do not see any such plot yet. But then again, you never know who might think of such a course of action. This is why we have to leave Master Katsuyori in Suwa. As long as he is in Suwa, he will be safe."

Princess Yuu was gazing off into space with her pale face; she then said, "That I understand.... Even I wanted to kill...my lord."

"Princess!" Kansuke stopped her words.

"We are not in the forest any longer, where we were completely alone, and there are things you can say and things you cannot say."

With Kansuke's words, Princess Yuu closed her mouth obediently. Then she thought for a while and said in a low voice, "In that case, I shall leave Katsuyori here."

"That is a good idea. I assure you that all the people of Suwa will look after him from the bottom of their hearts."

"But, I still want to go to Kai."

"Even if you do not go to Kai, it will be the same thing if the lord visits you here often enough, will it not?"

"Will he come for sure? Will you make sure he will?"

"If we have wars in Shinano Province, the lord will be in Suwa all the time. There will be continuous battles for many years. We must fight against Murakami Yoshikiyo. After we conquer him, we have to cross swords with Nagao of Echigo. Therefore, the headquarters of Lord Harunobu will be placed in Suwa rather than Kofuchu most of the time."

Kansuke seriously believed that. For many years, the Takeda would have to fight difficult battles in northern Shinano. And whether they liked it or not, for the sake of Princess Yuu, the Takeda's strategy had to be directed toward the north at all times, Kansuke thought.

Chapter 6
I HAVE TO KILL HER ...

As Kansuke had predicted, Harunobu had to fight against his northern enemies after Princess Yuu's incident. Against fearless Murakami Yoshikiyo, who had always harbored intentions to attack the south, Harunobu had to engage repeatedly in life-and-death battles.

Murakami, who experienced fierce battles with the Takeda during the fight for Toishi Castle, gradually rearranged and prepared his troops and by the sixteenth year of Tenbun, his fighters started to show their readiness all over the district of northern Shinano. In response to these movements, Harunobu also repositioned his troops. As a result, he often stayed in Suwa Province.

Under these circumstances, Lord Harunobu and Princess Yuu carried on their lives seamlessly. Kansuke visited Princess Yuu occasionally in the Kan-non-in Temple.

"It is nice to hear that you are feeling well, Princess."

At the same time Kansuke looked at Princess Yuu's face intently. When her beautiful visage looked happy and calm, he felt relieved.

"Please let me know whenever anything is unsatisfactory," Kansuke said searchingly.

"I have nothing to complain about, except I am concerned that Katsuyori is not very healthy and he is quite irritable lately. I wonder if the weather of Suwa does not suit him."

It was true that on observing him, he was obviously a sickly child. He cried fitfully for unimportant reasons. The strange thing was that, no matter how loudly he howled, he never shed tears. He cried, trembling and twitching his body, turning his face purple; yet he never actually wept.

Kansuke rather liked him because of that. He felt it showed his strong personality, which was different from others.

"Do not worry about him, Princess. When he grows up he will be like Marishiten[43] or Ashura[44] because he has something which is different from other children," Kansuke told her. He really believed what he said.

But, he said this only in front of Princess Yuu. In front of others, he stated that Master Katsuyori was very sickly and he did not have the personality to be a strong samurai. This was much safer for Katsuyori's sake. Only Itagaki Nobukata saw through Kansuke's facade. Maybe because he was looking after Princess Yuu and Katsuyori, Itagaki gradually started to be fond of both of them.

Somehow, it started to form a pattern that through Princess Yuu and Katsuyori, Itagaki and Kansuke, who lived in Suwa, were confronted with many high-ranking samurai who supported the Takeda's consort in Kofuchu.

It was August of the seventeenth year of Tenbun. Harunobu destroyed Shiga Castle in the Shinano district and entered and stayed at Komuro Castle with 10,000 troops.

Murakami found it a rare opportunity, with Harunobu staying in the northern part of Shinano, and took this advantage to determine the winner in their conflict. With 7,000 troops he left Katsurao Castle and waded across the Chikuma River. When the lovely breezes of autumn were felt, the plains of Uedahara became the site of a decisive battle.

Harunobu came out with a unique strategy inspired by Kansuke's idea. This was the unusual formation called *Shimarino sonae*.[45] Itagaki Nobukata led the vanguard. Obu Toramasa, Oyamada Masatatsu, and Takeda Nobushige led the second formation. The third formation was led by the Itagaki's retainer Baba Nobuharu and Naito Shuri. One mile behind them, Hara Toratane led the last formation with 300 horsemen.

The battle started at the hour of the Sea Horse on August the twenty-fourth. Itagaki's vanguard of 3,500 men formed six tiers, advanced toward the front, and stood facing the enemy.

Immediately, they started fiercely shooting arrows and firing guns against the Murakami vanguard.

Kansuke felt at ease with Itagaki, who had excellent leadership skills. When it came to a disorganized battle, Itagaki had some problems and showed weakness, but in the early stages of the war he had enormous strength that nobody could exceed. He always gained the advantage at the beginning of the battle and made an extraordinary charge at the enemy. It was the same thing with this battle. Within a couple of hours Itagaki crushed the Murakami formation and led his troops to attack the enemy. It was an impressive scene to watch how he handled the conflict.

Eventually, the battlefield became quiet. Far away on the plains, they could see the separate moving groups of warriors in the recesses of the hills, the routed Murakami army and Itagaki's warriors chasing them. It was rather quiet, quite unlike a normal battle scene.

In less than an hour, Kansuke was sitting beside Harunobu on the hilltop where their headquarters were situated. Suddenly he stood up. "General Itagaki is dead!" He was sure he had heard somebody yelling that. No, it can't be! But the voice was approaching closer and closer.

"General Itagaki is dead!"

Kansuke saw a horseman galloping up the slope of the hill toward them. Kansuke suddenly felt a cold gust of wind blowing into the core of his heart. He felt as if Princess Yuu, her son Katsuyori, and himself were isolated from the rest of the world and left alone in the middle of the vast plain.

"General Itagaki is dead!"

The horseman approached, yelled the last word, and fell from his horse with a thud.

Kansuke stood fast on the hill with his legs apart, his spear in his right hand, as he watched over the Uedahara Plain that spread out beneath him.

Itagaki's troops, who had lost their leader, were retreating in different directions up hills or down valleys, which looked like rising and falling waves. Kansuke also saw the major power of the

Murakami troops, who had cut Itagaki's formation in half and were surging toward Kansuke's position like storming clouds. One or two hundred horsemen formed each group, and many such groups were heading his way, making a stream like a black line. They were no longer paying attention to Itagaki's fleeing army. It was very clear that their intention was to attack the Takeda's headquarters at once.

"Can we stop them with the second formation?"

Harunobu, who was watching the plain while sitting on a stool, asked the same question that Kansuke had asked himself. Since the vanguard of the Itagaki army was broken, it was the second formation led by Obu, Oyamada, and Nobushige, which had to face the enemy.

"Well…" Kansuke could not answer.

"They don't seem to be moving, do they?" Harunobu spoke finally. The Takeda soldiers, who were forming the second config-uration at the bottom of the hill where headquarters was located, kept silent as if they were holding their breath. Not a single samu-rai moved. Harunobu was visibly concerned, seeing that they did not act immediately.

"I am quite sure that General Obu has some ideas," Kansuke said. When it came to stopping an enemy which was charging aggressively, Obu Toramasa fought a splendid battle. He showed great strength in this type of situation. This is why Kansuke placed him in the second formation.

Suddenly, they heard war cries all over the hill. Both the troops of Oyamada and Nobushige deployed the formation right in front of the enemy. At the same time, the mounted party of Obu initiated a charge on both sides of the enemy. The flags of the Takeda were shining like ears of pampas grass. The war cry, the sound of drums, and the blaring roar of the conch shell rang out clearly in the turbulence taking place below.

Instantly, the plain transformed itself into a scene of carnage. Many thousands of warriors and horses crashed into one another. Watching from the hill where headquarters was situated, it was impossible to tell who the enemy was and who were the allies.

Occasionally some new horsemen of Obu were led into the bloody chaos of the battle.

"It seems like we have a fifty-fifty chance of winning. But our troops will win. They will win but…" Kansuke started to comment, and then all of a sudden he stood up, his face paling considerably.

"Yoshikiyo is going to attack here!"

Yes, his army was on its way. Yes, his army was losing the battle, but there was a totally separate group coming from a different direction. About 300 horsemen were trying to break the formation of Oyamada's army in half. They were pushing desperately, hoping to open a way through. Obviously, they were aiming for the headquarters on the hill.

"How about moving your troop three quarters of a mile?" Kansuke suggested, but Harunobu did not answer. Harunobu obviously wanted to attack rather than retreat.

"You must move your troop a little!" Kansuke said it rather forcefully this time. Considering the situation, they had the third formation prepared by Baba Minbu with Naito Shuri at the rear.

Harunobu remained silent. He might be thinking that it was a disgrace, as commander-in-chief, to be chased away by the enemy with only a party of 300 mounted soldiers.

"If you retreat now, Murakami Yoshikiyo's group could be attacked."

"By whom?"

"Our backup horsemen, or the Naito's troops. Those backup troops are there for this purpose, my lord. This is a great opportunity for them to attack Yoshikiyo."

Kansuke was desperate. The 300 horsemen were rushing up the hill extremely quickly. If they retreated, the mounted party, known as the most skillful among the Takeda's men, would attack the enemy from the right and the Naito's men would charge from the left, and they would bring down the enemy's entire cavalry.

"Can't we attack them here, at headquarters?" Harunobu said.

"Of course we can, but what good will that do? Then, what is the use of having a strategy? We set up the third formation for this purpose. It is the mounted party and the Naito's troops who were supposed to attack them. It will not give you any honor even if you attack them."

"All right, then we shall retreat!" Finally Harunobu reluctantly agreed.

The drums were beat to announce the advance of the Naito army. At the same, time the banner of "Furin Kazan" swayed and the flags on the warriors' backs, who were stationed at headquarters, started to move slowly to the eastern slope of the hill. Kansuke wanted to move as quickly as possible. But, Harunobu moved slowly and unwillingly.

Kansuke, who happened to look down on the plain, was shocked. He saw a group of horsemen dashing through the foothills. That was the enemy's group. The allied backup army had just started to transfer to their position.

"My lord!" Kansuke brought his horse up right next to Harunobu's. "We are too late to retreat. The enemy has broken the formation at the bottom of the hill. Yoshikiyo obviously made up his mind to fight directly with your army. In this situation, you must do whatever I, Kansuke, ask you to do, otherwise we will be in trouble."

At the instant he said this, Kansuke ordered Harunobu's army to be ready to counterattack the enemy's troops. He could no longer pay attention to Harunobu.

Kansuke stayed right beside Harunobu and held a moment of silence.

On the peak of a small hill, about two and a half miles away, the enemy's mounted party appeared and then galloped down to the valley. Soon they would be climbing up to Harunobu's position. There would be a little while before the backup mounted party and Naito's troops arrived from the third formation.

Soon the war cries and the sound of horses hooves arose, and in no time the place transformed into a scene of carnage and mortal combat.

Kansuke tried to go down the hill with a hundred horsemen surrounding Harunobu, but there was a big difference between the attackers and the defenders. Sixty of the enemy's horsemen surrounded Harunobu, at the same time the hundred horsemen around Harunobu dispersed. After that, the battle degenerated into total confusion.

Kansuke stayed right beside Harunobu and dealt with two attackers, throwing them down from their horses. He looked around for Harunobu, who, in the interim, had moved away from him.

Then, Kansuke saw that Harunobu was crossing swords with an enemy horseman. Harunobu was about fifty yards away, mounted on a black horse and wearing white armour with a blue lining, the color of a *unohana*,[46] and the helmet of "*Suwahosho*.[47]" Both warriors were fighting as gracefully as if they were dancing *Noh*,[48] riding their horses with ease. When they came close to each other, they engaged in fierce battle. Both lost and gained ground equally.

Kansuke thought the opposing horseman had to be the enemy's leader Murakami Yoshikiyo. The distinguished and brave fighting style was obviously Murakami's. They were no longer the heads of their entire armies. They were simply combatants seeking the life of their opponent. It looked as if they were isolated from the general battle, away from the scenes of carnage, just two of them fighting for their lives without interruption.

Between Kansuke and the two noble combatants, many hundreds of enemy and allied samurai were engaged in combat. Kansuke bent low on the back of his horse and steered its head toward the two commanders-in-chief. Pain ran through his shoulder. He must have been attacked from the side.

While Kansuke had composed himself, many enemy and allied warriors surrounded Harunobu and Yoshikiyo again. The backup mounted party had just arrived at the scene. Yoshikiyo's horse leaped high, and Kansuke saw that Yoshikiyo had fallen to the ground. The enemy's sixty horsemen rushed to pick him up. Quickly they lifted him up on their horses and galloped down the hill in one cluster. They were swift to attack but also swift to retreat.

"My lord," Kansuke pulled himself close to Harunobu.

"Damn it! I missed him!" Harunobu said.

"He must be thinking the same thing, my lord."

Kansuke gathered Harunobu's army around him and trotted down the hill. Constant war cries were heard. The backup horsemen and Naito's troops must have been shifting into pursuit.

When the battle was over, it started to rain. In the fine rainfall, the head count was recorded. The enemy corpses numbered 2,919, and the allied corpses were some 700 men.

Soon after the battle, the whole army came together and raised their victory cry; Kansuke advanced in front of Harunobu and said, "My lord!"

"Don't say it," Harunobu stopped his words. Harunobu thought that Kansuke was going to lecture him, but Kansuke had no intention of doing so.

"Yoshikiyo will never recover again. I expect your next battle to be with the great leader on the other side of Murakami's land."

"Who is it?"

"It is Nagao Kagetora,"[49] said Kansuke.

"Why?"

"I believe that Murakami attempted his final attack today. It was not a regular attack. But now that he has failed in his strategy, he will not try to take us on alone again. He will come with the army of Nagao Kagetora and that time his target will be you, assisted by the power of Kagetora."

That was all he said, and then Kansuke excused himself from Harunobu's presence, took Itagaki's head under his arm, mounted his horse, and left the field to return to the Suwa, leading Itagaki's warriors ahead of the rest of the army. The sadness of losing Itagaki, forgotten during the fierce combat, returned and swept into Kansuke's heart along with the wind that carried the bloody smell of death.

The battle of Uedahara created a great gulf between the influence of Takeda Harunobu and Murakami Yoshikiyo. Both Nishina and Sarashina districts became Harunobu's territory and consequently, all the castles in these districts such as Kousaka, Inoue, Men-nai, Suda, Takanashi, and Seba fell into the Takeda's hands. The Takeda also swallowed up Kotani Castle, and the power of the Takeda increased significantly.

On the other hand, Murakami's power decreased notably after the battle of Uedahara after his losing major high-ranking samurai, and as a result he could not regain his power nor stand up again on his own.

Harunobu suffered two cuts from this battle but recuperated quickly. Kansuke added several cuts to his already unique features, but they also healed rapidly.

At the end of September, one month after the battle of Uedahara, a large funeral for Itagaki Nobukata was held in Suwa. Itagaki's legitimate son, Itagaki Yajiro Nobusato inherited his father's position and started to govern the Suwa district. The wind of the fall of the seventeenth year of Tenbun felt exceptionally cold to Kansuke's heart. He stayed at Takashima Castle after the battle without going back to Suwa for the preparations of Itagaki's funeral and the other religious ceremonies, which followed.

The death of Itagaki was a heavy blow to Kansuke. Itagaki was not necessarily always on Kansuke's side, but since he was the one who had helped Kansuke enter Harunobu's service, he was not Kansuke's enemy. He was the only one who understood Kansuke's personality as both a schemer and a loner who did not compromise. However, it had to be Princess Yuu who received the heaviest blow from Itagaki's death. Only Itagaki, Harunobu, and Kansuke knew the real reason why she became a concubine for Harunobu and why she moved to the Kan-non-in Temple in Suwa. So it was quite natural that Kansuke was feeling totally isolated and lonesome without Itagaki.

On October the eleventh, three messengers arrived on their post-horses, one at a time at short intervals. They were from the mansion of Harunobu in Kofuchu and brought the following orders: "Nagao Kagetora of Echigo [later known as Uesugi Kenshin] is planning to march to the Shinshu district along with a large army, accepting a proposal from Murakami Yoshikiyo. Tomorrow, on the twelfth, during the hour of the Monkey, I will leave Kofuchu with my main army. On the fifteenth or the sixteenth, we will arrive at Komuro where we will make camp and receive Kagetora's army at Un-no-Daira. The Itagaki army of Suwa should head to Komuro along with Kansuke."

What Kansuke had mentioned to Harunobu right after the triumphant victory at Uedahara Plain became a reality within two months.

Kagetora was only eighteen years old, but he was already known for his bravery as Lord of Echigo. Up until this time, because Murakami was situated between them, Harunobu and Kagetora had had no opportunity to come into contact. Now Murakami was defeated, and Kagetora and Harunobu's two great camps had to fight a decisive battle. Whether he liked it or not, Kansuke had known that they had to face this situation someday, but he never expected this day to come so soon.

Takashima Castle, after the arrival of the post-horses, turned into a town of preparation. Kansuke directed the entire procedure, encouraging the new young General Yajiro Nobusato [Itagaki's son]. They decided to leave the next morning, the twelfth, at dawn.

Later that night, in the hour of the Dog, Kansuke somehow felt like visiting Princess Yuu. He himself did not know why, in the midst of this chaos on the eve of taking the field, he had a strange premonition that he had to visit Princess Yuu, but he was anxious to take his horse out to Kan-non-in Temple.

Once the idea entered his mind, he could no longer wait. He took his horse out and galloped unattended along the shore of Lake Suwa. As at the time Kansuke had come to Takamatsu Castle as a messenger, bonfires were set along the lake and the flames reflected over the water. The late fall wind was cold on his cheeks.

Kansuke kept his horse at a strong gallop without resting it and arrived quickly at Kosaka Kan-non-in Temple. The mansion among the thick trees was quiet, and it seemed as if everyone were asleep. Kansuke peeked in at the guard station next to the priest's residence. Two samurai, who were night duty watchmen, came out looking surprised.

"Nothing new?" asked Kansuke.

"No, sir."

"Make sure you patrol around the mansion."

"Yes, we will sir."

"How is the princess?"

"She has retired to her bedchamber, sir."

"All right then."

Kansuke got ready to go back. He desperately wanted to glance into the princess's room, just to see her, but since he heard that she was already in her bedroom, he decided to go back without speaking to her. There was nothing in particular to discuss even if he had an audience with her. He had no special reason to come. He simply had wanted to see her. The warriors came to see him off at the bottom of the slope, where he mounted his horse.

"Make sure that you look after the princess," Kansuke said and returned the same way he had come.

When he entered a small village about two miles away from the temple, Kansuke saw a procession of about twenty people passing by. They looked like strong samurai carrying a palanquin with a few female attendants among them.

Since samurai surrounded the palanquin, naturally the person inside had to be of high birth. Seeing some female attendants indicated that there was a lady inside the palanquin. Kansuke felt strange. If anybody of status was passing by, Kansuke, who lived in Takashima Castle, should have been notified. Besides, it was so late at night. It seemed to be a secret journey of some sort.

Who could it be? Kansuke followed them on his horse from a vantage point of about a hundred yards behind them, going neither closer nor falling behind.

The procession stopped suddenly in front of a farmhouse. For a while, only the palanquin was carried into the front yard of the farmhouse, which was just a bit off the road.

Kansuke dismounted, tied his horse to a tree at the side of the road, and entered into the estate from the side entrance. When he went close to the main residence, where light was coming from, the sliding door of the entrance was opened. A young lady was sitting on the elevated wooden floor by the large opening. A few steps behind her, three samurai and an old woman were kneeling down on the dirt floor. The people in the farmhouse were all bunched up in the corner of the wooden-floored room, and a woman who looked like the wife of the owner of this farm was serving tea to the lady on the elevated wooden floor.

Kansuke was watching the young lady. She looked two or three years older than Princess Yuu. She might be twenty years old or so. Kansuke sensed that she was calm and gentle. Every time she sipped the tea, she looked around the house curiously. She did not have the striking beauty or the sophistication of Princess Yuu, yet Kansuke was amazed at her beauty. Her rosy cheeks were full, and her large innocent black eyes looked as if she were dreaming. Her beauty presented a striking contrast to Princess Yuu. Figuratively speaking, the beauty of Princess Yuu was ardent, while the beauty of this lady was vivacious.

"Princess, are you ready to leave?"

"Yes."

"Or would you like to stay a little while?" she was asked again by the old woman.

"Yes," she repeated without changing her expression. The wife of the house had already offered her fresh tea several times, constantly looking at her admiringly. The young princess picked up the fresh tea bowl. She held it in her hands for a while, as if to warm them, but did not drink from it. Then, she placed it on the floor and said, "No more, thank you."

She smiled graciously at the wife of the farmhouse.

Who could she be? She must be from a rather powerful family, but where was she going?

Soon, when the three samurai and the old woman stood up, the young lady also stood up slowly. Only the old woman stayed behind.

"I am sorry to disturb you without any notice, but since the princess wanted to drink hot tea, we had no choice. This is simply to show our appreciation," said the old woman and placed some money wrapped in a small folded piece of paper on the floor. The farm woman refused to take it, but the old woman ignored her and asked, "Is there any road to Nirasaki without passing through Takashima Castle?"

As the farmwife was explaining how to get there, Kansuke could not hear her, but the old woman's question "without going through Takashima Castle" caught his attention. Kansuke left there immediately through the hidden door beside the storage building and came out onto the road. The procession had started already, and the old woman who came out last had to run to catch up, about a hundred yards ahead of her. Kansuke left his horse there and ran after the old woman.

"Excuse me," Kansuke called after her. She turned her head, surprised. Suddenly Kansuke's hand reached out for her, and she fell backwards into Kansuke's arms.

Kansuke held the old woman and looked around him. He then carried the helpless woman into a grassy area and made her sit on the wet ground that was covered in night dew. Then he shook her body violently.

"I have no intention of harming you, but I would like to ask you several questions," said Kansuke.

"Who are you?"

Though she looked scared, her tone was firm. Without answering her question, Kansuke asked, "Where are you going?"

"We are heading for Kai."

"Where in Kai?"

"That I cannot tell, because we were told not to by our superior."

"Who is the person in that palanquin?"

"I cannot tell."

"It must be a woman?"

"No, you are wrong."

"There is no use telling me a lie. I saw her with my own eyes."

Kansuke felt it was not going to be easy to deal with this woman, and then he said, "If you do not tell me the truth, I am sorry, but I will have to take your life."

"For goodness sake, who are you?" the old woman asked him again. "Would you like some money?"

It was an unexpected question for Kansuke, but the idea sounded rather convenient for him.

"Yes, you are right."

"How much do you want?"

"After I learn who is in the palanquin, I will decide the price."

Then she realized that Kansuke was a blackmailer of some sort and suddenly acted high-handedly.

"It is the daughter of the Aburagawa Gyobu-no-kami."

She spoke in a tone that would discourage anyone from doing any harm to this great family. Then she ordered Kansuke, "Leave!" and she stood up to emphasize how serious she was.

The daughter of the Aburagawa Gyobu! Aburagawa used to be a powerful and well-known family in the district of Shinano. But that clan should have been destroyed by now. Kansuke sat there for a while. The daughter of Aburagawa was on her way to Kai, furthermore, at night, with twenty samurai. And they were trying to avoid taking a road that would pass through Takashima Castle!

Kansuke knelt tensely. What does this mean?

"Wait!" Kansuke shouted at the old woman who was about to leave. He thought he had to force her to tell him everything, or else.

"It does not make any difference whether she is of the Aburagawa or not. Nobody is allowed to pass through the Suwa territory without permission, though obviously you are taking advantage of the dark night."

She responded with silence.

"This is the territory which I am looking after by the order of the lord."

"Then, do you belong at Takashima Castle?" She changed her haughty tone and said, "I am advising you to be careful. You might as well leave right now, because I am also here by the order of the lord."

"What?"

"We are going to Kofuchu, on an order from the lord in Kofuchu. Leave!"

This time the old woman started to walk away. She was going to Kai by the order of Harunobu! Kansuke too stood up, but did not call her back, nor did he chase her.

Kansuke returned to the place where he had tied his horse and mounted it. Then, he whipped his horse and galloped away. Soon he could see the procession, but Kansuke rushed without slowing his speed until he was right beside them. Then he increased his speed even more until he reached Takashima Castle.

The number of bonfires around Takashima Castle had increased. When he could see them, he came to his wits for the first time. He turned around and galloped away from the castle for about a mile and again turned back and headed slowly to Takashima Castle.

This can't be! Kansuke was possessed by one idea. His body was soaked with perspiration. No, it couldn't happen that Harunobu was trying to take Aburagawa's daughter as another concubine, disregarding the beautiful Princess Yuu! However, this was the only reason he could think of, otherwise why would the daughter of Aburagawa be going to Kai in the darkness of night?

If that was the truth, it would be unfortunate for her, but I, Kansuke, would have to take the life of that beautiful woman. I have to kill her for the sake of Princess Yuu, Katsuyori, and the Takeda!

Without knowing it, Kansuke was already at the gate of Takashima Castle. The courtyard was so filled with armored samurai standing shoulder to shoulder that they could hardly move. Countless bonfires were burning, and drums were beating constantly. When he was passing there, he thought of the twenty-eight-year-old Harunobu's young and energetic face and body and felt depressed. Is there anything that he could do to prevent any woman but Princess Yuu from approaching him! Perhaps let him be ordained into the priesthood? That would not be enough. Would there be any way to make him swear to lead an ascetic life? Kansuke was seriously thinking about such things. Up until this time, a flash of Harunobu's eager eyes and his strong and energetic body, which seemed as if it never experienced fatigue, were the subjects of Kansuke's admiration. Those were the qualities that Kansuke always felt promising and reliable in Harunobu as a lord. But now, to the contrary, he felt those were the qualities which were a nuisance and troublesome.

When Kansuke rode through the jostling crowd and came out in the square of the castle, two or three samurai clung suddenly to the bridle of his horse; and one of them said, "It is time to take the field, sir. Please go and get ready!"

"I know!" said Kansuke and slid his small body down to the ground.

"Yes, I have to dispose of that life, I have to end it with my own hands," he said so loud that people around him were shocked. In his vision, a young Lord of Echigo, Nagao Kagetora, whose face Kansuke had never seen, and the face of Aburagawa's daughter, mingled together, confusing him. Who were his immediate enemies?

Chapter 7
NAGAO KAGETORA THREATENS

IT WAS IN THE AFTERNOON on the sixteenth day when the Itagaki troop of Suwa arrived at the camp in Komuro.

The main army from Kofuchu had already placed the first flag at the bottom of the northern hill on the previous day and waited for the troops from the other allied castle towns.

As soon as Kansuke arrived at Komuro, he visited Harunobu.

"Thank you for coming. What you said at the battle of Uedahara was right."

Just the way he said it was slightly different from his usual way of speaking. The normal intensity of his voice was not there. His tone was rather hesitant, and what he said actually sounded somewhat gentle.

When Kansuke saw him, there were so many things he wanted to tell him. He wanted to accuse him for his conduct with the daughter of the Aburagawa, forgetting his responsibility toward Princess Yuu and Katsuyori.

"My lord, I must advise you that it is very important to think only of the battle for a long while."

"That is all I think of," said Harunobu without batting an eye.

"Don't you think of anything else?"

"Not at all."

"The lord Aburagawa's…" started Kansuke, and at the same time he looked up and watched Harunobu's expression intently.

"What about Aburagawa?"

"The daughter of the Lord Aburagawa Gyobu-no-kami…"

"What!?"

By his expression, it was quite obvious that he had never heard of her before.

"So! What about her?"

"You do not know her?"

"Not at all."

"You have never seen her?"

"No." Then he added nonchalantly, "What is the matter with you today, Kansuke?" and laughed. The doubt that Kansuke had harbored since that night disappeared like a mist dissipating as the sun rises. Kansuke suddenly felt great.

"What's so special about the daughter of the Aburagawa?" inquired Harunobu mildly.

"Oh no, nothing at all, I just heard something about her, that is all."

"I've often thought that I should meet the family of the Aburagawa. I think of that occasionally but have never had the time to do so. If he has a daughter, I wouldn't mind meeting her."

No, absolutely not! Kansuke thought, who knows what would happen if Harunobu had the opportunity to meet such a beautiful young woman.

"Well, we will be at war for a long while, sir," Kansuke tried to change the subject as he gazed at the capable general filled with youth and vigor.

His doubt over Aburagawa's daughter dissolved momentarily, but he looked at Harunobu as if he was watching someone new and dangerous, who he had never seen before.

"So, finally, we are warring with Nagao Kagetora. Where do we begin?" Kansuke asked Harunobu.

"How about Un-no-Daira?"

"That will be a fine location."

Kansuke felt very proud of his young lord. He was happy to hear him say Un-no-Daira without any hesitation.

Since it was a battle in the Shinano district, it was natural for him to want to attack the enemy first, but to the contrary, he was clearly trying to let *them* make the first move and then intercept them at Un-no-Daira. This proved that Harunobu had confidence in his battle ability.

In everyone's opinion, Kawanakajima[50] was the most suitable location for the battle. A battle at Kawanakajima could be decisive for either side because of its geographic formation. For Harunobu to avoid fighting at Kawanakajima proved that he was cautious. To set the battlefield at Un-no-Daira was a good choice, because it would be convenient for both, the enemy and Harunobu's forces, to retreat, if they had to.

Although preparations were already complete for the upcoming battle, Harunobu did not move his army. They spent the sixteenth, seventeenth, eighteenth, and nineteenth at Komuro doing nothing.

On the night of the eighteenth, they heard the sound of conch shells. Their plan was to begin battle as soon as they arrived at Un-no-Daira. At about the same time as the Kai army's arrival, the enemy army of Echigo was supposed to appear at the same place.

At dawn, the three samurai, Kansuke, Obata Toramori, and Hara Toratane had left camp and galloped ahead to scout the enemy. This was the first time that Harunobu had ordered three high-ranking samurai to join together on one mission. They galloped in silence, keeping about two meters' distance between their horses. Kansuke was riding in front. He knew exactly what the other two samurai were thinking. Kansuke thought that both of them must have been wondering why Harunobu had asked three of them to patrol, when one of them was sufficient to do the task. Both of them were the type to be dissatisfied for not being chosen as the sole patroller.

But Kansuke was very satisfied with the cautious way Harunobu was acting.

"Our lord has acquired the experience to face any opponent now, hasn't he?" Kansuke stopped his horse as he turned toward Toratane.

"You are right. When it comes to strategy, nobody can exceed his ability," answered Toratane. It seemed that Toratane

believed what he said. Kansuke, however, thought that he himself excelled far more when it came to strategy. But he noticed
Harunobu's caution, which had never been evident before, and
was satisfied with this improvement.

About the time that day broke, the three of them split up and
went in separate directions. Kansuke urged his horse into a gallop
and followed along the rubble of the Chikuma River where there
was no shelter. Away ahead of him, he could see the figures of
several mounted men as they appeared and disappeared in the
mist of the river. They appeared to be enemy patrols. Kansuke
casually entered into the mist with the sound of his hooves echoing on the rocks. When the mist disappeared, no one could be
seen. They must have retreated.

Kansuke climbed up the hill from the riverbank. Far, far
away he could see a black line of people and horses extending its
wings toward his position.

Kansuke halted his horse and watched with great interest. It
was the army of Nagao Kagetora [later known as Uesugi Kenshin]
which Kansuke had never seen before. It was the appearance of
the opponent, he thought, one day they had to defeat. Theirs was
a very quiet way of moving the army, compared to the way the
Kai army had done it. It was not a commonly used way of keeping
the main part of the army invisible. Kagetora had the main body
of the army marching in a dignified, grand style, in plain view of
anybody watching.

The commander-in-chief, Lord Kagetora, had to be merely
eighteen years old. He was one decade younger than Harunobu.
For a long time Kansuke watched the army which was led by this
young leader. Kansuke watched the enemy lines in elation as
they advanced ahead of him, taking the same bend as the wind-
ing river. As the current of the Chikuma River was very natural,
the army of Echigo was marching in a very natural line. It had the
same pliability and gentleness as the water.

It was the hour of the Snake when Kansuke rode back to
Harunobu. He was in a cedar grove, about 300 yards from the
beach on the Chikuma River. Harunobu had dismounted and was

sitting on a stool. Both Hara Toratane and Obata Toramori had arrived earlier, and they were sitting in front of Harunobu, waiting for Kansuke's arrival.

"Tell me what you have seen, Kansuke," Harunobu asked before Kansuke had time to say anything.

"Have you already heard from both Lords Hara and Obata?"

"I have."

"I believe then it is sufficient. They hardly make any mistakes. The number of warriors is about 6,000."

"Six thousand. That is exactly what they said," Harunobu replied.

"I am not surprised. Our enemy is advancing. They have not created any formations yet, but most likely they intend to start fighting as they are marching now. They seem to go into war in a natural sort of way, which is quite different from our previous enemies. Their structure is extremely rigid."

"Both Toratane and Toramori also agreed that they would start a battle in the same form that they march in now," Harunobu commented in satisfaction.

"I believe that I will be different from them in one way—how we should fight against such an opponent. Most likely both of them are thinking that we will attack them first seeing that we have a much larger army of 15,000 men. However, I believe that it would be beneficial for us to take a defensive strategy rather than an offensive one. If we defend for a longer period of time, our enemy with fewer warriors will be weakened eventually and then victory will be ours. If we attack them, taking advantage of our larger numbers, it will turn into a disorganized combat, and that will be our loss. Kagetora's bravery is well known. If the battle turns into a melee, he and his direct retainers will try to do combat with you and your direct retainers. Then, you will end up crossing swords with the eighteen-year-old commander-in-chief of Echigo just as you did with Murakami Yoshikiyo," said Kansuke.

A scowl came over Harunobu's face at the mention of his previous combat, but he said despite his anger, "I shall take Kansuke's suggestion." Whenever the last battle with Murakami was mentioned, he was completely under Kansuke's thumb and this was why he agreed to his suggestion.

The battle began at the hour of the Bull.[51] The Takeda's formation was shaped like the wings of a crane. The main power of the army was placed in the body of the crane and on both sides of the body, the bands spread its wings by gradually advancing slightly ahead of the main body. Oyamada[52] Masatatsu led the right wing and the left wing was led by Oyamada Nobushige. Sanada Yukitaka led the forward defence. Five hundred yards away from the main formation, on the right side, was Obu Toramasa.

Six battalions led by Baba, Naito, Hyuga, Katsunuma, Anayama, and Nobushige defended the rear of the formation. They followed like a flock of wild geese. And further back, Hara Toratane led the final rear defense with his 9,000 mounted men.

Kansuke was in the main body next to Harunobu, waiting for the start of the battle.

"Please do not think that you have to attack Kagetora today. Just learning the way Kagetora handles battle is more than sufficient," Kansuke cautioned Harunobu.

In reality, Kansuke felt that he was more excited than Harunobu. Although Kansuke was telling Harunobu to be patient, Harunobu was more composed and confident than he was at the previous battle with Murakami.

Kansuke took precautions, thinking how futile it was to get too excited. In the near future, Kagetora would have to be defeated. If we defeat him, the power of the Takeda will extend to the Sea of Japan. Harunobu will rule the main body of the mainland in its entirety.

The battle was started by the troops of both Oyamada and the forward armies of Nagao of Echigo by advancing closer and starting to fire guns.

The sound of guns lasted for only a short while. Soon war cries roared through the heavens. The troops of Oyamada

Masatatsu were dashing across the plains along the Chikuma River with spears in their hands.

"Well, what do you think?" said Harunobu.

"The troops of Oyamada will win. They will put the enemy's forward armies in retreat. But at the next line, they will most likely retreat. It presents that type of formation."

There was no other way. Both of them had perfect formations without faults. It was the type of the formation that one side will win, then in the next battle, the victory would be promised to the other.

The troops of Oyamada were pushing the forward lines of the enemy back. Perhaps because of the way the wind was blowing, the cries of battle were heard from a totally different direction: the lower current of the Chikuma River.

Eventually, as Kansuke predicted, the forward armies of the enemy could no longer resist the Oyamada troops, and their lines were routed. They retreated about two hundred yards.

The troops of the forward armies on the left wing led by Oyamada Nobushige began to fight with the left forward armies of the enemy, but his troops were pushed out and retreated gradually before them.

"It is interesting, is it not?" asked Kansuke, who was captivated by the battle. He had never seen such an interesting conflict. The troops of Oyamada Masatatsu, who had just won, would soon retreat before the enemy's new line and the enemy's left forward army would defeat the troops of the Oyamada Nobushige, but would eventually be defeated by the new allied line.

War cries thundered constantly and shook the air over the plains. The frenzied neighing of the horses echoed sorrowfully throughout the countryside.

The sunset crept over them. When the sun disappeared, the plain of Un-no-Daira was rather oppressive. The low wavy hills were covered with tall weeds, and the late autumn wind was blowing over them.

Kansuke sighed loudly. "My lord," Kansuke called. Harunobu was watching the battle intensely without answering him.

Then he turned to Kansuke and said, "A battle with no outcome as of yet, is it not?"

"Exactly, My Lord."

"How will the battle finish?"

"The army with the larger numbers will win. Obviously more of our warriors will be left."

"Humph!"

"This will be a battle with a large death toll. The enemy has 6,000 warriors and we have 15,000. So if each army loses 6,000, they will disappear, and we will be left with 9,000."

Harunobu made an expression of disgust. He obviously did not appreciate this type of battle.

"However, I don't believe that Kagetora will attempt such a thoughtless battle. The earlier he withdraws his army, the better off he is. You watch, My Lord, he will undoubtedly withdraw.

Kansuke had not even finished his sentence. The conch shell's eerie call drifted over the gloomy field of Un-no-Daira. The troops of Kai had never heard such an unusual call. When Kansuke heard this, he said quickly, "Excuse me My Lord," and lightly bowing to Harunobu, he mounted his horse. He galloped down the hill and rushed in the direction of the battlefield. In the meantime the conch shell was still echoing high and low. That must be the sign for retreat of their army. Kansuke wanted to see with his own eyes how the Echigo army would withdraw. It was not an easy task for every single warrior to retreat in the midst of a battle in which they were wielding their spears and swords frantically. This was exactly what he wanted to see.

When Kansuke's horse climbed up onto the small plateau, the sound of the conch shell stopped suddenly. Although he was still over a hundred yards from the battlefield, he held his horse right there. From the high plateau, it was more effective to simply look down on the battlefield.

At that moment Kansuke could see the two cavalry battalions start to gallop from the enemy's camp. Their skillful maneuvres were breathtaking.

Each horsemen held a baton.[53] Conducting their batons skill-fully they galloped around the battlefield forming a large half circle and then they dashed like an arrow in the direction of their headquarters at full speed. In an instant their figures were get-ting smaller and smaller, as they disappeared from sight.

One of the horsemen who was leading this maneuvre must have been the commander-in-chief, Nagao Kagetora, Kansuke thought. The one who followed him had to be the notable and brave General, Usami Suruga-no-kami. He could not think of anybody else who could lead that skillfully.

Kansuke realized the sound of the conch shell, which indi-cated the withdrawal, was also booming from the camp of the Takeda. Harunobu must have given the order. Judging from his personality, Harunobu must have been dying to attack the routed enemy; however, he must have controlled his desire and ordered the blowing of the conch shell. Knowing Harunobu so well, Kansuke was quite surprised, but that was the way to respond. We should await some other opportunity to attack Kagetora, he thought. If we attack the routed enemy, we might kill a hundred or two hundred soldiers. It would be wasting our own warriors by simply demonstrating their skill at pursuit.

Then from the headquarters of Harunobu, where Kansuke had just left, he could see several mounted men were rushing down the hill. Every one of them was bending low over his horse's neck, clinging very tightly and lifting his rear so as not to fall from the horse. Each horse dashed down the hill like a gust of wind, and at the bottom of the hill they headed in different directions and dispersed.

Two horsemen among them galloped past Kansuke with incredible speed. As both of them were bending low parallel to the horses' necks, the flags attached on their backs flapping in the wind. All of the mounted men were called "*mukade no sashimono*."[54] They belonged to the special group of samurai who were called *mukade*, a centipede, and the one sentence that could describe them was "one warrior is worth a thousand war-riors." They were chosen from a group of extremely efficient young warriors to give an absolute command to each battalion not to attack the routed enemies.

Kansuke remained there for a while, watching the retreat. War cries were still echoing, but gradually it became quieter. Now the war was ending in a strange way. The sun was still behind the clouds, and no matter where you looked, the plain was still in the shade.

From now on Harunobu would have to fight a painful war against Kagetora, which could be quite different from previous battles. It could last five years or even ten years. No matter how long it took, it would be a very good match. Harunobu was twenty-eight years old, and Kagetora was eighteen. Although there was a large age difference, both were as strong as tigers, and neither of them was stronger than the other. As long as I am with him, Harunobu will win, Kansuke thought. Then, someday the time will come that Kagetora will no longer be able to show that leadership to anyone. A few years from now, the Takeda Clan will have to take that young general's life.

Kansuke turned his horse and let it walk slowly back to camp.

The encounter between the two powers had started at the hour of the Bull and ended at the hour of the Sheep. It was an extremely short battle. In this battle, the Echigo army lost 236 warriors; the allies lost only 132 warriors. The death toll was recorded and it was the hour of the Monkey, when the victory cry was raised.

Harunobu kept silent until all the troops gathered in the new battlefield. It seemed as if the first battle with Kagetora had turned him into an extremely shrewd leader.

The Takeda army stayed on the plains of Un-no-Daira until the twenty-third. The reason for this was that the Echigo army had not retreated from the area and did not show signs of leaving.

The next day, Harunobu received several messages brought by post-horses. They were from the generals who were protecting their fortresses, and each of them notified him of their victories over the enemy in the small-scale battles at each. They were taking advantage of the large battle of the Un-no-Daira, and the troops who were protecting the castles whose masters were fighting with Takeda Harunobu also engaged in battle with the enemy in near-by areas. Of course, this was done in accordance with orders from Harunobu.

Akiyama Nobutomo, for example, was to protect the castle from the Ina, and he had a minor battle with Ina troops. He captured seventeen cavalry, twenty-five foot soldiers, and gained territory worth 3,000 kan.[55] The two generals, Amari and Tada, who were placed at Shimo Suwa and Shiojiri Guchi, reported that they attacked the clan of Ogasawara in the middle of the night and captured ninety-three Ogasawara troops. General Komiyama and General Asari, who were placed at Fuefuki Sunset Point, engaged in battle against the Uesugi army and captured thirty-three soldiers.

After all this good news was brought in, a post-horse arrived from Kofuchu on the morning of the twenty-third. The message was from a man who was in charge of the Takeda household, Yamashita Ise-no-kami. It said that in the afternoon of the nine-teenth, a fire broke out in the main part of the Takeda's mansion, but everybody worked hard to prevent it from spreading. As a result, the damage was only to a small part of the building. In addition to the report, he also mentioned that while the fire was burning, two large white eagles flew out of nowhere and perched on the roof of the mansion and stayed there for three days and three nights, even after the fire was extinguished.

Harunobu believed that it was divine protection from the Iwashimizu Hachiman Shrine in Suwa, that although his mansion was exposed to fire in his absence, it was saved from major damage in the end and those white eagles might be the incarnation of the divinity. Harunobu made everybody face in the direction of Suwa and say a prayer.

After finishing this ceremony, Harunobu called two young samurai who excelled in the art of horsemanship and made them pay a visit to his mansion at Kofuchu. Both samurai received letters from Harunobu and immediately left Un-no-Daira and headed to Kai.

Suddenly Kansuke experienced an uneasy sensation in his heart. He had no idea what had caused this sensation. Some time after the two young samurai left, Kansuke fleetingly looked up at Harunobu's face.

There was nothing suspicious about sending a letter of inquiry to Kofuchu, but why did he need to send two messengers with two letters? He felt that some unnatural plot existed there.

As soon as Kansuke left Harunobu's presence, he nonchalantly mounted his horse and chased after the two samurai who had left for Kofuchu.

After galloping for about an hour, the two small figures on horseback came into sight.

"Hey," Kansuke yelled as loud as he could and dashed after them. The two horses stop immediately. As he approached, two horsemen dismounted and waited for him.

"Let me see the letters which the Lord Harunobu handed you," Kansuke said.

"Yes, sir."

Without any hesitation, they handed over the letters, which they carried attached to their waist.

"You are going to give them to Yamashita Ise-no-kami, is that correct?"

"Yes, sir."

"Make sure you do not make any mistakes," said Kansuke while he glanced at the envelopes. One was for his legitimate wife, but the other was for somebody else. It was addressed "To the Lord Aburagawa."

As he expected! Harunobu had played the innocent saying he had never seen the daughter of Aburagawa, even that he did not know of her. The color had started to drain from Kansuke's face, but with his usual dignity, he returned the letters to them and said, "There was nothing for the lord to worry about, now you may go carefully."

The two samurai bowed to Kansuke and mounted their horses. When the sound of the horses' hooves was gone, he realized he was standing in a field of *susuki*[56] that were as high as his own waist. On his right-hand side was a mountain, and its slope was descending gently toward where Kansuke was standing in the valley.

The wind was blowing up from the valley and gently cradling the ears of susuki. Poor girl, but I have to kill her now without being seen by anyone, Kansuke thought.

I will take the life of the daughter of Aburagawa. And from now on I have to watch my lord day and night so that he will not approach any other woman. But where on earth did he meet the daughter of Aburagawa? I cannot take my eyes off of him for even one moment. He conducts an ingenious war, but obviously it is not only in wars that he plays ingeniously. Kansuke recalled Harunobu's face on the day they set up camp at Komuro. That day, Harunobu betrayed Kansuke with a face so innocent that he looked as if he could not kill even an insect. Nevertheless, he thought, how can I get rid of that girl?

Kansuke started to walk in the fields of susuki, pulling his horse along by its bridle. This was much more difficult than the battles. It was my mistake that I mentioned the name of Aburagawa's daughter to Harunobu that day. If I kill her, he will know right away that I did it. No matter how skillfully I do it, suspicion will be placed on me. He was more intent on arranging his strategy in this minor court intrigue than in any other battle he had faced before.

The next morning, they received news that the army of the Uesugi was withdrawing to Echigo and vacating the camp at Kawanakajima. Therefore, Harunobu decided to return with his army to Kofuchu. Even though, the battle of Un-no-Daira did not go any further than the first small skirmish, its impact was still great. Before this battle, the powerful lords in northern Shinano, such as Nishina, Un-no, Urano, and others, were not quite sure with whom they should be allied, but now every one of them sent hostages to Harunobu and became subservient to him.

Harunobu issued the order of withdrawal and headed to

Kofuchu on the twenty-fifth. Kansuke placed himself alongside Harunobu in the main army and joined the triumphant procession. Sixteen thousand warriors formed a long procession and headed north into the fields and mountains of Shinano in the early winter.

Since Kansuke was heading towards the Suwa with Itagaki's troops, he had to leave Harunobu half way through. It was three days after they left Un-no-Daira.

"Soon I shall visit you in Kofuchu," Kansuke said to Harunobu.

"I am looking forward to seeing you. Next time when we meet, I would like to hear your opinion in detail on the strategy of Nagao Kagetora," said Harunobu cheerfully.

Kansuke, along with the Itagaki troops, departed from the troops that were heading to Kai in the mountainous area.

About one hour after Kansuke had left the main army, he told Itagaki that he forgot to mention an important fact to Harunobu; therefore he had to catch up to the main army.

"Should I give you several warriors to accompany you?" asked Nobusato, but Kansuke refused his offer politely.

"Oh, no. I think it is better being alone. But please make sure to look after Princess Yuu when you get back."

Immediately after saying this, Kansuke left the procession of Suwa troops. It was at the foot of a small oak forest where the brown leaves were rustling in the blowing wind.

When he was alone, he dropped the heavy things he was wearing or carrying in the underbrush. He had to sprint on his horse to Kofuchu. He had to enter the castle town of Kofuchu at least one full day before Harunobu's main army arrived. His intent was to take the life of the daughter of Aburagawa Gyobu-no-kami.

Kansuke avoided the main road as he galloped along on his horse. It was a narrow road at the foot of many small mountains. Kansuke did not meet a single person until sunset. He kept galloping on his horse, kicking up the dead leaves. When he was about to reach the highland where the land almost seemed to be leaning toward the south, the darkness of winter was ready to swallow him.

While he was galloping, he heard the sound of horses hooves from afar, which differed from the sound of his own horse. He dismounted from his horse and hid himself using his horse as a shield. Soon, he saw three horsemen riding like a gale of wind not even three yards away from his horse. It was quite clear who one of the horsemen was. He had a unique style of riding. He was leaning forward and touching his face to the right side of the horse's neck. Nobody rode a horse like that but Harunobu. It had to be Harunobu. But it was unbelievable that the commander-in-chief of the army of 16,000 was taking such an independent action. It could not be done!

But he was in no doubt that the rider was Harunobu. Harunobu was also trying to get into the castle town of Kofuchu ahead of his own army. Kansuke thought this young general might have sensed Kansuke's intention. Kansuke thought for a while and then decided to take a different road. No matter what, Kansuke had to reach Kofuchu ahead of those three horsemen, otherwise Harunobu would hide the daughter of the Aburagawa someplace where Kansuke would not find her.

Knowing Harunobu, Kansuke was afraid that he would do anything to succeed. Kansuke always felt that it was worthwhile risking his life for his master, but his lord was also a very trouble-some person. Kansuke mounted his horse. Then, for the first time he noticed that crickets were making soothing noises all over the large field.

Chapter 8
PRINCESS OGOTO

IT WAS DAWN when Kansuke entered the castle town of Kofuchu, after sprinting through the fields day and night. The entire area was still asleep.

He went through the lower part of the town, where the artisans and merchants lived, and entered the samurai residential area. In the center of the area, there was a wide street going upwards with a gentle slope. At the end of this central street was Takeda's mansion that had survived many generations.

Kansuke took a side street alongside the moat of the mansion and kept his horse at a slow gallop until he reached the rear of the mansion higher up on the hill. From the top of the hill, the cold wind of early morning was blowing right into his face. As the slope steepened, his horse slowed noticeably. It was laboring every step of the way and breathing heavily. No wonder, Kansuke thought, he had forced his horse to gallop all the way from Shinano to Kai, hardly feeding or resting him at all.

Kansuke appeared on the foothills of Mt. Yogai, the summit of which had fortifications, and he kept climbing up the mountain. Halfway up the mountain, there was a small temple called Sekisui Temple, built as if it was to be intentionally hidden in the dense forest. Kansuke suspected that it had to be near here where the daughter of Aburagawa Gyobu-no-kami was sheltered. Harunobu had ridden his horse day and night over these foothills. He had always done so since his childhood. There was no reason for anybody to feel suspicious whenever he rode here. Since this area was opposite the castle town, even if he secretly left his mansion at night, nobody would have noticed. Kansuke suspected that there had to be new construction within the compound of the temple. The new building would have been recently completed so that Harunobu could send for the beautiful princess.

Kansuke's guess was correct. Not at the entrance of the Sekisui Temple, but opposite it, further up the mountain there was a brand-new gate suggesting a back entrance to the temple. Kansuke had ridden around here several times previously but did not think he had seen a gate at that time. There was no reason for such a gate here.

Kansuke dismounted. The sound of rapids could be heard nearby. Kansuke pulled his horse to the forest opposite the Sekisui Temple and walked down in the direction of the sound of the rapids. The rapids were quite narrow, but the rushing water, which ran down a steep slope, was pounding onto the rocks. It was the upper stream of the Ai River. There, Kansuke let his horse quench his thirst. He then tied his horse to a tree along the rapids. He looked to the east and saw the sun beginning to rise and break up the greyness of the early morning.

Again, he returned to the back gate of the Sekisui Temple and pushed on the gate. It was bolted tightly from inside. Reaching to the top of the mud wall, Kansuke quickly climbed over. Jumping to the ground, he slipped stealthily through the compound of the temple and came out at an attached building connected by a small corridor to the main residence of the monks. He circled the attached building once. Avoiding the small entrance to the building, he stood in front of the open veranda.

Kansuke knocked twice at the door lightly and called out in a low voice, "Princess."

There was no answer from within. He knocked twice at the door again.

"Princess."

Then he sensed somebody was getting up. He heard the rustling of a silk kimono. After a while, he heard a very clear voice saying, "*Jiiya?*"[57]

Kansuke did not answer.

"Jiiya?" with the voice, the door slid open smoothly from the inside.

"It is I, Princess." Kansuke said kneeling down to the ground.

"Ah!?" she gave a startled cry and said, "How careless of me, I thought it was Jiiya!"

He lifted his face and looked at the princess. It was unmistakably the daughter of Aburagawa Gyobu-no-kami. She must have felt the air of the dawn cold, because she placed one side of her kimono over the other, holding it tightly in the front with her delicate hands. She had a full and round face. Her black eyes were large.

"It is I," Kansuke repeated.

"I don't think I know you at all. Are you a messenger from the lord?"

"Yes, Princess. It is an urgent message."

"Oh, I am sorry to put you to so much trouble, I shall wake somebody up. You can come inside from the front entrance since it is very cold."

Kansuke was planning to slash her throat right there at once. There were ample openings if he wanted to. But he couldn't. That was because his opponent did not have the slightest bit of mistrust toward him. She was almost unthinkingly naive.

"No, I would rather talk here. Please do not wake anybody," Kansuke said in a hoarse subdued voice.

"All right, then I won't bother waking anybody up," said the princess. Kansuke's hand slowly crawled to the haft of his sword. Then, suddenly, he heard the cry of a child.

"It seems the princess is awake. She has been colicky lately and she was crying all night."

"Pardon me?"

Kansuke was taken aback. He never even dreamt that there had been a child by the princess and Harunobu.

"When was she born?" Kansuke asked.

"The one who is crying now is the older one."

"I beg your pardon!!" He could hardly believe what he had

just heard. "Older one? That means…"

"Yes, the older was born last spring, and the younger one was born this summer, so we named them Princess Haru[58] and Princess Natsu.[59]

He could not believe that this princess who was standing in front of him was the mother of two children.

"Are they really your children?" Kansuke asked in astonishment.

She laughed and said, "You say funny things, Jiiya."

In no time, Kansuke had become an old servant for her. Since the dawn was still grey, she probably had not seen his face clearly. Therefore, she must have sensed by his way of talking and moving that he was an old man.

"As I am cold, I would like to close the door. Would you please go to the other door, since I think the cold air is not good for my unborn child."

Now this was the third blow that caused Kansuke to lose his presence of mind.

"Unborn child?!"

"This time I have to give birth to a male child, you know. Therefore, I have to look after myself."

"All right, in that case I shall come in the other entrance."

Kansuke was drawn away totally from his intention to assassinate her, and he was somehow exhausted. There was no way he could bring himself to murder this beautiful young women.

Kansuke did not know what to think of Harunobu. He made Aburagawa's daughter produce two children, and she was pregnant with another. He had kept such a reckless secret from Kansuke and Princess Yuu.

He had to wait at the entrance hall for a while, and then a maid took him inside. He sat on the wooden floor at the entrance of the room. The princess appeared in the room and sat facing Kansuke.

"Oh, for heaven's sake, what did you do to your face?" the princess asked candidly with surprise when she saw Kansuke's face for the first time. "Does it hurt?"

"No, it does not hurt. Yes, I was injured several times, but all the injuries are healed. I was born this way, for the most part."

"You were born that way? Oh, how sad!" she frowned in her distress and added, "Oh, I am so sorry to hear that you were born that way."

"Princess, you were born beautiful, and I was born ugly," Kansuke said gently and calmly. Strangely, no matter what she said, it did not seem to disturb him at all. It was like a punishment of being beaten with a flower petal and it was not accompanied with any pain at all. "Princess!" Kansuke lifted his face and said sternly, "Please make everyone leave the room."

The princess called out to the next room, "I wish all of you to leave the house for a while." Again, the princess revealed her qualities of total trust.

When the two young maids were about to leave the room, Kansuke said, "Leave the door and sliding inner doors open."

From the veranda where the doors were wide open, the white light of the morning was coming into the room. The *shoji* [60] was beginning to look white also. Kansuke made sure that no one was hiding in the three other rooms. When he was quite sure that they were alone, he opened his mouth and whispered, "You told me that you were pregnant. Would you like a prince this time?"

"Since the two older ones are princesses, I wish I could have a prince this time."

"You will suffer a lot if you have a prince."

"Why so?"

"His legitimate wife, Sanjo, has two sons. Prince Yoshinobu and Ryuho."

"Yes, I realize that, but..." The princess lifted her head slightly and hesitated for a while, then said, "But I intend to have a strong son. A son who will be able to carry the name of the Takeda family."

"I see."

"My lord also told me that he really wanted at least one strong son."

"But, he has one strong son," said Kansuke bluntly. "Do you know anything about Princess Yuu?"

"No." She was visibly shocked by his question.

"Princess Yuu has already produced a son, named Prince Katsuyori; he will be the strongest warrior in all of Japan.

"No, it can't be!" she said in exasperation. "Who is Princess Yuu?"

"She is a daughter of the late Lord of Suwa." He was determined to tell her everything, taking this opportunity, although he felt it was cruel. "Right now, she lives in the Kan-non-in Temple in Suwa. You are probably the only one who does not know about her."

"Oh, no." Then she asked him, her face pale, "Is she more beautiful than I?"

Kansuke did not know how to answer this question.

"It is hard to tell who is more beautiful. Both of you are very lovely."

"Is she that beautiful? But my lord said that I am the most beautiful woman in the world."

"Yes, you are beautiful. But Princess Yuu is just as beautiful as you are."

She suddenly bent her body and flung herself on the floor. Her body was writhing in agony.

"Will you hate your lord, Princess?"

In answer to his question the princess shook her head from side to side. She was not crying.

"Why do you not hate him?"

The princess lifted her head. With a blank expression on her face she said, "Because I love him."

"Even if you love him so…"

"Yes, I am the one who loves him more than anybody else. I was well aware of the existence of his wife, Sanjo. Although I knew that if I had his children, that might cause some problem within the Takeda family, I still wanted them. Now I have learned that my lord has another woman whom I was not aware of. But that will not change the way I love him. I realize that I have to suffer tremendously from now on. But it was entirely my fault; I cannot do anything but feel sad.

Her beautiful white face was expressionless, much like a Noh[61] mask.

"Do you realize why I am here?" asked Kansuke.

"No, I don't. But I feel something negative and fearful."

"I came here to take your life."

Kansuke expected her to be shocked, but she was not.

"I somehow sensed that."

"Then why were you not more cautious?"

"Because I felt that if it were the wish of my lord, I was willing to give up my life for him."

Women possess strange feelings, Kansuke thought. That type of self-sacrifice was something which Kansuke himself could not even dream of.

"This has nothing to do with your lord. I came to take your life of my own choice without your lord even knowing."

"Then why did you not kill me?"

For the first time, her tone was fiery. Her beautiful eyes were staring at Kansuke's face.

"Because I felt all of you, your two princesses, the child in your body, they will all be an important asset for the Takeda family. All of your children will be good brothers and sisters for the son of Princess Yuu, Katsuyori."

"I am not sure about that. They might cause some problems for the peace of the Takeda family."

"No, if the children were brought up by you, I believe they will be the treasures of the Takeda family. I am very certain of that," then Kansuke added, "I am the one whose name is Yamamoto Kansuke."

"I know. When you came into this room, I thought you must be."

"From now on, I shall help you. I shall protect all of you, the princesses and the child in your body, with all my life. No matter how much you suffer and feel sad, you must suffer for the future of this house. You have to realize one thing, though; since Prince Katsuyori was born one year before your son, you have to recognize him as your son's elder brother.

The princess looked at Kansuke, sadness creeping into her eyes.

"If you can accept that, I shall protect him."

The princess kept silent for a while, and then she said in a low voice, "As you wish," and bowed lightly.

"I'd prefer it if you do not mention to your lord that I was here. For the time being at least."

"I understand."

"I have one more request; please do not…" he wanted to tell her not to chop Harunobu's head off while he was asleep, but he felt it was unnecessary advice to this princess. "Please do not hate your lord. It is… it is his body that has a problem. I have to do something about it."

"To hate my lord…" though her expression was sorrowful, it was far from showing hatred.

"Excuse me, but what is your name, Princess?"

"My name is Ogoto," she said.

"Princess Ogoto. It is such a beautiful name."

Kansuke stayed in her detached residence for about an hour and then excused himself from Princess Ogoto's secret house.

On his way back, his horse did not gallop. Princess Ogoto did not show her feelings very much in front of Kansuke, but after all she was a woman. Kansuke thought she could be a very difficult person to handle at times. But it would be with Princess Yuu that Kansuke would face a more difficult challenge. If she learned about this, she would not leave Harunobu or Princess Ogoto alive, knowing her temper. But someday she will find out about Princess Ogoto, somehow. It would be better for Kansuke to tell her at the right time to avoid an undue shock.

Now Kansuke was in the position of protecting two princesses from Harunobu's legitimate wife, Sanjo-no-Uji. But Kansuke did not think that that was much of a burden. If he could steer the situation into an advantageous position for Prince Katsuyori by showing Princess Ogoto how to bring up her children, it should work out well for the young prince.

He stopped at a farmer's house and filled his stomach, then returned the same way he came.

His horse galloped for seven miles without any rest and entered the village of Nirasaki. When he came to the other side of the village, he saw three horses resting on the big bank of the Kanna River. He could not see their riders anywhere. They must have gone to have something to eat. He rode his horse in the opposite direction, away from the bank. He knew it would be a detour, but Kansuke simply did not want to see Harunobu here. Someday, Kansuke would have to have a very meaningful talk with Harunobu and somehow deal with his lust.

From Nirasaki to Takashima Castle was about thirty-two miles. Kansuke kept his horse at a gallop, without any rest, for the duration of the journey.

He was anxious to see Princess Yuu and her son Katsuyori. Besides, he had to direct the army of Takashima Castle that had just come back from Un-no-Daira to go to the district of Takato before they took off their armor. Kansuke was determined to make these areas part of the Takeda's territory.

And once they won the Takato district, he thought about placing Princess Yuu and Katsuyori there.

There were many small-scale battles from the fall of the seventeenth year of Tenbun to early in the eighteenth year. Before they met Nagao Kagetora of Echigo again, they had to clean out all of the Takeda's enemies from the Shinshu district. Kansuke attended many of the small battles throughout Ina, Kiso, and Matsumoto and anticipated the stabilization of the power of the Takeda in these areas.

In early August, Kansuke had the opportunity to spend several days of freedom and rest without armor. At this time, a messenger was sent from Princess Yuu to Kansuke asking for an urgent visit to the Kan-non-in Temple. Kansuke had not seen Princess Yuu for about three months, so he quickly took his horse and hurried to the mansion of Princess Yuu.

When he placed one foot in the gate of the Kan-non-in Temple, Kansuke sensed a somewhat different atmosphere from the usual. Kansuke went straight to the next room, Princess Yuu's living room, and sat there.

"Princess!" he called.

"Please come in."

With that, Kansuke opened the shoji. Princess Yuu was sitting there with a pale face, and her bedding was behind her. As soon as she saw Kansuke's face, she said, "Can you look me directly in the face?"

Her voice was trembling.

"I beg your pardon?" answered Kansuke, unconsciously casting his eyes down. Kansuke kept no secrets from Princess Yuu, except for the matter of Princess Ogoto. And he believed that there was no way that Princess Yuu could get any information about her. Never mind Princess Yuu, there were very few people at all who knew anything about Princess Ogoto.

"Can you look straight into my eyes, Kansuke? Answer me!"

Kansuke did not answer her, but looked straight into her eyes.

"I cannot tell whether you are looking at me or not with those eyes of yours," Princess Yuu said crossly and continued, "Are you aware of the fact that my lord has a concubine whose name is Ogoto and she delivered a male child in Kofuchu about a month ago?"

It was the first time that Kansuke had heard of this occurrence. Although Ogoto was nearing the delivery of her child, he had not had the time to visit her in Kofuchu because of the constant battles.

"I was not aware of this fact."

"What does it mean? Does that mean you have heard about the birth of the baby for the first time?"

"Yes, that is what it means."

"Then, I shall ask you whether or not you knew that Ogoto was going to deliver a baby? Now tell me the truth. If you tell me a lie, I will never forgive you."

Kansuke stared at her in silence, a slight fear in his eyes.

"Do you know a woman whose name is Ogoto?"

As long as she knew her name, Kansuke felt it was no use hiding the fact. However, he could not figure out from where the information had leaked. It was strange and also uncanny. Kansuke said decidedly, "Yes, I have seen Princess Ogoto."

"Why did you keep that secret from me?" Princess Yuu met Kansuke's silence with another question, "Can you tell me why?"

"I am more interested in who told you about her."

"It was my lord who told me."

He held his breath for a few seconds in surprise.

"Lord Harunobu actually told you such a thing…."

"Do you think he would not tell me such a thing?"

Princess Yuu did not change her expression at all. Then with a cold smile on her lips, she said, "I pried it out of my lord, the same way that I pried it from you now."

Kansuke kept silent. All of a sudden, he was cautious about what to say.

"My lord is more honest than you are, Kansuke. He also told me about you visiting her hiding place in Sekisui Temple."

"Ohooo," Kansuke groaned. "My lord knew about it!"

"That is not my problem."

"How did you know about Princess Ogoto?"

"Would you like to know?" Suddenly Princess Yuu's body was magnified in front of his eyes. At least, Kansuke felt that way. "You would not even dream how I learned about it. It was the smell of incense. I have heard that his wife (Sanjo-no-Uji) did not like incense. In spite of that I often smelled strong incense."

"Well, well." Kansuke was speechless.

"I simply sent somebody to Kofuchu and had him follow the trail of the smell of incense."

Kansuke had never felt this much fear in front of Princess Yuu before.

"Kansuke!"

"Yes."

"I have a request to make of you. Please bring Princess Ogoto here."

"If I do bring her, then what will you do?"

"I have not thought about it yet. I will think about it then. I just want you to bring her here."

Kansuke kept silent again for a long time.

"If you do not do what I ask you to, I will do it myself."

Kansuke believed that she would. She was the type who would accomplish what she wanted to regardless of how hard it was.

"I understand. I will bring her here," Kansuke answered.

"When will you bring her?"

"Well."

"I will allow you one month," she snapped.

"I understand," he said it again.

That day, after he left Kan-non-in Temple, he stayed overnight at Takashima Castle and left for Kofuchu in the morning to see Harunobu. Once he reached this point, there was no other way but to discuss it with Harunobu, who was solely responsible for the whole thing. He had to decide what to do. Kansuke was going to take this opportunity to advise him to control his lust.

As soon as he had arrived at Kofuchu, he went to Harunobu's mansion to see him.

Harunobu was unusually happy.

"You must realize what I am here for, My lord," said Kansuke sullenly.

"It must be about when we should fight Kagetora."

"Not at all."

"Then what?"

"I think you know. Because this whole thing was caused by you."

"I don't know what you are talking about."

"It is about Princess Yuu and Princess Ogoto."

"You knew it!" said Harunobu, surprised. He suddenly looked embarrassed, "That is not good, is it?"

"It is not a joke, My lord. Don't you realize that I am in trouble?"

"I don't know anything about your trouble. How did you learn about it? What can I do?" said Harunobu.

"What could you do about it? You told her yourself. I was totally beaten by Princess Yuu because of it."

"Oh no. There must be some mistake. I never said anything to Princess Yuu."

"But when she tried to pry it out of you, she said that you told her everything."

"Do you think I am stupid!" said Harunobu. And in his expression Kansuke detected no deceit.

"She must have tricked you, Kansuke."

"I don't think so, but…" Kansuke started to feel helpless. "Are you sure, My Lord, that you did not tell her anything?"

"There are things you should say and things you should not say. I believe I know the difference."

"Well, then that was my mistake," Kansuke said uncontrollably, "But she even knew the fact that I visited Princess Ogoto."

"You did!?"

"Yes."

"When did you visit her and why?"

"Are you sure you knew nothing about it?"

"No, I didn't know anything about it."

"Well, I am in trouble."

"It is I who is in trouble," said Harunobu.

"Princess Yuu ordered me to bring Princess Ogoto to her."

"Well, that is between you and Princess Yuu. Don't involve me in that." Harunobu laughed aloud then added, "Tell her that I have returned Ogoto to the House of Aburagawa in Shinshu.[62] It is as simple as that." Harunobu laughed again.

Kansuke was having a hard time trying to figure out what was the truth and what was a lie, but there was nothing else he could do but trust Harunobu in the interim.

"Tell her so; then you will be saved from immediate trouble."

Somehow the tables had turned on Kansuke and Harunobu actually was helping Kansuke instead of Kansuke helping Harunobu. Kansuke was going to question him about Princess Ogoto and lecture Harunobu about his behavior in the future. But he was given no opportunity to do so.

"Once we decide to return Princess Ogoto to Shinano, I have to ask you to keep her three children, Kansuke, since I don't know anybody but you who can look after her children."

"Yes, I will take care of her children."

"Tomorrow you leave here with the three children."

That day, Kansuke left Harunobu's mansion wholly confused and bewildered.

The next day, when he went to the castle again, three palanquins waited at the gate. The two little princesses and the newborn baby were each held in the arms of the three maids who were sitting in the palanquins. Kansuke left Kofuchu along with twenty samurai to guard his charges. The strong sun of midsummer was beating upon the palanquins with its full strength. Kansuke once went to Suwa guarding the palanquin with Princess Yuu in it, and now he was going to Suwa again with the children of a different mother.

When he thought about it, he had difficulty in understanding why he went to Kofuchu. Without having any opportunity to deliver his advice to Harunobu, Kansuke ended up straightening out the aftermath of Harunobu's affair. When it came to capturing a castle or fighting a battle, he could see things so clearly, as if a morning mist was dissipating in the sunrise, but when it came to the problems of men and women, he could not see a thing in front of him.

The only thing he could think of was that he had to capture four castles. Suwa was for Katsuyori, the castle in Takato was for the baby cradled in the palanquin, or possibly even the other way around. And, the princesses were also entitled to castles. Oh, I am going to be so busy. While he was thinking about these things, a post-horse passed Kansuke's group from behind, making a loud clattering sound of horse's hooves echo around the area. Soon a second post-horse passed by. When a third one appeared, Kansuke brought his horse right next to it and galloped beside it.

He yelled at the messenger, "What's happening?"

"Nagao Kagetora is about to invade northern Shinano. Lord Takeda is leaving Kofuchu tonight."

"All right, go!" said Kansuke and dropped back. The body of the post-horse was shining with sweat, as if someone had poured a bucket of water over it. The horse and rider quickly disappeared from sight.

Kansuke trembled briefly. But it won't be a big battle, Kansuke thought, since Kagetora's army would be weak in the hot summer. Unlike a few minutes ago, his brain was clearing up as he thought of an impending war.

Chapter 9
RENOUNCE THE WORLD

FROM THE EIGHTEENTH to the nineteenth year of Tenbun, the Takeda army had been in constant battles from which they did not even have time to rest their horses or themselves. They took a stand against Nagao Kagetora several times in northern Shinano district, but these skirmishes never turned out to be big wars. Most of the time, Kagetora withdrew his army at an opportune time. The way he retreated with his army was always enviably skillful and beautiful to observe.

In the eighteenth year, when both armies confronted each other on the plains of Un-no-Daira, a messenger was sent from Kagetora, bringing a letter to Harunobu. It said:

> The reason why I send my army to the land of northern Shinano all the way from Echigo is not because of my ambition to conquer your territory but because I was asked to by Murakami Yoshikiyo. Therefore I am obligated to challenge you simply to maintain the way of the samurai. But if you will accept Murakami Yoshikiyo, whom you drove away from Shinano and let him live in northern Shinano, I will never invade this land.[63]

In response to this letter, Harunobu promptly took out his writing brush, without even consulting Kansuke, and wrote:

> It is out of the question to invite Murakami Yoshikiyo back to the land of northern Shinano, and I will never do it as long as I live. Therefore, I must reject your proposal. If you would like to fight us, we are ready anytime.

After he finished writing this letter, he called Kansuke and handed it to him to read. Kansuke said after reading it, "This is fine except that I would like to suggest you add one more line after 'If you would like to fight us' to include 'I would like you to be the one to wage the war.'"

"Why?" Harunobu asked with a tone of dissatisfaction.

"It is better not to provoke Kagetora at this moment. It is important to give him the impression that we have no intention of fighting against him. You should repeatedly emphasize this point."

"We don't have enough power to fight against him, you mean?"

"No, I don't mean that at all. We do have enough power to defeat Kagetora right now. But when we defeat him, most of the Takeda generals will be killed in the battle. What I am afraid of is the aftermath. We should try not to provoke him now, but we should stabilize the entire Shinano district, meaning we should conquer Kiso[64] so that we have nothing to regret after the war; then we can challenge Kagetora and attempt to win a great battle, something which we have never before attempted."

"When will that be?"

"I am not certain yet."

Harunobu laughed and said, "Kansuke, are you going to live forever?"

"Me?" Before he was aware of it, Kansuke had passed sixty years of age. Since he had begun service for Harunobu, six years of warfare had transpired.

"I cannot die until I achieve three things."

"Three things?"

"One, a decisive battle with Nagao Kagetora. I would like to present to you his head. Though I do not know when this will be, I am looking forward to this opportunity."

"What is the second thing?"

"The second thing is the first campaign of the young prince of Suwa."

He lowered his voice when he said this. They were dangerous words to be said if anybody overheard him. The young prince of Suwa was, needless to say, Princess Yuu's son, Katsuyori. To this, Harunobu said nothing. He only looked far away.

"And number three?"

"The third, well, it is difficult to say," said Kansuke rather suggestively.

Then Harunobu started to laugh. "I know. I know what you mean. You have to wait at least two or three years for that."

"Two or three years are too long. It is necessary for you to make up your mind much earlier."

The third thing Kansuke wanted to accomplish was to make Harunobu renounce the world and become a priest.[65] Every time Kansuke saw Harunobu, he requested this of him. Kansuke's point was that he would also renounce the secular world and shave his head. Therefore, Harunobu should do the same.

This was not really a fair bargain. There was a significant difference between Harunobu, who had just passed thirty, shaving his head and Kansuke, who had just passed his sixtieth year, shaving his head and renouncing the world.

Harunobu resisted this request with excuses of many kinds and did not listen to Kansuke. But he could not flatly refuse, since he had been letting Kansuke look after Princes's Yuu, Princess Ogoto, and their total of four children.

Although Kansuke said that he could not die unless he accomplished these three things, he actually had one more thing which he had to achieve before he died. Of course he had never mentioned this to anyone nor was this the kind of thing he could tell anyone. The only other thing he wanted to do before dying was to dispose of Harunobu's legitimate son, Yoshinobu. As long as Yoshinobu was to inherit the Takeda family, Katsuyori would have no future.

Kansuke did not like either Yoshinobu or the faction that supported him. This faction around him was the type that would disappear like the mist if Yoshinobu were no longer the heir. It was a strange group, motivated by his position in society.

The first goal to make Harunobu renounce the secular world; the second, to eliminate the legitimate son, Yoshinobu;

then let Katsuyori performs glorious deeds at his first campaign. And, when he had accomplished every one of them, then he would kill Kagetora. Kansuke had no idea which would come first, killing Kagetora or the first campaign of Katsuyori. But Kansuke knew one thing: destroying Kagetora was not as easy a task as Harunobu thought it was.

This was why Kansuke always tried to make sure that the two commanders-in-chief didn't face each other in straight-out battle. The war between Harunobu and Kagetora had to be postponed until the day that the Takeda's power reached the peak of its strength.

In the nineteenth year of Tenbun, when Kagetora set up his battle camp at Mt. Zenkoji, Kansuke detained Harunobu, who was eager to start fighting, by forcing him to write a letter to Kagetora and sending it through a messenger. The contents of the letter were as follows.

> When we do not have any personal grudge, it seems to be a waste of effort to stand and face each other on the battlefield. What are your thoughts on the matter? If someone tries to invade my country, Kai, I shall have no hesitation in waging an unprecedented war, no matter who attacks me, but I have no intention to force you into a war.

One day after the messenger had left Harunobu's camp, at the hour of the Bull, Kagetora broke his camp promptly and sent his army back to Echigo.

Kansuke was apprehensive about this type of conduct by the young Kagetora. This was not the conduct of a twenty-year-old commander-in-chief. It looked as if he were trying to agitate Harunobu by setting up camp in northern Shinano so many times, to taunt Harunobu so that he had no choice but to bring out his army to protect his land. Thus, Kagetora was waiting for the most suitable opportunity to wage a war.

In January, in the twentieth year of Tenbun, Kansuke visited Kannon-in Temple after being invited by Princess Yuu. It had been a year and a half since she had questioned and embarrassed him about Princess Ogoto in the summer of the eighteenth year. She had never asked about Princess Ogoto since then. Taking advantage of this fact, Kansuke never brought up the subject of the other princess in front of Princess Yuu.

But this time, Princess Yuu brought the subject up. "How are Princesses Natsu and Haru and Prince Nobumori doing? Are they all healthy?"

"Yes, they are doing fine," Kansuke answered. He did not dare tell Princess Yuu that he was looking after the three children of Ogoto, but he figured by now that Princess Yuu must have heard about it, so he was not particularly surprised when she mentioned it to him.

"Could you give Katsuyori a chance to meet them formally sometime? Since you mentioned that they will be good friends for Katsuyori, I would like to see it happen."

Kansuke had no objection to this, but he felt a little uneasy because of the expression on her face and the way she said it. Kansuke was right in his judgment, because she continued, "I have suffered tremendously for a year. I have had enough suffering; I will no longer endure it. In the past I often thought of chopping my lord's head off, but I no longer think that way."

Kansuke lifted his face up and looked at Princess Yuu, but he did not understand what was in her mind.

"I am quite certain that Princess Ogoto is feeling the same way," said the Princess.

"Yes," said Kansuke, feeling as if she were accusing him of this.

"Therefore," Princess Yuu continued, "both Princess Ogoto and I have decided to retire from the position of the lord's concubine. And I am thinking of living with Princess Ogoto peacefully here at Kan-non-in Temple."

"What does Princess Ogoto think of this idea."

"I have already sent a messenger to her and received her agreement."

"What?!" Her statements often shocked him, and this was no exception.

"Did you send a messenger to the Aburagawa family?"

"The Aburagawa family?"

Princess Yuu laughed a little with a strained voice.

"Kansuke, did you really believe that Princess Ogoto has been returned to her family?"

"Yes, I did believe she had."

"You are very naive, Kansuke!"

She laughed again, then stopped suddenly and said, "It really does not matter. But I would like you to tell Lord Harunobu of our decision."

"Yes, Princess."

There was no other way for Kansuke to answer. He did not understand the situation very well. However, he was amazed at how Princess Yuu had received all this information secluded in the Kan-non-in Temple.

"So you are going to live together here?"

"Yes, we plan to."

"It must be difficult." Kansuke felt that the two princesses living together was not something he was looking forward to.

"You do not have to worry about us, because both of us are going to be nuns."

"What!?"

"Yes, we have decided."

"Why? What made you decide on such a drastic change, so suddenly?"

"My lord has been wrapped up with the idea of conquering Kiso. You probably would not understand why he is so much involved in this idea."

"That is because I suggested that he should do so."

"Yes, you are right, but the lord has something else in mind," she said implicitly. After a few minutes silence, she continued, "I have heard that there is an exceptionally beautiful woman who is a cousin of the Lord of Kiso's wife."

"There might be such a lady, but what does that have to do with Lord Harunobu?"

"His main target is not Kiso, but this woman."

"It cannot be," said Kansuke. But then, knowing Harunobu, he could not deny her idea totally. When he thought of it now in this new light, there was definitely a different enthusiasm in Harunobu's way of handling this battle from his previous approach to conquering other fiefdoms.

Despite his realization of the truth, Kansuke still refuted the idea to Princess Yuu, "I know Lord Harunobu very well. As far as the Kiso invasion, I believe it is...."

"A groundless suspicion, wouldn't you say?"

"I do not say groundless, but I think you are simply worrying too much."

Without commenting on this, she said, "Well, what did he do when my father lost his territory? You are very well aware of the circumstances of that time. So, I presume you are going to go to Kiso to pick up another woman for the lord? You must be very busy!"

Kansuke was speechless when she referred to her own experience.

"Anyway, I shall talk to the Lord Harunobu about this. But no matter what you do, you should not trifle with the idea of becoming a nun." Kansuke was afraid that if both Princess Yuu and Ogoto became nuns, Harunobu would, no doubt, look for a new concubine.

"All right, in that case, the choice is his, either he will stop his invasion of Kiso or we will become nuns."

"To stop invading Kiso, that..."

"Cannot be done?"

To take over Kiso was an urgent necessity for the benefit of the Takeda Clan. It was unthinkable to stop the invasion.

"I shall discuss it with Lord Harunobu," Kansuke answered.

The next day, Kansuke went to Kofuchu to meet with his master. He thought he would suggest to him to renounce the world and become a priest. Harunobu had to shave his head and commit to vows of chastity so that Princess Yuu would no longer doubt his conduct; then he could keep on invading Kiso. There was no other way, Kansuke thought.

It was in the dying hours of the afternoon when Kansuke met Harunobu. He asked to have a private talk with him.

"My Lord, I have something that I must ask of you," said Kansuke. He was going to get to the point and get it over with quickly.

"Where did you hide Princess Ogoto?"

Harunobu's face showed an expression of impatience, but he answered strongly, yet indifferently, "She is still at the Sekisui Temple."

"You told me that you returned her to her home in Shinano. I remember that clearly, but that was a lie, then, was it not?"

"Well, I was going to send her back, but Ogoto refused to go so she is still there."

"All right, that is fine. But Princess Yuu knows about it, and she has made a decision to become a nun along with Princess Ogoto."

"Hmmm."

"What are you going to do about it?"

"Well, it is troublesome, isn't it?"

"What would the people of the other fiefdoms say if they heard that two of your princesses became nuns?" Kansuke continued without softening his expression. "There is no other way but for you to become a priest and renounce the world. If you do that, the princesses would not come out with such a distasteful idea."

"A distasteful idea?"

Kansuke did not explain it right away.

"What is this abhorrent idea?"

"It is not only these princesses of yours. It is necessary for you to renounce the world to free yourself from public suspicion…"

"What is this public suspicion?"

"The general public always thinks of something that you could not even imagine doing. They say that the reason you are trying to conquer Kiso is because of a beautiful woman," said Kansuke as he lifted his face to gaze at Harunobu. Kansuke kept his focus there. Hard as it was, Kansuke's trained eyes saw the complexion of Harunobu's face change.

"Maybe it is not the general public's opinion, Kansuke. I think that it must be your own opinion."

"If that is only my opinion, your princesses would never have come up with the idea of becoming nuns."

"But, I am not interested in renouncing the world," Harunobu said carefully. He was unusually cautious about not allowing Kansuke an opening to challenge his decision.

"I would like you to think about it until tomorrow," said Kansuke and left.

That night he settled himself at Itagaki Nobukata's previous mansion where he always stayed whenever he came to Kofuchu over several nights. Late at night, he visited a priest, whose name was Tosho-an, who lived in the town of Katagawa. He asked him to recommend to Harunobu to renounce the world and to give up his carnal desires. Kansuke had held a close and friendly relationship with this priest for the last two years, and he trusted him.

Tosho-an said that he was not very good at persuasion but knew a priest called Choshuza in Ashikaga whom he respected immensely. He suggested issuing an invitation to this priest and having him recommend this course of action to Harunobu. Then, the lord might listen to him.

The next day Kansuke took his horse to see the priest, Choshuza, in Ashikaga. He felt it would be quicker than sending a messenger.

It was early February when the two priests Tosho-an and Choshuza visited the mansion in Kofuchu together. Choshuza said to Harunobu, "My Lord, we came here together to tell you something important. We recently read your future, and it turned out that your ancestors were born from a great and affluent family, but it showed that the early part of the day presents good omens, but the latter part of the day presents the word 'a bad omen.' This is why we are here to tell you to be cautious about this."

Kansuke who was present watched Harunobu's expression in silence. Harunobu was listening to the priests' words with a displeased look.

Choshuza continued, "The early part of the day means the early part of your life, and the latter part of the day means the rest of your life. We consider a human life to be sixty years; the early part of the day is up to thirty years old. My lord, you are now over thirty, and you have entered into the latter part of your life. If your fortune tells you that negligence exists in this latter part of your life, you must think about your actions very carefully."

"So what do you suggest?" asked Harunobu.

"This is the time, My Lord, you should resign yourself to heaven's will and renounce the world. If you look at the entire country, many families of great antiquity have been overthrown. It would not be strange if someday the Takeda family were overthrown in this warring era of Gekokujo. For generations the Takeda family has been successful in keeping its power with the bow and arrow; therefore if in your generation…"

"I understand," said Harunobu.

"No, you don't, not that well, My Lord."

"Yes, I do understand, I do. So, I renounce the world and become a priest and submit myself to Heaven's will; then everything will be fine, right?"

"Even if you renounce the world, if it is merely for form's sake and you don't really mean it, it will be of no use to you. Once you renounce the world, it is desperately important for you to make up your mind not to have any new women around you." Kansuke was determined to say everything to him at this opportunity.

It was February the twelfth, at the hour of the Monkey, when Harunobu renounced the world and renamed himself Tokueiken Shingen with the religious name Ikuzan. Now Harunobu would be known as Shingen.

The generals who shaved their heads along with Takeda Shingen were Hara Toratane, Yamamoto Kansuke, Obatayama Shiro-no-kami, and Nagasaka Saemon-no-jo. Hara Toratane was named Nyudo Seigan, Kansuke was named Doki, Obatayama Shiro-no-kami was named Nyoi, and Nagasaka Saemon-no-jo was named Chokan.

On February the twenty-third, Kansuke went back to Suwa. A few days later, he visited Princess Yuu in Kan-non-in Temple.

Kansuke sat in front of Princess Yuu and announced to her that Harunobu had shaved his head. Princess Yuu watched Kansuke for a short while, suppressing the temptation to laugh. She then said, "Thank you very much for everything. It was too bad that even you were involved, Kansuke!" and she burst into laughter.

"Well, now you do not have to be a nun, Princess."

"A nun? My goodness, did you really believe such a thing?"

"Then was it a lie when you told me that you were going to be a nun?"

"Whether it was a lie or the truth, I never even dreamed of being a nun. If I did become a nun, it would have meant that I was defeated by my lord, would it not be so, Kansuke?"

"Then was it also a lie about Princess Ogoto?"

"I do not know anything about Princess Ogoto, although she may be a nun by now."

"What? You ruthless bitch!" was what Kansuke wanted to say. Instead, he said, "If Princess Ogoto has already become a nun...."

"Most likely she has, because I ordered her to."

"Then you tricked her!"

"Kansuke, which side are you on?"

"Me?" Kansuke could not respond.

"Kansuke!" Princess Yuu said in a strong tone, and then she changed her mind and said quietly "Kansuke, would you like to walk outside? Let's enjoy the peach blossoms."

Kansuke followed Princess Yuu as she walked down the slope in front of the Kan-non-in Temple, which came out onto the street. At the joining of the Tenryu River and one of its smaller tributaries, they walked along a path. In that area, there were many peach trees. Light crimson flowers were blossoming in the woods and mountain valleys, although the cold air indicated that winter had not left completely.

"Kansuke, I do not think I will live much longer," Princess Yuu said as she continued walking, "Look, my arms are becoming so thin."

When she mentioned it, Kansuke had to agree. Her original slim arms looked much thinner. The skin there was so pale they looked almost painful.

"You are not cold, Princess?"

"No, I am not cold." Then she added, "Am I a bad woman to make my lord and you renounce the world and trick Princess Ogoto into becoming a nun?"

"No, never..." answered Kansuke. He could never think that she had done something wrong. Whatever she did, or thought, it was impossible for Kansuke to blame her for doing anything wrong.

"What lovely flowers the peaches have! But it seems that this will be the last year for me to enjoy them."

"Don't ever think such a thing."

"But to be honest, I really do not want to live any longer. To be a woman is a pitiful thing. I realized that not long ago. When I found out about Princess Ogoto, I was disgusted with my lord. Then I became used to the idea and lived until today being caught between his wife and Princess Ogoto. And when my lord will have a new lady in the future, something I have no doubt will occur, I will have to live in agony and sorrow. Yet, when my lord visits me, I still try to please him. I've just had enough of that kind of life!" Only her last words were emotional.

"You do not have to worry about it any longer, he has renounced the world."

With this, Princess Yuu laughed. The laughter sounded cold in the air of early spring, "Just because he has renounced the world you think it is going to make a difference? It simply means that he receives the title of daisojyo[66] from the Capital. A daisojyo! My lord being a daisojyo, it's comical!" This time her laughter differed slightly from her previous outburst.

"Princess!" Kansuke thought she had gone insane. The way she acted, anybody might have thought the same.

"I like my lord only when he is ready to go into battle. I like him when he is not thinking about things like his wife, Princess Ogoto, or even me. He is best when he thinks about nothing but war. Any other time I do not like him. I would like Katsuyori to take from my lord only bravery as his birthright. Kansuke, please help Katsuyori to be a great general at war like my lord. I beg you, Kansuke."

"You do not have to worry about that. It is so obvious that he will be the greatest archer in the whole country. He will be the greatest general anybody has ever seen. Just imagine him with the helmet of the Suwa Hossho."

When Kansuke thought of Katsuyori in Suwa Hossho's helmet, he just about fainted with joy. It was also his greatest dream to see Katsuyori at his coming of age.

Kansuke liked Harunobu and Princess Yuu. He loved both of them more than anybody else on earth. But to protect this child, who had inherited the blood of the two people he loved more than anyone and to bring him up to be a great general was his only goal from here on.

"Kansuke, shall we go back?"

Until called by Princess Yuu, Kansuke's eyes had been focused on the slope of a far away hill. His eyes saw nothing as he dreamed of the future. There were a lot of things to think about.

Then, a young samurai approached, his horse galloping at full speed. When he came near Kansuke, he dismounted and said, "The lord will be here very soon."

"What, the lord! I will return immediately," said Kansuke. It must be another war, Kansuke thought.

The news of Shingen's visit visibly put life to Princess Yuu's face in an instant. The change was quite obvious to Kansuke.

"We must go back to the Kan-non-in Temple quickly," he said to her.

"Kansuke, please go and get a branch of peach blossoms. I have no reward for him who renounced the world at my request. So I shall show him peach flowers, at least."

Kansuke was enchanted by her beauty as her face lit with joy. This time, he thought, yes, definitely she is more beautiful than Princess Ogoto. And, he was satisfied with this thought.

Kansuke and Princess Yuu went back swiftly to the Kan-non-in Temple. Kansuke thought it had to be another war for sure, but

Shingen sat on the veranda of the mansion and looked unusually relaxed. Looking at the peach flowers which Princess Yuu brought he said, "Peach blossoms. Blooming already?"

"The peach blossoms have been blooming for over a month," said Princess Yuu.

"Is that right? I have not noticed them at all," answered Shingen. He had been too busy, spending day and night plotting strategy, to notice the peach blossoms, which covered the entire mountain and the fields of the Shinano and Kai districts.

Shingen, with his shaved head, looked rather cold. He must have appeared funny to Princess Yuu's eyes. She looked as if she was suppressing laughter, but she resisted the temptation and did not bring up the subject at all.

"I thought you were taking to the field again," said Kansuke.

"Taking to the field? Give me some time to rest," he said in disgust. Then he looked at Princess Yuu and said, "Would you prepare for a banquet?"

Kansuke was about to withdraw and leave the two of them alone, but Shingen said heartily, "How about drinking sake together, with us for a change, Kansuke?"

This was the first time that all three of them had drunk sake together and it was quite a surprising request coming from Shingen.

The surface of the lake darkened as the day waned. The lake was unusually calm and not a ripple marred the placid surface. Across it, the summit of the mountains was still covered with snow.

"Well, we both have renounced the world, what should we do now?" Harunobu asked jokingly. "I will do anything that you tell me to do, Yuu. If you tell me to attack Kiso, I will do that. If you tell me to conquer Echigo, I will do that too."

"You will do as I tell you!?" she said it quietly, then added, "Why do you say such a sweet thing to me today, My Lord?"

"There is nothing sweet about it. Since I am in doubt about many things that I ought to do, I would like to decide my course of action by following your requests. I am facing the most difficult time in my life. Although lately I have been thinking things through thoroughly, it does not seem to solve any of my problems. That is why I would like to hear your opinion. Both Kansuke and I have exhausted all of our thoughts."

Shingen's tone was more serious this time. Listening to his lord's words, Kansuke agreed that half of what Shingen was saying was true. It was the most difficult time for the Takeda family. But deciding his course of action from Princess Yuu's suggestions sounded like Shingen was trying to quickly put Kansuke in checkmate.

Shingen's true wish was to destroy Kiso, Uesugi, and whoever else stood in his way, utilizing his mighty power, as quickly as possible. But Kansuke had always been holding him back, and Shingen did not like that at all. Therefore he was going to use Princess Yuu's request as the supreme order, without letting Kansuke interfere, and carry out her plans immediately. Kansuke could see right through his lord's scheme so easily.

No matter what the princess demanded, this young general who had just renounced the world, had the confidence to win wars without fail.

"All right. Then I shall request…" Princess Yuu opened her mouth without a moment of hesitation. Kansuke lifted his face and watched Princess Yuu.

"Why do you not conquer Kiso? That is what you always wanted to do, is it not? To subjugate Kiso." There was a slight tone of cynicism in her voice.

"Kiso?" said Shingen with a frown.

"Yes, you conquer Kiso, and then why don't you marry your daughter to the Lord of Kiso? Up until now you took hostages from the families who surrendered to you, as in my case…" said Princess Yuu and laughed a little, "but I think it is dangerous to bring home a blood relation from the family you have destroyed. In my case, My Lord, you were lucky since it was I. You were let off simply by having your head shaved. If it were anybody else but I, I guarantee you would have lost your life," snapped Princess Yuu.

"Don't be silly," Shingen was dumbfounded.

"I am serious. Kansuke knows my feelings very well. I am not saying this because I am jealous of the women of Kiso. If you are planning to carry a beautiful woman from Kiso to Kai in a palanquin, you are going to regret it. You will quickly lose your life. There is no other person but myself who understands the feeling of having your whole family destroyed. Instead, I suggest that you send a hostage to the enemy.

"Hmmm," Kansuke mused. It was unthinkable for a conqueror to send a hostage to the enemy. However, as Princess Yuu suggested, it could be a very effective strategy which nobody had ever thought of before. It was an idea only to be thought of by someone who had experienced being a hostage.

"Hmmm," Kansuke mused again.

Shingen seemed to be taken aback by her words, and with an expression much like he was choking on a large piece of food, he said instantly, "All right, I shall conquer Kiso." Then to Kansuke he said emphatically, "Kansuke, is it all right with you?"

"I agree with your idea of settling the Kiso affair before Echigo, and along with conquering Kiso, it is important to form an unswerving alliance with Imagawa and Hojo.[67]

A small flame, which was ignited in Kansuke's mind through Princess Yuu, was about to blaze in every direction.

To stabilize the alliance with the Hojo, it was necessary to marry Shingen's eldest daughter, from his legitimate wife, into the Hojo family. Then Hojo would marry his daughter to the Imagawa and Imagawa's daughter would marry into the Takeda family. This stratagem, which Kansuke had schemed up several years ago, came out with new meaning. Kansuke's eyes started to shine. If we can execute this plan, the three families of the Takeda, the Hojo, and the Imagawa will be relatives of each other. Then, Shingen can face Kagetora without any fear of these families at all.

In August of the twentieth year of Tenbun, Nagao Kagetora received the title of daimyo[68] and the surname Uesugi Norimasa.[69] Since then he has been called Uesugi Kenshin Kagetora.

Kansuke explained this to Shingen in detail. Shingen thought about it for a long time in silence and did not respond immediately.

Suddenly Shingen ordered Princess Yuu to leave the room. "Princess Yuu, would you leave us alone?" Princess Yuu left obediently.

Kansuke was left alone with Shingen. Before they were aware of it, the sun sank below the horizon and darkness began to surround them.

"Shall I light a torch?" asked Kansuke.

"No."

Shingen shook his head and asked wearily, "The alliances between the Imagawa, the Hojo, and the Takeda, will they last forever?"

"Well, I am not certain whether they will last or not. However, if you follow through with the strategy I just explained to you, they will last at least until we destroy Uesugi Kenshin Kagetora. Once we bury Kagetora, even if the alliances are broken..."

"It does not matter, right?"

"No, it is not a difficult task, then to conquer the Hojo and the Imagawa in that order."

"Kansuke!" Shingen called out sharply. "Then, what will happen to my daughter who marries into the Hojo Clan? And my son Yoshinobu who will receive the Imagawa's daughter?"

Kansuke started to tremble slightly. It looked as if Shingen was seeing through Kansuke's scheme. Shingen continued, "How about my other daughter who will go to Kiso as Princess Yuu suggested? In that case, Yoshinobu and his two sisters are..." Shingen's words died out halfway through his sentence. He then added, almost as an afterthought, "Poor souls."

"My Lord," said Kansuke quickly.

But before he could continue, Shingen interrupted him solemnly, "Don't worry. I just mentioned that that could be one of the possible outcomes. But for the Takeda family, it will be most effective to execute the scheme that you just mentioned. For the fortune of the Takeda in this warring era, it must be executed. I would like you to translate your scheme into action immediately."

At this moment, for the first time, Kansuke felt in awe of Takeda Shingen. He looked at Shingen as a dangerous enemy to

Princess Yuu and himself. He was well aware of the fact that the children of his legitimate wife were facing danger, and, over and above that fact, he was willing to take this risk and put Kansuke's stratagem into practice. Until this time, Kansuke considered Shingen as a young inexperienced leader. Although he respected him as an exceptional commander-in-chief, the knowledge that he was much younger than Kansuke was always there, and thus he always thought that Shingen was not as mature as himself. But that idea was completely erased at this moment.

Kansuke was not certain whether Shingen loved Princess Yuu or not. It was not only in the case of Princess Yuu, but also in his own case in which he was uncertain. He knew that Shingen trusted him, and yet there was something which kept Kansuke on guard toward Shingen. Yet, his feelings toward Shingen were also complicated. Kansuke had no regrets in risking his life for Shingen. He was willing to do anything to support him in conquering the entire country. But when Princess Yuu was added to their relationship, things were not as easy. Kansuke could not deny the fact that he was trying to protect Princess Yuu and Katsuyori from Shingen.

A few days after Shingen had returned to Kofuchu from Kannon-in Temple, Princess Yuu and Kansuke got together, and Princess Yuu asked him, "Kansuke, what did you talk about with the lord, after he made me leave?"

"It was nothing special. He ordered me to execute my scheme of the alliances of the three families, the Imagawa, the Hojo, and the Takeda."

"I believe that my lord is well aware of the disadvantageous positions that his legitimate wife and children will be in if this plan is brought to fruition," Princess Yuu said.

"How do you know?"

"Oh, I knew just by watching the expression on his face. He looked weary and worried, but he also knew that it was necessary for the Takeda family, so he decided to risk the dangers that the plan suggests." Then she added, "Another thing is, although he did not mention it, he also knew somehow that my life would not last very long. If he thought that I would live longer, he would never have decided to do this. He could see that my life would not last much longer and therefore I will not be a source of misfortune toward him. That is the reason why my lord has decided to take this step."

"If you are healthy, why would you be a source of misfortune?" asked Kansuke bluntly.

Princess Yuu answered with a sad expression on her face, "If his children from his legitimate wife gain advantageous positions, I will never leave them alone. I love my own son, Katsuyori. I detest the children of his legitimate wife. Even though they have my lord's blood, I still hate them. Oh, Kansuke, I am ashamed of myself!"

"Princess, your voice is too loud. You should not say such things."

"But it is the truth."

"If it is the truth, that is all the more reason that you should not mention it."

"But Kansuke!" said Princess Yuu, "I say such horrible things simply because I love my lord. Before I often thought of taking his life. But now I do not think about it. Now I would like to take his children's lives, those who were born between my lord and other women."

"Don't ever say such a thing."

"There is nobody listening to us. Kansuke, am I not dreadful? Of course, my lord knows my dreadful personality. He is afraid of me. But again, he knows that I will not live very long."

Suddenly she stood up and started to laugh as if she had gone mad.

"You should not talk about your life so lightly. You have to be healthy and live long, so that you can see Master Katsuyori…"

Kansuke realized that he was also wishing fiercely the same thing as Princess Yuu. And he desperately wished that Princess Yuu's life would last longer than she had predicted. Kansuke could not even contemplate the consequences of her death. The world without Princess Yuu did not exist for him.

Chapter 10
PRINCESS YUU GOES HOME

IT WAS AT THE END of the twenty-first year of Tenbun when
Takeda Shingen took Imagawa's daughter as the wife of his legitimate son, Yoshinobu. During July of the twenty-second year of
Tenbun, the daughter of Hojo Ujiyasu married Imagawa's son, thus
the union with the two families became reality. And in December
of the next year, the Takeda's eldest daughter was sent to Sooshu[70]
to become the bride of Hojo Ujiyasu's son, Shinkuroo. It had taken
close to four years for Kansuke and Shingen to bring about the plan
that they had discussed in the Kan-non-in Temple with Princess Yuu.

The bridal procession from the Takeda to the Hojo was simply
magnificent. Over 10,000 people joined the procession. Among
them were 3,000 mounted samurai, who guarded the front and the
rear. The saddles, palanquins, and the large oblong bridal chests
were all either covered or trimmed with gold, which shimmered
under the weak, winter sun. In the twilight of a cold, winter day,
the procession entered into the castle town of Odawara.

Kansuke joined the bridal procession. Everyone who came
from the Takeda stayed in Odawara until the New Year; everyone,
that is, but Kansuke. He went back to Kofuchu and reported to
Shingen on how the procession went.

"Well, finally we have nothing to worry about. Now we can
plan the campaign for the Kiso invasion."

"When will be the best time to attack Kiso?"

"I believe that around August will be the best time. The Kiso
River will be filled and flooded with snow-fed water until April,"
answered Kansuke.

So until August, the preparations proceeded for the campaign to attack Kiso.

When Kansuke returned from Kofuchu to Suwa, he visited Princess Yuu. By this time, she had lost even more color, and her skin was so white that it was almost transparent. Her dark eyes looked large and her beauty was so striking that it would have brought any man to his knees. From that position Kansuke told her, "The daughter of our Lord's legitimate wife has married into the Hojo family."

"The next obstacle will be the war against Kiso and then the war against Echigo.[71] I would like to live until that time," said Princess Yuu gravely.

"What are you saying? You have to be strong. Once we conquer Echigo, then we will attack the Hojo, then the Imagawa."

"I will not be alive when you attack the Hojo and the Imagawa."

"If you do not live until then, you will not be able to see Master Katsuyori inherit the Takeda."

"I would love to see that," Princess Yuu cast her dreamy eyes skyward for a moment.

"You have to tell yourself that you are going to live until then." Recently, even in Kansuke's eyes, the approach of her death was clear.

It was at the end of August of that year when Shingen moved his first army into position to attack Kiso. Since Seba, a castle town which was right at the entrance to the Kiso district had surrendered, Shingen had pulled his army back to Kai for the time being.

The next year, the twenty-fourth year of Tenbun, when the leader of Seba visited Kofuchu to give his New Year's greetings to the Takeda, his procession numbered 213 retainers. Shingen attacked them and destroyed every single one of them. Although Seba had surrendered, Kansuke was afraid that when the time came to attack Kiso, there was a good chance that Seba would betray the Takeda and try to take the side of Kiso. This was why Kansuke suggested this attack to Shingen, although it was cruel, to remove them.

On March the seventh, Shingen raised his army for a full-scale attack against Kiso. The Takeda army pushed through the Kisoniekawa River, over Narai Sunset Point, and made camp at Yanehara. Kansuke had realized that this was the best place to build their fortifications.

While the Takeda were preparing for the Kiso attack, Uesugi Kenshin Kagetora entered into the area of Kawanakajima. Shingen sent an army to northern Shinano to prevent Kagetora's advance, but nothing serious happened. As soon as Kagetora withdrew his army, Shingen settled his camp at Yanehara and began, once again, to prepare for the Kiso attack. Amari Saemon-no-jo was assigned commander-in-chief of the vanguard, and Baba, Naito, Hara, and Kasuga were appointed the four commanders of the second formation. The Takeda army targeted a castle in the Ontake Mountains as their first point of attack.

From the beginning, the Takeda's forces had been swallowing up their enemies with ease. This war was no different. The Takeda's army overcame all the notably difficult cities and castles such as Kokiso and Mizoguchi and stampeded toward Kiso Yoshimasa's Castle. They advanced and charged as quick as lightning and as swift as the whirling wind. Within a day's battle, the castle fell and Kiso Yoshimasa, who had been resisting the Takeda for a long time, finally surrendered.

Shingen gave his second daughter from his legitimate wife, Sanjo-no-Uji, to Kiso Yoshimasa as his wife and promised the security of his land. In November of that year, the Takeda marched to their home of Kai in triumph. As soon as Kansuke returned to Kai, he led his own 500 troops to northern Shinano.

Over ten years had passed since Kansuke had begun his service under the Takeda. To him, this expedition was the most brilliant moment of his life. Now Uesugi Kenshin Kagetora in Echigo was the only enemy which the Takeda had to face and destroy. For a long time, they had been prudent and cautious and had restrained themselves, taking a passive strategy against the Uesugi army, but it was no longer necessary to do so. Kai, of course, and the entire area of northern Shinano had all submitted to the powerful Takeda army. In addition, the Takeda had very strong alliances with the Hojo and the Imagawa. Right now, the Takeda's only worry was Uesugi Kenshin. The time for an aggressive strategy had come.

Kansuke led his troops into northern Shinano despite the fact that there were no indications of Kagetora invading Takeda's territory. Kansuke was determined to fight a great war leaving his fate to providence. This was why he wanted to survey the prospective battlefields of all of northern Shinano from a totally different point of view.

When Kansuke's troops entered Komuro and made their camp on the gentle slopes of the district, a messenger arrived on a post-horse from the Takashima Castle of Suwa. It was a messenger from Princess Yuu. The letter said:

> *Your presence is requested as soon as you can possibly come. I would appreciate your presence.*

Kansuke had just settled at Komuro, but without a moment of hesitation he decided to go back to Suwa alone. He was not expecting a war at this moment, and there were no indications that the army of Echigo would attack northern Shinshu.

It was three days later that Kansuke entered Takashima Castle. Princess Yuu was waiting for him there, having come from Kan-non-in Temple. Kansuke went swiftly to her in her room.

"I am very sorry to have summoned you all the way from Komuro," said Princess Yuu quietly. "I have really nothing special to talk about. I simply wanted to see you."

Sake and food were brought in. Kansuke lifted his cup as Princess Yuu served him sake, and he immediately poured it into his fatigued body.

"How old are you now, Kansuke?"

"I am sixty-three years old."

"It has been ten years since I first saw you in this very castle," said Princess Yuu with emotion.

"How old are you now, Princess?"

"I am twenty-five."

"Well, time goes quickly, does it not?"

"Katsuyori is ten years old."

After saying that, Princess Yuu had her maid bring Katsuyori into the room. Kansuke had seen Katsuyori only two or three times a year in the past ten years. He was too busy with the constant wars his master was involved in; he had no time to spend with the boy. This was only the second time that Kansuke had seen Katsuyori this year.

The prince came in after he was called by his mother and sat beside her in silence. Although he was a reticent and delicate-looking boy, to Kansuke he looked excellent in every aspect. He did not resemble Shingen at all, except for his eyes. They were the exact replica of his father's eyes.

"Please look after him," said the princess. "This is what I wanted to say to you tonight. I suddenly had a desperate urge to ask you to do this. I am so sorry to make this demand of a sixty-year-old man who has just come back all the way from such a far away place. Please forgive my selfishness."

"I am used to your capricious behavior, Princess," Kansuke answered with laughter. Although he did not say it, there was nothing which made Kansuke more joyful than Princess Yuu's whimsy.

That night Princess Yuu did not look sick at all. Her face was radiant, and her eyes were luminous and lively. Kansuke stayed at Takashima Castle and early the next morning, he galloped back to Komuro where he had left his troops.

When he returned to Komuro, naturally he was exhausted, and he slept like a log in a small room in a temple where they had made camp.

Early the next morning Kansuke awakened. It was already fairly bright outside, and the morning light was beginning to stream into the room.

"There was a warning that the enemy's patrols are advancing toward the camp from Un-no-Daira," Kansuke heard a voice from the next room.

"What! The enemy's patrols?"

"Yes, it is believed to be the Echigo troops."

"How many?"

"There seems to be over 1,000."

"All right."

When Kansuke got up, his retainers were all assembled in full force. Their breath came out white on the cool November morning. Although it could be called a patrol, it was still an extremely large patrol. If they were advancing this way from Un-no-Daira, it was clear that they were willing to engage in battle.

"We shall retreat immediately," said Kansuke. Kansuke had no intentions of injuring his retainers for nothing, or to be involved in a meaningless minor battle. Kansuke cleared his camp from Komuro, and they started on their way south. He believed that as long as his troops were retreating, the enemy would not chase them.

When they had marched about three miles, an arrow flew into the rear part of his army. Kansuke was quite upset about the tenacity of the enemy samurai. But he had no intention of responding to it.

They quickened their pace and continued south along the foot of the mountain. A post-horse appeared in the distance in front of him. The mounted samurai galloped right up to Kansuke, who was in the middle of his troops, and almost tumbled off the back of his horse. He said, haltingly, interrupting himself to gasp for breath, "Last night Princess Yuu passed away."

It was a very unexpected message from Suwa, and Kansuke doubted the validity of what he had just heard.

"Say it again?!"

"Last night Princess Yuu…" He repeated the same sentence.

"Princess Yuu has passed away!? The princess!"

Kansuke nearly fell off of his own horse, which suddenly kicked its hind legs high with a violent neighing. An arrow struck the rump of his horse.

"The princess has passed away, the princess!"

Several arrows whizzed by around him.

Shouts were heard from afar.

"Retreat!" Kansuke sternly ordered his troops while his horse remained motionless. After a few seconds of deep thought, he dismounted and pulled the arrow from his horse's rump. His retainers were retreating at full speed, quickly passing Kansuke by.

"Retreat, Retreat!" Kansuke kept yelling.

When he remounted his horse, unexpectedly he saw, from the other side of the hill, a group of the enemy numbering about ten or fifteen. They were closing in quickly and each of them had his sword drawn.

"This is absurd, the princess has not... no, it cannot be!" Kansuke could not think of Princess Yuu's death as reality. Several arrows went by him. Shouts were rising from every direction. Kansuke dashed off to the west, and then suddenly he turned all the way around. The group of warriors was quickly closing in on him. He steered his horse in all directions uttering the same words repeatedly, "The princess, the princess!"

But suddenly, the realization struck him that the enemy's samurai were rushing toward him from every direction, and for the first time he recognized clearly in what circumstances he found himself. Extreme hatred arose up in him. He threw himself flat onto his horse's back, clasping his spear tightly. He was determined to fight his way out. He never thought of the danger to his life, nor was he afraid. He simply felt an extreme hatred toward the enemy's samurai who were about to swarm around him.

He wanted to be alone as quickly as possible.

Once he had decided on the way out of his predicament, he turned the horse's head toward his chosen direction with a determination that he was not going to allow any of the enemies to prevent his escape.

Some of Kansuke's samurai must have returned, worrying about his life, since there were several who were locked in battle, their bright swords flashing in the early morning light.

Kansuke stabbed one enemy and kicked another. A spray of blood splashed onto his horse's stomach. Taking that as a signal,

Kansuke jumped over something black, something that he could not determine exactly what it was. It had a face like Ashura.[72]

He kicked and scattered the enemy in front of him and found his way out. He directed his horse north. It dashed across the open field like an arrow, galloped up and down the hilly area of northern Shinano and kept heading northward.

"The princess!" When he shouted the same word again, which he had repeated hundreds of times, the horse neighed aloud and bent its front legs as it fell on its side to the ground. Kansuke was thrown off, rolled several times in the grass, and came to a stop at the root of a shrub.

The princess!

He sat up and looked around him. He searched for the messenger who had brought the news of Princess Yuu's sudden death. There was no one to be seen anywhere. He saw no human figures in the vast field. Kansuke felt the feeble sun of midday in winter around him, but only the golden susuki, their ears sparkling with frost, felt it with him. There must have been no wind, as the flag-like ears were standing still.

Kansuke, for the first time, rolled the words out of his mouth, the words which he had heard from the messenger not long ago, "Last night the princess passed away."

He had heard those words for sure. Princess Yuu had left this world. This meant that she had stopped breathing and her soul was gone. No, it is absurd, for such a beautiful and precious creature to have disappeared from this world.

No matter how hard he tried, Kansuke could not believe it. Indeed, Princess Yuu's body was so thin that he could have clasped her waist between his hands, and her large clear eyes were more radiant than a candle. All this made everyone who saw her think that she would not live very long. Even Kansuke himself felt that. But no, not that precious thing…

Kansuke stood up from among the dead weeds. The horse was unrideable. From afar, he could hear the sound of a conch shell that was ordering an assembly. It sounded like an allied conch shell.

All through that day, Kansuke walked north as if he were mad, rapidly some of the time and at other times slowly.

He passed several villages. Those villages seemed to be ghost towns. Not a single person was visible. The front doors were tightly shut. Except for the occasional bird, which flew by, each of the villages was as quiet as death. Each and every village was the same. Whenever Kansuke entered the village, he drank water from somebody's well and kept walking, using his bloody spear as a cane.

Once, as he was passing through a village, he yelled out suddenly, "Princess!" It was a desperate cry of anguish. The stone tip of his spear sank about two inches into the dry dusty ground. Just at that time, inside the wall where Kansuke was standing, somebody shrieked. At the same time, Kansuke heard the footsteps of many people who were running away from him. It was not a ghost town. Not only this village but in all of the villages that he passed, people were hiding in their houses, the doors tightly shut, to avoid a confrontation with this ghastly looking old man who had a face like Ashura.

Without his even noticing, evening fell on the exhausted Kansuke. He was in a walnut grove. The blue light of the winter moon was scattered as he peered at it through the leaves of a huge walnut tree. "Princess!" Kansuke screamed. Suddenly several night birds flew away, flapping their wings.

Two days and two nights had passed, yet Kansuke continuously walked.

"Where are you heading?" Kansuke recalled somebody asking. He could not remember when and where it was. He just remembered that somebody had asked.

It was midnight when he woke up. He had fallen asleep in a dry riverbed. Wherever he looked, there was nothing but white stones. They were scattered around everywhere. There was not a single plant in view. And far away from this massive white field of stones, a stream of blue water was running, shimmering under the bright light of the moon. On the other side of the stream there also spread a field of white stones.

"Hmmm." Kansuke sat on the riverbed and placed his fists over his eyes. The sudden urge to cry came upon him, and although he could not stop his body from trembling, he tried to control his sorrow.

Princess Yuu is dead. She no longer exists in this world. No matter where he looked for her, he would never be able to find her beautiful figure, face, hands, eyes, and black hair again. For the first time Kansuke accepted her death and the sorrow started to numb his body.

…The princess has passed away.

Tears filled his eyes. He sat cross-legged and placed his hands on his knees, and then he lifted his face and let tears run down his cheeks. This time, he wept openly.

The next night, he came out to the east of Lake Suwa. He did not know where or even in which direction he had walked. He took the road to the north and kept walking toward Takashima Castle. When he came close to the castle, he saw a line of bonfires burning across the lakeshore. It looked like the bonfires were placed from the castle town of Takashima all the way to Kan-non-in Temple. Each bonfire was reflected on the surface of the lake, and it was so beautiful that it looked as if it belonged to another world.

To one of the first samurai he met when he entered the boundaries of Takashima Castle, he asked when the funeral was held.

"It was at the sixth hour of this evening," the samurai answered politely, realizing it was Kansuke.

"Did the casket leave from Takashima Castle or Kan-non-in Temple?

"It left from Kan-non-in Temple."

"Where is my lord?"

"According to rumor he is at Kan-non-in Temple."

"Good!"

The samurai, released by Kansuke, ran swiftly to the castle.

He must have been reporting Kansuke's return. For when Kansuke reached the gate, there stood many samurai waiting for him.

"I am going to visit Kan-non-in Temple directly," said Kansuke to them and walked in the direction of the temple without entering the castle. Somebody offered him a horse, but he refused. Several mounted retainers came behind Kansuke and passed him. Kansuke walked slowly dragging his tired legs on the road, alongside the lake which Princess Yuu used to enjoy watching.

Along the slope to the Kan-non-in Temple, many samurai were waiting for him to appear. Kansuke did not even acknowledge them and kept walking, leaning against his spear, which he used as a cane. Suddenly he stopped and called one of the samurai over to him. He handed him his spear and adjusted his disordered armor with both hands.

He heard the chanting of the Buddhist sutra and felt vibrations from Kan-non-in Temple. Kansuke entered the main entrance, walked through the corridor, and advanced to the innermost room that was the living quarters of Princess Yuu.

There were many people in the room. Every key vassal of the Takeda Clan was there. The Buddhist altar was placed in the *tokonoma*[73] and the vassals were sitting on both sides of it.

"You have come back, Kansuke!" It was the voice of Takeda Shingen.

"Yes, My Lord," Kansuke said as he knelt to.

"Princess Yuu will no longer return, but I believed that you would."

"Yes, My Lord, I have."

"You must be exhausted. You should have a good rest."

Kansuke stood up and walked to the altar and burned incense for the repose of the departed soul. On the mortuary tablet it was written Shukoin Koran Seigen Daitei.[74]

Kansuke stepped back from altar and sat in front of Shingen. He was about to offer his condolences, when before he could open his mouth, Shingen said. "The people of Ina[75] are in an uproar."

"Ina? Why wouldn't you suppress them?"

"Nagano Shinano-no-kami in the Joshu[76] district and Ota Nyudo of the Bushu[77] district would not leave us alone."

"Then, you should destroy them too."

"Destroy them?!"

"Yes, anybody who opposes you, My Lord, should be destroyed."

"But it will delay the attack on Kenshin Kagetora."

"I don't think it will delay it that much. Suppress Ina, destroy Joshu and Bushu, and immediately after we will extinguish Kagetora's life," Kansuke lifted his head straight up and stared at Shingen. "Within the next three to four years, we have to kill this man."

"Three to four years!? You are too hasty Kansuke."

"But if you don't do it, I am sure you will not feel safe either, My Lord," said Kansuke. Shingen did not respond to him this time. To destroy Ina, Joshu, and Bushu and at the end of it all destroy the ultimate enemy Kagetora were his goals for the next few years. He could not think of any better way of living. Kansuke felt Shingen had much the same goals.

"Kansuke, you injured your face again. How many scars do you have?"

"I believe thirty-six scars. How old are you now, my Lord."

"You must be getting senile, forgetting my age. I will soon be thirty-six. The same number as your scars."

Only the people who were sitting near them heard the conversation between them. The rest of the people could not hear because the chanting of the sutra swallowed up the conversation.

This year, the twenty-fourth year of the Tenbun era was the turning point to the era of Koji[78] and the first year of the Koji was about to end in fifteen days.

Kansuke left the room and went to the veranda. The bonfires along the lakeshore were still burning brightly. He thought he had no other way to fill his empty days without Princess Yuu but by fighting his enemies. He was satisfied with the fact that Shingen also agreed.

Kansuke went toward Katsuyori's room. Katsuyori was asleep from fatigue, as he had not slept for two days and nights. Kansuke entered his room very quietly.

"Who is it?" with an awe-inspiring voice, ten-year-old Katsuyori sat up. Kansuke felt that was a very promising sign.

"I am the old man, Kansuke."

"*Jii* [old man], you are alive!"

"How could I die? How can I be happy in another world if I die before I see your first campaign?"

"Fastidious Jii is still alive. Since my mother died, I thought you might have died too. If you are still alive, I want you to live at least another five years."

"Why five years?"

"I will be fifteen then. I, too, want you to see my first campaign.

"Oh!" An emotional feeling went through Kansuke's old body. "Your Jii, Kansuke, will…" He could not continue any longer. A violent wave of emotion swept over him like a flood. He was imagining Katsuyori in his first campaign. In Kansuke's mind, a young girl whom he saw ten years ago for the first time in Takashima Castle replaced the young face of Katsuyori. He could not tell the difference between the two faces. The faces of Princess Yuu and Katsuyori were mixed up in his imagination. It was like the princess who had disappeared from this world had been revived again.

Princess Yuu is still alive. She is still alive. It was as if a beautiful beam of light had entered from nowhere into the coming miserable days and nights of battle after battle, which were to follow in the next few years.

WHILE SHINGEN STILL MOURNED Princess Yuu's death, his army quickly advanced to Ina. In March, the second year of the Kouji,[79] Kansuke also took part in the campaign.

At the time of the battle against Kiso, in the mountains, they could still use horses, but on this campaign their horses could hardly be used at all. The troops marched in single file on the steep mountain paths, alongside sheer cliffs overlooking the torrents of the Tenryu River.[80] They climbed over several mountains, which had never been crossed before.

One by one, the Takeda armies attacked and captured the small castles that were scattered throughout the Ina valleys. Two weeks into the campaign, they received a report that Uesugi Kenshin Kagetora of Echigo had started his own campaign in Kawanakajima. The Takeda army was stationed in a small village in which several farmhouses were built close together on the corner of a vast, dry riverbed off of the Tenryu River. As soon as they received the information, they immediately held a meeting to discuss how to deal with this new situation.

"I don't think this is anything serious. Let us ignore them for now and continue capturing all the castles and forts in the Ina district. When Uesugi marches down from the north, then we can withdraw all our troops from Ina and fight him," said Shingen. The Takeda's confidence in his armies was quite evident.

"I agree with you," said Kansuke. To the other generals, Kansuke's response to his lord's words was totally unexpected. As a rule, it was Kansuke's custom to contradict Shingen's bold ideas and come out with more cautious strategies.

Yamagata Masakage was the first samurai to oppose the idea. "For any enemy other than Kenshin Kagetora, I would agree with you. But, I strongly suggest that you avoid using such a strategy with Uesugi Kenshin," said the young officer, who had a fine record in warfare to support his words. Akiyama Nobutomo also supported the words of the young officer. Shingen seemed hesitant to abandon the subjugation of the Ina district at this point, as he did not want to be intimidated by the news of the appearance of Uesugi Kenshin.

"All right," Shingen attempted to camouflage his feelings of disappointment by asking Kansuke, "Kansuke, what do you think?"

"I do understand General Obu's opinion, although I do think the same way as my lord, if everybody agrees. But, if there are some other opinions, we should take them into consideration."

"Well, then what do we do?"

"Taking General Obu's words to mind, we should send half of our army to northern Shinano," said Kansuke. He was very compliant. There was a huge difference in personality between Shingen and Kansuke.

"Who will go?"

"I believe, it is you, My Lord, who should go."

"No, not me," said Shingen, "This will be simply for intimidation; therefore there won't be any fighting there."

"You are absolutely right. It is not like Uesugi Kenshin to attack you, just because it is the commander-in-chief who is leading the troops."

"I am not interested in going. I would prefer it if somebody else would go."

"Yes, but if somebody else goes, it will become a battle. Then, we will be in trouble. So it must be led by you, My Lord."

Kansuke believed it. The idea of not sending anybody to northern Shinano was fine. But if they were going to send somebody, it had to be the commander-in-chief, Shingen.

When the meeting was over, Shingen left for Kawanakajima, leaving part of his army in Ina. It was decided that Kansuke would stay there and continue capturing castles.

As Shingen expected, there was no declaration of war at Kawanakajima. Uesugi Kenshin never moved from his camp in Zenkoji Temple, while Shingen settled in his camp on Chausu Mountain. Neither yielded for over a month, and on May the first, Uesugi Kenshin finally broke camp and left for Echigo. Following Kenshin's lead, Shingen also marshalled his troops and went back to Ina.

While Shingen was in northern Shinano, the Takeda's armies, under the leadership of Kansuke, conquered the entire district of Ina. All who surrendered were forgiven, and all who did not were put to death.

"There is not a single territory in Ina which does not bow to you as their lord, My Lord." said Kansuke,

"How about Mizoguchi, Kurokawaguchi, and Odagiri?"

"They were all put to death."

"How about Miyata, Matsushima, Tonojima?"

"I also put them to death."

"How about Hanyu, Inabe, and… ?"

"They also…"

"Killed?"

Kansuke did not change his expression at all. It gave Shingen an eerie feeling.

"It means you put every one of them to death."

"Yes, since they all showed indecisive attitudes toward your leadership, I felt it better to cut off the evil at its roots. But the ones who surrendered, I did not harm at all."

As Kansuke had mentioned, the great numbers who surrendered were several times more than Kansuke's troops, and they were all gathered on the dry riverbed of the Tenryu River. The other generals were having difficulty understanding how Kansuke, alone, with his small army could conquer so many fortresses in Ina, which had resisted the Takeda for so many years.

That night, the army of the Takeda gave a feast in honor of the victory.

Akiyama Nobutomo was ordered to take charge of the Ina district and protect Takato Castle. Yamagata Masakage became a general of 500 mounted samurai and Kasuga Danjo-no-Chu became the successor of the famous family name, in the Shinano District, Kosaka. He called himself Kosaka Danjo-no-chu and was transferred to northern Shinano as the leader of 450 mounted samurai. The lineup was complete; Akiyama Nobutomo was holding Ina in check, and Kosaka Danjo-no-chu was keeping an eye on Uesugi Kenshin of Echigo.

That evening and until late into the night, Shingen and Kansuke faced each other in the inner guest room of a farmhouse in their main camp.

"Now, what should we do?"

"Let's attack Joshu."

"How about Bushu?"

"Fine, we'll attack Bushu too."

"Don't you think somebody else will disagree with us again?"

"I don't think so."

Their eyes met. Shingen smiled, but not Kansuke. For a while they looked each other straight in the eyes.

"You are not fair," said Shingen suddenly.

"What do you mean?"

"At the time of the subjugation of Ina, you drew the better straw."

"I could not help that."

"This time, I will go and fight, and you cannot prevent me from doing so."

"I shall not say a word, but I will go with you too. I beg you not to leave me here as a housekeeper; it is so boring."

They both started to laugh and just as quickly as the laughter started, it stopped. They both felt a sudden sadness at the absence of Princess Yuu. It was as if a gust of cold wind had blown into the room at just that moment.

From the fall of that year, the banner of Furin Kazan never stayed at Kofuchu for more than half a year. Like the starving tiger seeking food, thus the Takeda army sought war. They repeated the process of war countless times, riding out in all four directions, fighting, winning, and returning, once more, to Kofuchu.

It was in the third year of Koji when Shingen marched his army over Fuefuki Sunset Point and headed to the Joshu district where he crushed the large army of Nagano Shinano-no-kami at the battle of the Kamejiri. Even before this battle was over, Shingen received information about Kenshin appearing at Kawanakajima, and he moved his army to northern Shinano.

As usual, both armies avoided a battle and spent the summer and autumn months standing toe to toe, neither budging and as Kenshin withdrew his army, Shingen also assembled his troops for withdrawal.

In the fourth year of Koji, the name of the era had changed to the first year of Eiroku.[81] In April of that year, Uesugi Kenshin entered the province of Shinano with 8,000 warriors and set fire to the plains of Un-no-Daira, which were under control of the Takeda. Shingen was stationed at Komuro Castle at that time, but he ignored Kenshin's threat and concentrated his attention on the reinforcement of his fortresses. There was an ominous silence between the two armies. To all, it was clear that a great collision between Kai and Echigo was imminent.

In August, Shingen unexpectedly received a confidential letter from the Shogun[82] Yoshiteru[83] suggesting that negotiations for peace between the armies of Kai and Echigo should be undertaken.

The contents of the letter was the following:

What is the use of sending your armies out every year to fight Uesugi Kenshin and destroying the peace in your boundaries; this does not produce anything for your people but suffering.

Shingen showed this letter to Kansuke.
Kansuke asked immediately, "Did you respond to this letter?"
"Yes, I did."
"What was your answer?"
"Here." Shingen showed Kansuke a long letter in a printed style of writing on official letter paper. It was, however, not an answer to the Shogun Yoshiteru, but a prayer for the security of the province of Shinano dedicated to the Togakushi Shrine.

There was nothing more comical and meaningless for Shingen than the advisory letter from the Shogun.[84]

Judging from the last part of the advisory letter, which said, "I shall advise Uesugi Kenshin in the same fashion," it was presumed that the Shogun had sent a similar letter to Kenshin. But there was no response from Kenshin to Shingen. Most likely Kenshin must have also felt that it was comical and meaningless.

In February of the next year, which was the second year of Eiroku, a priest named Zuirin visited Kai as a messenger from Shogun Yoshiteru. At the same time, it was said that Oodate Harumitsu was sent to Kenshin in Echigo from the Shogun. Shingen did not say anything specific to him, although he dealt with him tactfully.

In early April, two months after the arrival of the priest, Shingen suddenly summoned Kansuke. It was midnight as Kansuke visited Shingen in his mansion; Shingen was grinning and said, "I have received information that Uesugi Kenshin just left to go to Kyoto to be received by the Shogun." Then, his body shook for a moment, giving the impression that he wanted to attack Echigo immediately.

"Indeed, there is no better opportunity than now. We have to make use of this efficiently. However, it is not yet the time for a decisive war," said Kansuke.

Kansuke believed that the war with Kenshin had to take place on the fields of northern Shinano. Providing that they charge, into Echigo now while Kenshin was in Kyoto, the Takeda might be able to cause such extensive damage to the army of Echigo that they would never be able to recover again. But, it would make it very difficult to kill Kenshin himself.

Kansuke mentioned his thoughts to Shingen.

"Then, how will we use this golden opportunity?" asked Shingen

"I would like you to order Kosaka Masanobu to eliminate all of our enemies in the vicinity of Kawanakajima. Then, please allow me to build a castle right there. Once the castle is built, we will be ready to fight Kenshin at any time."

"Do you really need a castle?"

"Definitely, we do. I would like to have a castle in that strategic area along either the Sai River or the Chikuma River."

"All right, if you think so, go ahead," said Shingen quietly. He did not ask why Kansuke needed a castle there.

If it was to be a decisive war of life and death, a castle was not really required in the strategy. It was not the type of war from which they could attack from a castle, or from which they could retreat into the castle. But Kansuke wanted a castle. As long as it was strong, it did not have to be big. It only had to be big enough to accommodate 200 to 300 warriors.

The Takeda would most likely win. Uesugi Kenshin's army would begin to falter after being broken down. At that time, fresh troops from the castle would attack them from the side. The last decisive blow against Echigo had to come from this small number of warriors. And the commander of this most vital troop had to be the young Katsuyori in his first campaign.

Kansuke wanted a castle for Katsuyori; he wanted a castle in a strategically important location for Katsuyori's first campaign. Whether Shingen knew about Kansuke's plot or not, he readily accepted Kansuke's idea.

And that night, without wasting a second, the order to go ahead was sent to Kosaka who was stationed in northern Shinano. Post-horses were quickly sent one after another from Kofuchu.

Kosaka, who was at Amakazari Castle, followed his orders immediately and headed in the direction of the border between Shinano and Echigo. He quickly defeated and overtook several fortresses one after another. By May, he had captured Takanashi Castle, which was the foremost base of the Echigo army.

As soon as Kansuke was informed, he left Kofuchu and headed for northern Shinano. It was to forecast the probable position of the battle that he hoped would soon occur between the Kai and the Echigo armies. He hoped to build Katsuyori's castle right on this spot. Kansuke slowed his horse to a trot as he rode on the plateau along the borderline of Kai and Shinano where he had previously made numerous trips. In those days, he had ridden alone and galloped at an amazing speed, but now Kansuke was sixty-eight years old. Protected by over twenty samurai, he looked around at the spring scenery of the surrounding fields and mountains, resting his horse occasionally, as he relaxed in the saddle.

Once in a while he stuck his little finger into his ear. He constantly heard a drumming sound, and for Kansuke it sounded like battle cries from a distance.

The day after his arrival in Ueda found him following the Chikuma River. Kansuke met Kosaka at the junction of the Chikuma and the Sai Rivers. Kosaka was on the way from a triumphant battle. Kosaka stationed his troops on the beach of the Chikuma River and visited Kansuke along with a couple of his samurai, where he and his samurai were resting at one corner of the delta. Kansuke stood up and welcomed the young general who was about the age of Shingen. Kosaka was of small stature with a small face. An insignificant-looking samurai accompanied him.

"I am thankful for the trouble you have kindly taken in spite of your great age," mumbled Kosaka in a low voice.

"The trouble was yours; you have done excellent work. You must be quite fatigued," answered Kansuke with equal politeness. Now, all of northern Shinano belonged to the Takeda through the great efforts of Kosaka.

There the two of them sat, side by side on stools. The Sai River was flowing by four or five meters in front of them; the river beach was covered with reeds. Opposite from where they were sitting, the Chikuma River flowed. The spring sun was shining on the white stones covering the beach and also over the black ripple of the Sai River. It was peaceful.

In front of the two reticent, yet notable samurai, sake was served. It looked as if they were father and son.

Kansuke actually did not know him very well except that he was surprisingly good in battle. This young general hardly spoke out at any of the evaluations or planning meetings. To anybody, it appeared that he did not have his own opinion and was happy to let everyone make his decisions for him; he accepted any orders he received and accomplished them to perfection.

This type of personality was both advantageous and disadvantageous to him. People trusted this young samurai, but they never considered him a great general. Even Shingen felt the same way. Whenever there was a problem with a slight difficulty or nuisance, he simply said, "Let's send Kosaka." This statement encompassed 80 percent trust and 20 percent insult. People thought that Kosaka was happy and satisfied as long as they gave him an opportunity to fight. At present, he was stationed at Amakazari Castle as the commander-in-chief of the front line against Echigo. Of course, nobody else but Kosaka was suited to this important task, but at the same time, the fact that he was sent to such a dangerous and remote area was proof that he was not considered a crucial leader among Shingen's staff who attended his war councils.

Kansuke always liked this samurai, although his perception of him was not much different from others. It was a pleasant experience for Kansuke to exchange cups of sake together with a man with whom he did not have to worry about his own silence for a lengthy time. Once in a while he picked up his sake cup and let his companion pour.

Then, suddenly this reticent samurai spoke, "There is something of which I would like to ask your opinion," said Kosaka and ordered his retainers to move farther back out of earshot.

"What is it?" Kansuke looked up and stared into the young man's eyes.

"I would like to have a castle built about two or three miles from here."

"Interesting," said Kansuke calmly, but inside he was startled since his own purpose for this journey was to locate an appropriate place to build a small castle.

"A castle?" Kansuke asked.

"Yes, a castle. I do want a castle. I have a plan for building a castle of my own, but I would like to have your advice on the subject first."

"Why do you need a castle?" asked Kansuke.

Kosaka lifted his face quietly and stared at Kansuke.

"I believe that the decisive battle against Echigo will be in this area."

"You are right."

"Around the Zenkoji Temple on the Uedahara Plain…"

"Maybe."

"The area between the Sai River and the Chikuma River."

"Indeed."

"I believe that the war will be at the end of this year, or next spring at the latest. I think we have enough time to build a castle here."

"Why do you think that we need a castle for this war?"

"Well," Kosaka stopped there and continued slowly, "I would like to place Master Katsuyori in this castle and support him so that he will survive through this war. We have to prevent the Takeda from being abolished in this war."

Without realizing, Kansuke was staring pointedly at Kosaka; the silence was deafening.

Kansuke also wanted a castle in which to place Katsuyori. But for Kansuke, his idea was to build the castle in anticipation of a victory. It was a castle to station a small troop of warriors who would deal the final blow to the retreating Echigo army. It was the castle which would give Katsuyori an opportunity of a triumphant victory and honor. But Kosaka had the exact opposite in mind. It was an idea built in anticipation of the Takeda's defeat.

"So, you think our allies will be defeated?" asked Kansuke.

"Nine chances out of ten. It will be difficult to win," said Kosaka without any hesitation.

"For what reason?"

"In this battle, there is no doubt that both the Takeda army and the Echigo army will fight to the last samurai. Judging from this endless confrontation and also from the personality of our lord and of Uesugi Kenshin, there won't be any possibility that either one of them would withdraw their army partway through the war."

"That is quite obvious. I believe you are right on that score."

"One has to win and another has to lose. And if one has to lose…"

"It will be our side, you think."

"Yes."

"Our Takeda will be defeated?!"

"The Takeda have not yet had experience in difficult wars. So far, we have always won battles through strategy; a smaller army winning over their larger enemy and destroying them with very little damage to our own army. However, with this decisive battle against Echigo, we will not know the result until the very end. Both will lose almost all of their warriors, and the camps and fortresses will fall into total confusion and disorder. Here and there, victory or defeat will be decided. A strategy will no longer mean anything. It will be a man-to-man battle of life or death. The Echigo army is used to constant scuffles and dogfights against the followers of Ikko Buddhism[85]; they will win and our inexperienced army that is not accustomed to this kind of scuffle will lose."

Kosaka stopped speaking right there. His words sounded insolent, but Kansuke admired him for having said them despite this.

Kansuke contemplated Kosaka's words in silence. He felt as if the young general, to whom he had never paid very much attention, had unexpectedly touched a sensitive spot. Kosaka continued, mumbling again in a low expressionless voice, "If the Takeda loses, excuse me for saying this, but it will be inevitable that our lord, Master Yoshinobu and all of his family members will die in the battle. But the youngest Takeda must live without severing the Takeda line. Master Katsuyori has to be saved. Nobody will blame him for the loss. To let him escape beyond the reach of his enemy, we need a castle to keep our enemies away, to allow the young master time to escape."

"I understand," Kansuke said bluntly. "I shall help you as much as possible to build the castle as you wish." Then he fell silent. Kansuke occasionally filled Kosaka's cup, and in return Kosaka filled Kansuke's cup. But, the silence continued unabated.

On the vast river beach, the warriors were scattered around, divided into several groups. A relaxed satisfaction was felt among those retainers who were on their way back from the triumphant battle. It was the first time that Kansuke had actually felt his age since he had begun his service under the Takeda. He felt he was no match for Kosaka.

Kosaka's words precisely pointed out the weaknesses of the Takeda army. Shingen had been conquering the surrounding fiefdoms by an ingenious strategy, and now on account of that the Takeda had fallen into a dangerous position. Nobody else saw it, but it was clear in Kosaka Masanobu's eyes.

Kosaka's words were also painful to Kansuke himself. Kosaka's words mercilessly criticized Kansuke's strategy, which he had provided until now to the Takeda Clan. Indeed, a strategy that would no longer be useful in the war against Kenshin. As a strategist, Uesugi Kenshin also excelled. As far as strategy was concerned, both Shingen and Kenshin were indeed equal. The fact, which would decide the winner, was the tenacity of the last samurai in a pitched battle. It depended on their ability to fight. As Kosaka said, Shingen and also his legitimate son, Yoshinobu, might die in the battle. Kansuke himself, as well as other old loyal servants, might expose their dead bodies on the battlefield at Kawanakajima.

Kansuke had never thought about defeat. In all of his previous wars, he had always thought only of victory. That confidence suddenly disappeared from his sixty-eight-year-old body as if an evil spirit that had possessed him for a long time had suddenly disappeared. Under the glorious spring sun, the small sake banquet lasted for about an hour longer. Neither of them spoke another word.

From there, Kansuke left for Amakazari Castle along with Kosaka. Kansuke wanted to stay with this young general a little longer.

Kansuke returned to Kofuchu afterward, and this time he took enough people to build a castle and left for northern Shinano again. It was June.

However, halfway through the construction, Kansuke had to go back to Kofuchu. It was because they had received news that while Uesugi Kenshin was in Kyoto visiting the Shogun, Nagai Masakage, who lived in Kasugasan Castle, had invaded the

Togakushi area, which was within the boundaries of the Takeda Clan. Northern Shinano, just recently conquered at the hands of Kosaka, was about to become a battlefield again.

In mid July, Kansuke left Kofuchu and stationed himself at Komuro Castle along with Shingen and his warriors. In the meantime, Uesugi Kenshin returned from Kyoto and joined those at Kasugasan Castle. At this point, it seemed inevitable that the clash between the two powerful daimyo would take place.

Kansuke, however, did not forget the words of Kosaka. Before the collision of both armies, a castle had to be built in the lands of northern Shinano. Although Shingen was eager to move his headquarters to Komuro rather than stay in Kofuchu, Kansuke held him in Kofuchu. He was afraid of provoking Kenshin.

The next year, on New Year's Day, in the third year of Eiroku, a New Year's banquet was held at the mansion in Kofuchu. Generals from every province gathered to attend. On this occasion, for the first time, Shingen informed his generals of the plan of moving his headquarters to Komuro. Under the expectation of commencing the decisive war against Kenshin, it seemed like quite a logical idea to everyone listening.

Kansuke alone disagreed with the idea.

"Sooner or later, we have to move headquarters, but you should delay the relocation a little longer."

"How long?" asked Shingen. As usual, he was not very happy.

"Wait until the castle is completed. If the castle is completed by March, you can make your move in March."

Once Kansuke spoke, he did not change his mind. For anyone listening in on the conversation, it would have appeared like the obstinacy of old age.

As usual, Kosaka Masanobu was sitting there saying nothing. Kansuke wished that Kosaka would say something to support his suggestion, but Kosaka, in line with his past practices, did not provide any supporting comments.

And yet, after the meeting, Kosaka ran after Kansuke and said, "Thank you very much, sir," and continued, lowering his voice. "There is a village in Matsui called Gokobuchi. I feel that that is the ideal place to build a castle. I would like you to visit there and see this place at once." He added, "The land is along the Chikuma River."

"Is that so?"

"It is perfectly ideal for defensive purposes."

"What about it's offensive capabilities?"

"Well, it is not that ideal for that."

"But if it is a good defensive position…"

"Yes, you would not find any better geographical features than these from the defensive point of view."

"In that case, it will be fine."

After a short discussion, they parted.

However, through the spring and into the summer, the Echigo armies intermittently invaded northern Shinano. There was no time to build the castle.

Kansuke could have built the castle whenever he wanted to if it were going to be built on his terms, but he wanted to discuss his ideas with Kosaka and include his ideas and plans as well. Kosaka simply did not have time to do this.

Kansuke made the journey to northern Shinano twice and examined the hamlet called Gokobuchi in Matsui. As Kosaka had suggested, it would have been impossible to find any better place than this when it came to defense.

It was the hilly areas along the Chikuma River that aided in the defense of the castle. Running from the northwest, it washed over the edge of the precipice and formed a great barrier to any-one invading from Kawanakajima. Over the northern and the northeast areas, mountains such as Mount Kanai, Senbyo, and Ugen were gathered together forming a natural obstacle. Besides this, it was possible to make a back road to retreat to Amakazari Castle. In the east, Mount Kimyo, Horikiri Mountain, and Tate-ishi Mountain towered over the castle-to-be like a folding screen, and they would not allow any mounted warriors to pass through. It was also possible to go to Komuro, their headquarters, through these mountains. To the west the terrain was high and mountainous.

The only open side was the northwestern side that spread out in the direction of Kawanakajima across the Chikuma River.

Kansuke had no objections to building a castle on this land. All he had to do was to wait for the battles in northern Shinano to settle down, so that Kosaka would have the necessary free time. When Kansuke saw this land, he thought of naming this castle Kaizu[86] Castle, because the current of the Chikuma River was flowing like an ocean and the castle would be built alongside that current.

It was September of that year when they raised the foundations of the castle. Kansuke was determined to build it within three months, working day and night. The situation at the time was so tense that they had to fight against the clock.

As he had planned, by November they were able to complete the castle. Besides the main castle and outer castles, the five towers were built and the Chikuma River and the outer moat surrounded them. The outer moat had a width of forty-seven feet at even the narrowest part. And at the northeastern end of the fortress, they built a shrine and brought in the divine spirit of Hachiman shrine[87] in Kongo.[88]

Since Kansuke was responsible for the building of the castle, Shingen ordered him to name it. As he had originally decided, he named it Kaizu Castle. As soon as the castle was built, Kosaka moved into it from Amakazari Castle as its representative. Oyamada Masatatsu, instead, replaced Kosaka in Amakazari castle.

The day Kosaka entered Kaizu Castle, Takeda Shingen, who had been stationed in Komuro for over a month, came to see it along with Kansuke. Kosaka, as the guide, Shingen and Kansuke climbed up onto the lookout tower at the northwest corner of the main castle. The field surrounding the Kawanakajima, which was considered to be the location of the decisive battle for both Echigo and Kai, spread out before their eyes. The flow of the River Sai divided the field in two with its gentle curve.

In late autumn, the three of them looked down upon the field, each one with a totally different emotion. Kansuke knew exactly where Kosaka was looking. The field, which was reflected in his eyes, did not bring positive thoughts to his mind.

Kansuke had different thoughts. While he was building this castle, he had had the same idea as Kosaka, but now that the castle was near completion, his idea had changed.

Suddenly the question of what the commander-in-chief of the enemy, Uesugi Kenshin, would think of this castle entered his mind. The fact that the Takeda built this castle right before the commencement of the war must have caused some reaction in Kenshin. The fact that a castle was built right here had changed the meaning of every single tree and blade of grass on the field.

Kansuke's eyes started to shine as they always did whenever he stood on a castle tower. He had to win, he thought.

Then suddenly Shingen opened his mouth, "None of the castles in this country could match this castle," he said quietly.

"Pardon me?" Kansuke asked.

"This will be an ideal castle to view the moon. Yes, the moonlight. How about having a banquet here every year under the moonlight."

When they thought about it, indeed, the view of the moon from here had to be the most beautiful sight they had ever seen. Kansuke felt so proud of his master. He was so impressed by his great personality that he was thinking of absolutely nothing concerning war, rather viewing the moonlight, when everybody was expecting him to focus only on strategy.

Kosaka was thinking of how best to call in the warriors in the event of a defeat. Kansuke was thinking of a strategy—no matter what the outcome or the situation called for, he had to turn this battle into a victory. Meanwhile, Shingen was thinking of a banquet under the moon.

IT WAS THE FOURTH YEAR of Eiroku. Kenshin postponed the battle against Shingen and turned his spearhead toward the Hojo in Odawara.[89] On New Year's Day, Kenshin was at the forefront, Umayabashi Castle and sent orders not only to the generals of the eight provinces in Kanto,[90] but also to several generals from Oou,[91] which was outside the province of Kanto, to join this campaign.

As soon as Shingen received this news in Kofuchu and realized the seriousness of the situation, he ordered his generals to assemble in Kaizu Castle.

If Kenshin destroyed the Hojo, it was quite obvious that his power would double and triple through a single battle. And it was clearly possible that, using the momentum of a victory, Kenshin would force his way into the Takeda's districts, Kai and Shinano. In this situation, it was absolutely necessary for the Takeda to gather their forces at the border of Shinano and Echigo and point their dagger to the heart of Echigo.

As soon as they arrived at Kaizu Castle, Shingen defined the stations for each of his generals and prepared for his advance on Echigo. The army had to be ready at a moment's notice. Shingen also sent a small troop of warriors to support the Hojo family.[92] He could not afford to send a large battalion, since he could only afford to place a small number of warriors in defense of Kofuchu. The power of the Takeda was assembled in the land of northern Shinano.

In March, Kenshin surrounded Odawara Castle with the 96,000 warriors assembled by his allied generals in Kanto and Oou district. Once the Hojo's Odawara Castle fell, without a moment's delay, Shingen was planning on advancing on Echigo. Throughout his forty-one years of life, this was the most eventful and uncertain time that he had ever experienced.

Kansuke kept silent during this time of preparation. He was just hoping that Odawara Castle would not fall. If it fell, whether they liked it or not, the Takeda army had to force a raid on Echigo, attacking in Kenshin's absence. In return, Kenshin would stampede to Kai. After that, how the state of this war would change was beyond prediction. It would no longer be strategy nor the skills of war that would result in victory. It would all depend on luck. Shingen's talent or bravery was no longer useful. He required neither Kansuke nor Kosaka.

Kansuke did not want to let Shingen fight with Kenshin in such a state of war. On March the thirteenth, Kenshin deployed a full-scale offensive at Odawara Castle. However, the castle was known for its unassailability, and besides, the warriors defended their castle in desperation with a mighty force—it would not fall that easily. Finally Kenshin gave up on this venture, and at the end of the same month he withdrew from his siege of the castle and returned his army to Echigo.

It was apparent that Kenshin, who had abandoned his assault on Odawara Castle partway through, might attempt to commence battle with the Takeda army again simply to save face. At the end of June, as soon as he returned to Kasugayama Castle where he resided, he rested his cavalry.

Kansuke suspected that it would be mid-autumn when Kenshin would advance with his army to northern Shinano. The Echigo troops, which had spent eleven months on their campaign in the Kanto district, required at least that much rest. But they would not wait till the next year, Kansuke thought. It was natural for Kenshin to wish to regain his honor as soon as possible. The shame brought on by his defeat at Odawara Castle was still fresh in everyone's mind.

On the night of August the fourteenth the general of Kaizu Castle, Kosaka Masanobu, received information of Kenshin's advance into northern Shinano. It was said that Kenshin was advancing with approximately 13,000 warriors. Having passed Tomikura Sunset Point, he had entered Obu,[93] heading in the direction of Kawanakajima.

Up on Noroshi[94] Mountain behind Kaizu Castle, a signal flare was sent up. A pillar of fire rocketed to the center of the sky and sparks of fire burned through the darkness of the night.

Signals were sent up one by one from one mountain to the next. This had been the prearranged method for sending information to the south. These were the Gorigatake,[95] Summit of Two Trees, Koshigoe, Nagakubo, and Wada Sunset Point. Pillars of fire were relayed from one mountain to another and shot up on the summit. Acting in unison with the signal, a group of post-horses dashed out in the darkness, with two or three warriors per group, from Kaizu Castle.

On the night of the fifteenth, Shingen learned the news from a fire signal sent up from one of the mountains. On the day of the sixteenth, he learned how many warriors their enemy consisted of, this through the express messengers. When the messenger arrived, the castle boundary of Kofuchu was already filled with samurai who were ready to leave for battle.

From then on, for three days, warriors left the castle town, divided into numerous groups and preparing their battle formations. It was the eighteenth of August when the last of the main army, led by Shingen, left Kofuchu.

Kansuke joined the very first group of the huge army as it marched out of Kofuchu. Close to twenty years had passed since he had first stepped here in the twelfth year of Tenbun. Kansuke thought that this would be the last time he left his footsteps on this great land. He foresaw the end of his long life. He could not predict which side would win, but he never thought that the Takeda would lose, as Kosaka Masanobu had predicted. This victory had to be placed on Shingen's shoulders. They had to win by any means possible.

However, for some reason, Kansuke felt that he would never set foot on the soil of Kofuchu again. If I do not die in this battle, I will never die in any other battle, he thought. He felt that he might live for a long time to come, if death did not come soon. But, he wanted to control his own destiny. Every human being has his own right time to die. The right time for him to die seemed to be in this battle.

Kansuke headed toward Takashima Castle in Suwa with his five retainers, leaving his troops, which were heading towards northern Shinano. Since Shingen's main army would not be leaving Kofuchu for two days, Kansuke thought of doing two things in those two days. One was to visit the grave of Princess Yuu, which was on the hill of the Kan-non-in Temple, and the other was to pick up Katsuyori. This was, of course, not only Kansuke's plan, but also Shingen's. He had agreed to select this war as Katsuyori's first campaign.

When he entered Suwa, Kansuke met many troops who were leaving to join the main army from Kofuchu. From the general who was leading the first troop, Kansuke learned that Katsuyori had been in the Ina district, not in Suwa, for the past six months. The representative of Ina was Akiyama Nobutomo, and he was in charge of protecting the castle in Takato. Therefore, Katsuyori had most likely heard the urgent news at Takato Castle and likewise, he must have left there along with Akiyama Haruchika.

Kansuke thought that Akiyama's army should pass this same road either that day or the next, so Kansuke could welcome him right there. Kansuke wanted to support Katsuyori's first campaign on his own. He wanted to march onto the battlefield beside him.

Kansuke turned his horse to Takashima Castle. Although he had entered the castle town, he did not go into the castle. Knowing that Katsuyori was no longer here, there was no use of going into the castle where the warriors would be in preparation for departure. Kansuke passed the front gate and continued along the shore of Lake Suwa. The six horses, led by Kansuke, galloped against the wind, all riders with their bodies bent in half.

The sun was just about ready to set, and its last glow was reflecting in rust-red tones over the lake.

Kansuke occasionally rested his horse. He felt excruciating pain when his horse galloped the whole way up. He could not overcome his age. When he rested his horse, he felt the cold wind on his cheeks. It was the cold autumn wind, come to chill his aching bones.

Princess Yuu's tomb was located halfway up the hill to the Kan-non-in Temple, where she had lived for a long time and died peacefully. Five years had passed rapidly since she had left this world.

Leaving his retainers outside, Kansuke went to the graveyard alone. He knelt down as if Princess Yuu was sitting in front of him.

"Princess," he called out loud, "Princess, it has been a long time. I am sorry for not visiting you more often, but I have been so busy with all the battles. You must have been awfully lonely. But please be happy. Finally the time has come for our lord to fight against Kenshin. Please watch from up there to see who will be the victor. Is it not impossible for our lord to lose? Princess, have you really loved our lord, or have you not? It will not be too long before our lord conquers the entire country. I have lived until today to face this war; otherwise, what was the use of my living so long? I would have died a long time ago if not for this war. I would have accompanied you when you left this world. Was it not a very cold winter, when you died? It must have been very cold to die on such a cold winter day."

Kansuke continued mumbling. Once he started to mumble, he could not stop. The words seemed to roll out of his mouth continuously.

Suddenly Kansuke lifted his face. Through the wind, he could hear the beat of horse hooves. It must be the hooves of the troop horses departing from Takashima Castle, and the sound must have come over the surface of the lake.

"Princess, I have to tell you one more thing. It is about the first campaign of your son, Master Katsuyori—the first campaign of the sixteen-year-old Master Katsuyori. Your noble Suwa blood is still running in his body. You have suffered extremely, Princess. You ran away from the castle on a snowy day and made me worry so much. It seems as if it were only yesterday. But now, you must be happy that the Suwa blood is alive in Master Katsuyori." Then, Kansuke suddenly ceased speaking. He felt as if he heard Princess Yuu's clear laughing voice.

"What are you laughing at, Princess?"

Then this time it sounded as if she were sobbing.

"Are you crying, Princess?"

Kansuke stood up, looking around him. Without his knowing, darkness had approached and surrounded Princess Yuu's tomb.

"Princess!"

But this time, Kansuke heard nothing but the sound of the wind, which was blowing over the hill from its base.

Kansuke stood there for some time. What does Princess Yuu think of this battle? The sound I heard, was it a crying voice or a laughing voice? Is she happy or sad about this war? He stood there feeling uneasy about the whole thing. Up until now, he was quite sure that Princess Yuu would be happy to hear this news, but now Kansuke was confused.

What does that cold, mocking laughter mean? No, maybe that was not laughter. If it was not laughter, then was it sobbing? If it was so, what does that imply?

Suddenly, from out of nowhere came a retainer's voice. "Can I have your attention, please!" Kansuke could not see him. He was swallowed up in the darkness. Kansuke turned and looked through the fence as if he were trying to see through the darkness.

"What is it?"

"Sir, at the bottom of this hill, a large group of warriors is passing by. I do not believe that the army from Kiso would take this road. Therefore, I believe they are the army of the General Akiyama of Takato, from Ina district."

His retainers knew that Kansuke was waiting for Master Katsuyori, who was with the Ina army.

"What, the Ina army?"

Although Kansuke thought it was still too early for the Ina army to arrive, he ordered the retainer to go and check. Indeed, the thunderous sound of hooves, which disappeared at one point because the direction of the wind changed, was heard again. Actually he could hear it approaching quite closely. The army must have been passing right under the hill.

"Yes, they are the army of Lord Akiyama Nobutomo, sir."

With that voice, Kansuke left Princess Yuu's graveyard and descended the hill, followed by his retainers.

Akiyama's army was quiet, a forced march in silence. There was an unending line of foot soldiers with groups of mounted warriors here and there. This was the army who was following the urgent message from Kofuchu and heading quickly to northern Shinano.

"Where is Lord Akiyama?" Kansuke yelled out the name of the commander-in-chief of this army at every interval of the line, as his horse galloped along the warriors.

But nobody seemed to know where he was. Some said he would be in the forefront of the troops, and some said he was at the rear. Kansuke advanced to the front.

"Lord Akiyama, are you here?" Kansuke shouted out regularly, quickly driving his horse forward.

Since the moon would not come out until midnight, it was pitch dark. He could see nothing but the dark reflection of the lake on the left.

"Is Lord Akiyama here?" After the tenth time that Kansuke yelled out his name, he heard a young voice calling right behind him, "Is that Kansuke?"

Kansuke brought his horse to an abrupt stop.

"Master Katsuyori? Is it the young lord?"

"Yes, it is. Is it Kansuke?"

"Oh!" Kansuke's voice trembled with swelling emotion. Then, one mounted horse left the line and came near Kansuke.

"Jii, aren't you?"

"Yes, I am. I have been looking for you."

"Kansuke, join the line."

"Yes, sir."

"Let's travel together."

Katsuyori went back to the line and Kansuke followed him.

"I am taking fifty mounted samurai," said Katsuyori proudly.

"That is wonderful!" responded Kansuke. He thought that Katsuyori was really protected by the fifty mounted warriors rather than being their leader. Suddenly, with uncontrollable force, Kansuke said, "You have to enter Takashima Castle with your fifty mounted warriors."

"What did you say!?"

"Master Katsuyori, it is far too early for you to join in your first campaign, you must wait another year."

"You must be joking! I have no intention of listening to you."

It was a stubborn young voice that would not move an inch.

"No, I am not joking, this is an order from my lord. I came all the way just to tell you his wishes."

"My father?"

"Yes, it is a strict order from your father."

"I am going to beg him again then."

"No, it is no use. Judging from my lord's personality, once he has spoken, he will not change his mind. You will have to wait another year."

It was cruel, but Kansuke stated this firmly. It was strange even to Kansuke himself that suddenly he felt the urge to keep Katsuyori from his first campaign. But Kansuke knew that he had done the right thing. After he said that, he felt unexpectedly relieved.

Suddenly for some reason, Kansuke was frightened to send Katsuyori to this battle. Somehow he had lost his confidence. This sudden change of mind was caused by his visit to Princess Yuu's graveyard. Kansuke felt that Princess Yuu was not necessarily happy about Katsuyori's first campaign. It was no use in sending such a young man to a dangerous battle such as this. He could make up an excuse for Shingen.

When they arrived at Takashima Castle, Kansuke took Katsuyori and his retainers out of the line and pulled them into the gate of the castle. Inside the castle, under the light from a bonfire, Kansuke saw Katsuyori's face was pale, and his mouth was firmly set. It was clear to all eyes that he was suppressing his angry emotions. His face was indistinguishable from Princess Yuu's expression when she had been upset.

"Won't it be better to go to war as Lord of Takato Castle of Ina, leading 2,000, than joining the campaign as a leader of fifty mounted samurai? I will promise at the risk of my life to ask your father that within one year, young Master, you will be the Lord of Takato Castle. I am sure your late mother would feel the same way."

No matter what Kansuke said, Katsuyori did not respond. Paying no heed to this, Kansuke took Katsuyori into the garden and said, "Please look after this castle, all right. Here I, Kansuke, will bid you farewell."

He felt it was no use staying any longer; he quickly returned in the direction of the castle gate. At the square, suddenly a woman called his name, "Kansuke!" Princess Ogoto stood there, one side of her face reflecting the light of the bonfire.

"Oh...oh..., it is you, Princess Ogoto."

"Please look after yourself, Kansuke."

Kansuke bowed and passed her by, but he came back to her again. He dismounted and said, "Please be helpful to Master Katsuyori from now on. Nobody knows who will win this war. If something happens, I would like you to look after him..."

"Why do you say such a thing so suddenly?" questioned Princess Ogoto. She continued, "I will not be able to be very much help, but there are two princesses and Nobumori. Nobumori is already twelve years old. As you mentioned to me a long time ago, I am sure they will be a good help to Master Katsuyori."

"I am glad to hear that. I will be able to go to war in peace," said Kansuke as he remounted his horse.

Once he left the gate of Takato Castle, he had no more regrets. He felt that he could die peacefully. His only remaining desire was to capture Kenshin's head with his own hands.

The main army of 10,000 warriors left Kofuchu on the eighteenth, as scheduled. It then passed over Daimon Sunset Point, where it added 3,000 warriors, and arrived at Koshigoe on the twenty-first and then stayed at Ueda that night.

Post-horses arrived one by one with messengers bearing urgent news. Shingen had learned that Kenshin had crossed the Chikuma River and flew his flag on Mount Saijo near Kaizu Castle. It was an extremely audacious and daring move. It was established tactics in a case such as this to set their camp across from Kaizu Castle placing the Chikuma River between them, but the fact that Kenshin had crossed the Chikuma River meant that he had cut off his own line of retreat.

Shingen acquired another 5,000 warriors at Ueda who came from several fortresses around northern Shinano. His total number of samurai had grown to 18,000.

Shingen left Ueda on the twenty-third; in the early morning they crossed the Chikuma River and set their camp opposite Kenshin's camp on Mount Saijo. They spent five days enduring an ominous silence. On the twenty-ninth, Shingen crossed the Chikuma River again and moved his entire army into Kaizu Castle.

In September, both Kenshin on Mount Saijo and Shingen in Kaizu Castle were still facing each other without movement on either side. Suddenly autumn was there, in the mountains and fields, the sunbeams weakened, and it became cold. On September the ninth, the day of the Chrysanthemum Festival, all the generals in Kaizu Castle gathered around the main part of the building and held a celebration banquet. Since it was a banquet in camp, everybody that attended was in armor. The subject of their conversation was when they would attack the Kenshin army on Mount Saijo.

"We have close to 20,000 warriors, while the enemy has only 13,000. If we dash out of the castle and push them as hard as we can, it is guaranteed that we will win simply through sheer numbers. I do not think it is a good idea for our fighting spirit to prolong this war," said Obu Toramasa. The argument was very much like Obu himself, who believed in regular tactics for attack. Akiyama Haruchika and Kosaka Masatada held the same opinion.

"What do you think, Kansuke?" asked Shingen.

"Well," said Kansuke, before answering. What he understood now was that as long as they shut themselves in the castle, they would never be defeated. Kaizu Castle was an absolutely invincible fortification which Kansuke himself had supervised the building of. It was solely for defensive purposes. They would never be defeated. This he was sure of. If they went out of the castle and blindly attacked, they might win, but they might lose as well.

"I do agree with General Obu, indeed we might win, but, we might lose too," said Kansuke.

"It is exactly true," laughed Shingen. He felt it was amusing that Kansuke had been so cautious and almost timid over the strategy of this war. First they had crossed the Chikuma River and set up their war camp with much trouble on the opposite beach. It was simply because of Kansuke's forceful recommendations that they had gathered all their armies and brought them to Kaizu Castle.

"All right, then what would you do to win?"

"Wait until they move. We will decide our strategy according to their moves. If we move before they do, the army of Mount Saijo will move accordingly. Then, it will be to their advantage."

"So, we have to wait forever, until they move, right?" laughed Shingen again. Shingen was always compassionate and protective of him. Kansuke's idea was not necessarily the same as Shingen's, but he always respected the suggestions of this old strategist even at the cost of suppressing his own opinion. He wanted to give the last opportunity of success to his retainer, Kansuke, who had lived through a tremendous amount of trouble for this very battle against Kenshin.

That night, Kansuke, who had retreated to his camp, received a visit from Kosaka Masanobu.

"Old master, I have something which you should know," he said.

"What is it?"

"Nothing much, but I believe that the allied troops will leave the castle and attack Mount Saijo in a couple of days."

"Is that right?"

"I believe that our lord is also inclined to do so."

"Hmm, for what reason?"

"All the generals in addition to both General Obu and Kosaka are pushing this idea."

"And you?"

"Me? I am not against the idea, sir. I am not sure if it was the war at Kawanakajima Island with the river in the middle, but in the situation we are in, I believe the superiority of numbers would give the advantage to us."

Kansuke was thinking in silence. Notable and skilled experts of war are all recommending this plan of action; Kansuke knew that it was a sound plan. And yet, he had no confidence that they would win. Maybe nobody had confidence in this war. But, if there is any hesitation, was it safe to risk the Takeda's fortune?

"If you think the same way, then I shall think about it more seriously. But I must meet my lord and discuss it directly with him," said Kansuke with a wan look. As soon as he excused Kosaka, he went to see Shingen immediately.

As Shingen saw Kansuke, he said abruptly, "You've heard it already."

"Yes, indeed. You too, My Lord, are thinking to attack them immediately?"

"Yes, I am."

"And the reason?"

"You ask me a difficult question. There is no reason. I just feel a need to attack them right away."

"I cannot find a good reason in such an answer."

"But that is the truth.... That is what you always wanted to do, is it not?'" Shingen laughed out loud.

"I beg your pardon, sir?!" Kansuke lifted his face quickly. "'That is what you always wanted to do, is it not?'" Kansuke murmured under his breath.

He locked eyes with Shingen for some time, a look of stout disapproval on his face.

"I have visited Princess Yuu's grave."

"Oh, is that right?" Shingen responded, "And I also heard that you locked Katsuyori in Takashima Castle."

"You've heard about it?"

"That kind of news travels very quickly."

"I have decided to have his first campaign postponed one year."

"What is the reason for this postponement?"

"This battle is a crucial battle, one in a thousand…"

"If you have prepared that well, why do you hesitate to attack? There is nothing left to worry about, is there? We have Katsuyori to continue the war!"

"Yes, My Lord."

"Princess Yuu had confidence and told me to do what I always wanted to do. 'Attack them, if you want to,'" said Shingen imitating Princess Yuu again.

Suddenly Kansuke felt as if new courage was springing out from him. He felt as if he also heard Princess Yuu's voice.

"My Lord!" Kansuke leaned forward and said, "if we are going to attack, we will divide our army into two. Then, with one army, we will attack Mount Saijo, and the other will cross the river and take up position at Kawanakajima. The Echigo army will come down to attack, abandoning their camp on Mount Saijo, and cross the Chikuma River. Then, we will put an end to them with our troops waiting for them at Kawanakajima."

"Hmm, and when will be the best time?"

"As soon as possible."

"Tomorrow night?"

"The day after tomorrow at night?"

"Well, if we are going to put this into action, it has to be tonight. If it is tonight, this plan will not have time to leak outside, since it is only you and I who are aware of it. Well, Princess Yuu might know it," having said this, Shingen stood up, about to leave the room, but he came back again and said, "whom do you suggest to lead the attacking troops for Mount Saijo?"

"How about General Kosaka?"

"Fine and how many soldiers?"

"Twelve thousand. Under the leadership of General Kosaka, they will leave the castle at midnight. All the troops under Obu,

Kosaka, Sanada, and Oyamada will join with Kosaka's team. We will have enough time to prepare them."

"The remainder of the army will be 8,000, then."

"Yes, My Lord, you will lead them, and before the sun rises you will cross the Chikuma River and set up camp at the Kawanakajima. Yamagata, Anayama, Naito, General Nobushige and Shooyoken, all of their troops will accompany you in the main army. Luckily the moon will not be up until after midnight, which will be ideal for Kosaka's early team. Besides, early in the morning, it will be very misty, and that will also be convenient for you to transfer your main team," said Kansuke as he excused himself from Shingen's presence.

In no time after that, every square in the castle was filled with samurai ready to leave. Nobody was allowed to utter a word; only the sound of clanging weapons and armor broke the uncanny silence.

It was before the moon rose when the large army of 12,000 soldiers led by Kosaka Masanobu left the castle. It climbed up the steep slope on Mount Saijo to attack Kenshin's camp at the hour of the Hare.

Kosaka came to see Kansuke on his horse.

"Dear old master, I shall leave the castle now before you," Kosaka said in reverence. In the darkness, Kansuke heard only his voice.

"I shall pray for your brilliant achievements."

"As do I, my dear Old Master."

Soon, Kosaka's horse was far away. It took a long time for the 12,000 soldiers to leave the castle. Once the first large group of the army had departed, it became quiet and felt like the entire place had been deserted. Kansuke was waiting for the time of departure of the main troop with his small group of retainers.

In two hours, nobody would be left inside.

Kansuke remained motionless for a long time. Eighteen years had passed since the twelfth year of Tenbun when the Takeda family had employed him. Scores of battles had filled these long years. There was nothing but war for Kansuke. Just like small and large stones rolling on the ground, wars had been rolling along all those years.

At the hour of the Tiger, the troops of Yamagata Masakage left the castle at the forefront of the main army. Following them, Anayama Izu-no-kami, Takeda Nobushige, and Naito Shuri and their troops left in that order.

Kansuke abandoned the castle following the main army of Shingen. When he looked back at the outer gate, the deserted fortress was standing like a black silhouette in the darkness. One side of the sky was slightly lighter than the other, but the land was still pitch dark. To everybody, the castle looked like a mass of blackness. However, to Kansuke it stood clearly outlined as if it were being seen in daylight. The silhouette of the main part of the castle, the subsidiary part of the building, and the five towers were clearly visible in front of him. This was because his own hands had made it.

They crossed the Chikuma River at Hirose. A thick mist was lying low over the flat fields. Shingen placed his war camp at Yahatahara. Several flags headed by Furin Kazan stood blowing steadily in the mist.

Chapter 13
CRY OF VICTORY

IT WAS SCHEDULED THAT, at the hour of the Hare, the 12,000 chosen warriors led by Kosaka Masanobu were going to attempt a reverse attack from the other side of the mountain on Kenshin's camp on Mount Saijo.

Shingen, who had set his camp on Yahatahara, was constantly sending patrols and watching carefully in the direction of Mount Saijo. Although the thick mist still remained and it was impossible to see even three meters ahead, it should have still been possible to hear the raging waves of sound as their allied army clashed with the enemy on Mount Saijo.

Almost at the same time that they heard the sounds of battle, the army of Kenshin would no doubt crumble and flee toward this camp, crossing the Chikuma River. Then the main army of the Takeda, which was waiting here, would attack them all at once. Shingen and Kansuke felt that it would only be a question of time until they could take Kenshin's head.

"Not yet?" Shingen asked several times whenever the patrols came back to report. Kansuke was sitting on a stool not even three yards away from Shingen.

Sometimes the patrolling samurai appeared almost crawling on the ground out of the mist.

"Nothing is observed yet in the direction of Mount Saijo. We could only make out a dim sign of a small fire of some kind in several spots."

Kansuke conveyed these reports to Shingen one by one.

"Our vanguard must be delayed because of this thick mist. It is such an unusual mist," said Kansuke.

"It really is an unusually thick mist, even for this area, but it could be an advantage for the allied troops, couldn't it?" Shingen answered.

"Indeed, it must be the divine protection of the Suwa's gracious deity."

"But what is advantageous for us could also be advantageous to the enemy, could it not?"

"Yes, that is, if they are also preparing an attack," suddenly Kansuke unconsciously lifted his hips from his stool as he said this.

"I shall immediately go to patrol myself," said Kansuke as he swiftly went down to the lower plateau of rice fields.

The mist started to lift slowly. Occasionally the dim shadows of the trunks of pine trees appeared in the mist, and, just as quickly, they disappeared again. Kansuke stopped after every three steps or so. It was as if he were swimming in the thick mist, and most of time it was impossible to tell what was ahead of him. Kansuke rashly walked further into the thick white wall ahead of him. Sometimes he tripped on tree stumps or roots and had to stumble before he could recover his footing. Kansuke was burdened with a significant uneasiness. It was no longer the thick mist, which was surrounding Kansuke, but an unidentified and painful apprehension. Now his allied troops were eagerly waiting for the moment to capture Kenshin's head. However, could it be possible that Kenshin was also keeping a vigilant eye out for an opportunity to prey upon his opponent's weakness in this mist and to capture his own victory? No, this could not be possible! —Then, what was the cause of this uneasiness? Where could this feeling of apprehension, which reverberated through him, be coming from?

Suddenly, Kansuke stopped and yelled out, "Who is it?"

It was because he heard the quick sound of horse hooves near him. It sounded as if somebody were riding his horse around and around on one spot.

"The wind!" yelled back his opponent.

"The mountain!" Kansuke responded.

"Stay away!" the horseman yelled and appeared out of the mist suddenly.

"I am Yamamoto Kansuke. Are you a patrol?"

"Yes, sir." With Kansuke's voice, the horse lifted its forefeet in the air.

"Sir, the rice field ahead of us is filled with hundreds of mounted horses."

"Are they our troops?" asked Kansuke in great agitation.

"They have to be, I believe, but I am not convinced."

The allied troops were preparing the war formation on both sides of Yahatahara field. Yes, they should be taking up their position further back in the field, but it was unlikely to think that they had advanced this far. Hence, there should not be a single warrior of the allied troops to the front.

"All right, return to your camp!"

As soon as Kansuke yelled at him, he himself also rushed to the main camp where Takeda Shingen was waiting. At about that moment, the mist started to dissipate with great rapidity. To their left and right, the branches and roots of trees started to appear.

By the time Kansuke arrived at the main camp, the numerous flags surrounding the main camp could be seen through the mist, looking like a thin white silk veil. And as each second passed, the veil was peeled away.

"My Lord!" called out Kansuke.

"How was Mount Saijo?" responded Shingen.

"Mount Saijo will probably be empty, sir."

"What!"

"Right in front of us, in this mist, Kenshin might be hiding."

"He can't be! What are we going to do?" yelled Shingen, his voice trembling.

Before long, the sound of a conch shell, which announced the shaping of the war formation, began to vibrate in a low tone. At just about the same time, three patrol horses dashed in one by one.

"Large military troops are forming war lines several hundred yards from here, and their right wing is about to start advancing," said one patrol.

"The left wing has started to deploy their mounted horses toward the east," reported the second patrol.

"I understand that the troops in front of us are the Echigo army. We assume that there are more than 10,000." When the third patrol said this, the violent explosive sound of guns was heard from the west.

Before they were aware of it, the mist dissipated. The low plateau, pine forest, rice field, roads, trees around the houses, and rivers which spread out across the vast plain started to appear as if they were emerging from the ground.

Kansuke saw them right away. What he saw was the most frightening scene that he had ever witnessed. Hundreds, no, thousands of mounted horses were stampeding, in three long lines of warriors, toward the Yahata field where Shingen and he were standing. Kansuke held his breath for a moment, overawed with the splendid form of the advancing enemies.

The next moment a war cry was raised from the allied camp. It was the left wing troops led by Takeda Nobushige. About 700 mounted horses were approaching in unity toward one of the enemy belts.

"My Lord!" said Kansuke, "I misjudged our enemy, and we put ourselves into an unexpected situation."

"Shall we win?" Shingen was as calm as ever.

"We must win."

"Yes, otherwise we will lose our lives."

"It's not our lives, but our ancestors lives to whom we owe this victory. It would be an inexcusable loss to them."

"Still I do not want to die yet. I am going to live," Shingen said as if it were a joke. He grinned fearlessly at his own words.

"Kansuke, until Kosaka's vanguard arrives, this battle is going to be a mess. Make sure you do not die in this."

"I give the same advice to you, My Lord," answered Kansuke, a smile on his face.

Kansuke agreed with Shingen. All of the most skillful generals among the Takeda army, such as Kosaka, Obu, Baba, and Oyamada, were all in the vanguard to attack their supposed enemy on Mount Saijo and the enemy was no longer there. The victory depended solely on when the Takeda's great army of 12,000 would be able to join them on this field of battle. If they could last until then, victory would be theirs. No matter what, I cannot let Shingen die in this field, Kansuke thought. He resolved to never leave the side of Shingen, save to die for him.

War cries were raised all over the battlefield. Yamagata Saburohyobei's troop arrived, cutting into the center belt; Naito Shuri and Morozumi Bungo's troops on the right wing were also attempting to cut into the enemy's massive lines.

Kansuke had never expected to deploy his warriors against Kenshin's army in this way in such a strained situation. He had been planning the strategy of this moment for such a long time. Yet what was actually happening in front of him was not what he had envisioned at all.

The fog had dissipated completely. The earth that was washed up by the mist presented a serene autumn morning. The sacred scarlet robe which Shingen wore was dazzling. He was sitting on a stool wearing armor stitched with woven black thread and the helmet of the Takeda Clan of the region of Suwa. Kansuke was sitting beside him. His ugly shaved head was tied with a white headband, and he was also wearing armor with black silk thread.

Suddenly, the war cries became louder, and the ear-splitting neighing of the horses was heard at the same time. Obviously both armies had collided at that moment.

From the beginning, it was a hard battle for the Takeda army. There was a large discrepancy in numbers between the two sides; the error of their strategy dampened the morale of the allied warriors. No matter what the situation was, the Takeda army had to face a sudden and surprise attack by the much larger and more powerful Echigo army.

They had to win. And to win, they had to overcome their inferior military position until the 12,000 warriors of the reserve allied army joined the battle lines. Kansuke had no other wish but this. There was no longer any room for strategy. It was simply a showing of power and pure brute force. Kenshin had outwitted Kansuke this time. The Takeda had fallen into the enemy's trap.

"How is Nobushige[96] doing?" asked Shingen. He was not looking at the war line; his eyes were half closed, and he asked his question in a less animated tone than usual.

"They have not yet reached the point of giving way."

"Hmm, they are withstanding well, aren't they?" said Shingen. Just the way he said it, there was a tone of warmth in Kansuke's ears. Even from there, Kansuke could see the desperate battle of Nobushige. With only 700 troops, they were hanging on with a firm grip against an enemy who was several times larger than they were. Although the allied troops were repeatedly pushed back, they rallied forward time and again and managed to push the enemy back every time.

Gradually, Kansuke sensed they were in danger, since new and fresh enemy troops continually advanced before them. Almost at the same time, Nobushige's troops, who had been withstanding so far, crumbled all at once. Once they fell apart, it was a pitiful site, since their numbers were so much smaller than the enemies'. In no time they were swallowed up by the billowing waves of enemy warriors.

Then, 1,000 warriors under Yamagata appeared from the side and tried to cut forcibly into the enemy's line. It was an excellent attack, which was an impressive sight from Kansuke's point of view.

"Lord Nobushige's troop crumbled, but…" Kansuke started.

"It's Yamagata, isn't it?"

"Yes, My Lord."

"We can depend on him on that side. How about the right wing?"

"Morozumi's troop is fighting desperately."

"Still withstanding?"

"Naito's troop is turning to the right. It is hard to tell who is winning."

It was not long before they heard news of the death of Takeda Nobushige.

"Lord Nobushige has passed away!" said the mud-caked messenger. The post-horse suddenly broke its front leg, and the mounted messenger rolled forward onto the ground holding his long sword in his hand. He stood up and yelled again, "Lord Nobushige has passed away," and again fell forward onto his face.

Kansuke rushed to the samurai and rolled him onto his back. Then he placed one leg on his chest and pulled out the arrows one by one. Three arrows had punctured his body. The samurai was already dead. Nobushige also must have lost his life just like this, Kansuke thought.

"Nobushige is dead, unfortunate man," said Shingen.

"I am so sorry," consoled Kansuke. Now Kansuke felt that he was responsible for everything, including Shingen's brother's death.

"Kansuke, I simply said that he was an unlucky man. Do not worry, today at the hour of the Sheep we will raise our shouts of victory."

"Yes, My Lord."

Kansuke could not lift his head. Is Shingen trying to cover up my mistake, thought Kansuke. Or does he really believe in his victory at the end. He never did blame Kansuke for his failures. A violent emotion struck him. He wanted to do everything he could to help. He was sorry that he had only one life to give to Shingen. Kansuke mounted his grey horse and looked around in every direction from the Yahatahara camp.

Now the battle lines were erupting into total confusion. There was no longer a distinct dividing line between the enemy and the allied forces. This was a battle to the death. Although the autumn sun was spreading its cold beams over the vast field, the place exuded a melancholy atmosphere. The sparkling swords and spears which could be seen everywhere were unexpectedly quiet.

If Kosaka were here! If Baba were here! If Obu were here! How many times had these wishes crossed his mind! The troops of the selected elite who excelled in riding and long spears were far, far away from the battlefield on account of Kansuke's own strategy.

Yamagata's troops which replaced Takeda Nobushige's troop had been attacking for a long time along the broad distance of the left wing and the center, but they too eventually fell back and were on the defensive; they were compelled to retreat step by step.

Under this situation, on the right wing, Morozumi Bungo-no-kami died in the melee. When their commander was killed, the right wing troop began to waver. At the moment he learned of Morozumi's death, Kansuke sensed that their main camp at Yahatahara would turn into a battlefield. Because of the defeat of the right wing, Yahatahara had lost its protection and would eventually be faced with the front line of their enemy.

"My Lord!" called out Kansuke. Shingen also realized the imminent danger and said, "Yes, Kenshin's main army will attack here, won't they?"

"I presume so."

"In that case, can we withstand for two hours?"

"Yes, we have to."

"If we can, we will win. By that time, our front line of Kosaka will arrive behind them."

"Yes, definitely."

Kansuke sent the message in every direction. They had to fortify Yahatahara. At the main camp there were only 1,800 warriors. One thousand reserve troops of the left wing led by Hara Hayato and Takeda Shoyoken and 800 of the right wing reserves led by Takeda Yoshinobu[97] and Mochizuki Kanhachiro advanced to the front. Thus, every last soldier of the Takeda camp was about to join the battle.

Soon Kansuke heard war cries which sounded as if they shook the earth. He saw 3,000 Echigo troops stampeding toward him over the plateau only several hundred yards away. It was exactly as they had expected.

For the first time, Shingen commanded. He ordered the entire army of the main camp to leave Yahatahara and to meet the enemy.

"My Lord, will you ride with your men?" Kansuke asked Shingen hurriedly.

Shingen was still sitting on his stool; he simply shook his head sideways. He did not move at all, sitting like a statue as if he were a warrior doll.

"My Lord, I am leaving."

Now Kansuke was determined to lead his troops into war.

"Do you see any vanguard yet?"

"No, not yet, My Lord."

"All right, then go!" said Shingen. The eyes of the young commander-in-chief were glaring.

Kansuke rode out onto the high field. He looked out at the far end of the vast space. He saw none of their allied warriors there. What has happened to Kosaka! How is Baba doing? Kansuke was about to be driven mad by despair.

Kansuke made his troop of 200 men remain where they were and waited for the right moment for his own troops to advance as the last shield to protect Shingen.

Stray arrows constantly hit pine trees and fell to the ground. The sound of gunfire was rampant. War cries were heard everywhere. A site of complete carnage was only a hundred yards ahead of him. Both armies were jostling back and forth and fighting for their lives.

Kansuke walked his horse back and forth over the same spot, time and time again, pacing. He was praying to God that a black speck of even the size of a poppy seed would appear at the far end of the plains. Their victory depended on those black specks. There was no other way.

"My Lord," Kansuke stepped up to him again.

Then Shingen said, "Was it not like this at the battle with Murakami Yoshikiyo? Not a single retainer was around me."

Yes indeed and yet didn't he raise shouts of victory at that battle with Murakami Yoshikiyo?! Kansuke felt that was what

Shingen was implying. Even in a melee like this, Shingen seemed to be thinking only of victory. There was no shadow of death, or despair, within him.

Meanwhile, the formation of the troops of Takeda Shoyoken had broken in two, and Kansuke saw the enemy's thirty mounted horses as the group dashed out of the split. They were advancing with full speed.

Kansuke gave an order to his waiting troops to advance. Now the time had come that every retainer, even to the last one, be committed to the bloody action.

The melee had been going on for over an hour. Kansuke had never experienced such a violent and difficult battle. The enemy was determined to destroy Shingen's main camp in a single attack. Groups of warriors cut into the defensive army of the main camp of the Takeda time and time again. Every time they did, a tremendous clash of shouts, cries, and the shrill whinneys of the horses rumbled through the earth. And every time the Takeda's forces made a daring attempt to surround them and kill every one of them. It was literally an awe-inspiring mortal combat.

Kansuke was constantly moving his warriors to the right and the left. It was his duty not to let any of their enemies come close to the main camp where Shingen was. Yet his retainers were constantly decreasing in number every time they moved.

Each time he paused for breath, he checked the main camp in the pine forest. In the midst of the field where over 20,000 warriors were fighting, only that one block was quiet. The many flags of the Takeda were standing straight. None of the enemies had broken in there yet. However, it was all a question of time. It was a battle against time. Soon Echigo forces would fill even this area.

"Yamamoto Kansuke!"

Kansuke turned around to the voice. It was Shingen's legitimate son, Yoshinobu dashing toward him. Twenty-four years old, this young general's forehead was cut open and his right cheek was covered with blood.

"Look after my father, Kansuke. Don't move from here."

"And you, Master?"

"I am going to attack the enemy's main camp. If we leave it, the allied troops will gradually be destroyed. Look after the rest. I, Yoshinobu, will attack the enemy's main camp."

Sink or swim, he intended to break into the enemy's main camp and aimed to capture Kenshin's head. But it was not going to be easy even to reach Kenshin's camp. Thousands of enemy warriors were blocking his way.

For a long moment Kansuke's eyes dwelt on Yoshinobu's face. He had long resisted the forces that surrounded this young man. From his forces, Kansuke had been protecting Princess Yuu and Shingen's illegitimate children led by Katsuyori and others. However, now Kansuke thought that he had hated this young general for the wrong reason, simply because he was the son of his master's legitimate wife.

The autumn sun was shining softly on Yoshinobu's helmet which was decorated with the Takeda crest, the dragon's head on a diamond shaped piece of metal. The purple woven thread with which his armor was sewn was torn, and his horse was already injured.

After a few minutes Kansuke said quietly, "I shall do that job instead of you. As you mentioned, if we leave it, we will not last even one hour. Our allied vanguard, which we have been expecting, have not arrived for some reason."

As he talked, he cast his eyes toward the horizon. Their 12,000 troops who were led by Kosaka had not appeared on the field, not even a single warrior.

"I, Kansuke, will attack the enemy's main camp. You, Master Yoshinobu, remain here, and when both the right and left wing can no longer withstand, you will take our lord and cut a way through the enemy and escape to Kaizu Castle."

"No," Yoshinobu shook his head vigorously and tried to say something. Kansuke interrupted him and said, "Do not handle your life carelessly. Your life is different from mine. You are an important legitimate son of the Takeda family." The very life Kansuke once wanted to destroy, for Katsuyori (Princess Yuu's son), he was now protecting. Unexpected and dangerous, destiny was approaching the Takeda. At a time like this, no matter who it was, as long as he has the Takeda blood, he must be protected.

"No!" Yoshinobu was not going to listen to Kansuke, and he tried to turn his horse's neck abruptly.

"Don't you understand?" yelled Kansuke. "Don't move from this spot. If you do not protect our lord, who else will?"

Kansuke slowly advanced, then turned around and started to climb up to the main camp where Shingen was watching.

Shingen was standing up straight, leaning his right hand on a pine tree. He was looking at the battlefield calmly with composed dignity.

My Lord, you certainly became a great commander-in-chief, Kansuke wanted to tell him. He had never seen him looking so magnificent. Up to this time, whenever a battle started he was always mounted on his horse. And he always wanted to direct and lead the troops himself. But today, in this battle in which he had a large chance of losing, he was very calm and composed right from the beginning, as if he were a different person. He left almost everything to his retainers, everything except the most important decisions.

Leaving his hand lightly on the pine tree, he was moving his eyes slowly from one side of the battlefield to the other as if he were sight-seeing. It was not the face of a commander-in-chief who was observing a losing battle. Kansuke wished he could show this Shingen to Princess Yuu. It was the face of the most notable commander-in-chief in the country.

Kansuke turned his horse around and collected all his surviving retainers.

"Now we are going to gallop through the enemy's field and attack their main camp. Simply gallop through to the main camp. Do not pay any attention to what is going on around you. Now your lives are mine!"

With the loud war cry of "Ahhhhh!!" there an indescribable uproar was raised among his retainers.

The next moment Kansuke was galloping to the opposite corner of the melee. Halfway through he turned his head and saw a group of his retainers, far larger than he had expected, following him.

Now enemies surrounded him. Kansuke was dashing and bending his body in half; he appeared as if he were licking his horse's neck. He held his sword at an angle, the tip of the blade beside his cheek.

Over the course of time, Kansuke felt pain all over his body. He was constantly cutting into an enemy and being cut himself.

When he chanced to look forward, it was into a wall of spear tips. Suddenly his horse jumped and changed direction and started to gallop as if it had gone mad. It kept running for about sixty yards. It stopped suddenly and bent its hind legs as if it were going to sit down. It was at the foot of a small hill.

Kansuke was thrown to the ground.

As he tried to get up, Kansuke held his breath. Surprisingly he could see the open field in front of him from where he was standing. He could see the rice fields and the plains filled with ears of susuki and a pond. And at the far end of the vast field he saw numerous black specks like poppy seeds spread all over the place. And they were spreading in all directions.

They are here at last, Kansuke thought. When he turned to see the pine forest, several mounted horses passed beside him galloping at full speed.

Kansuke stood up. Several enemy samurai pressed in on him from the right side. He started to walk toward them unsteadily. He killed one, but his shoulder was also cut. He killed another, but his legs were swept from under him and he sat on the ground.

My Lord, our vanguard has arrived. Now you will win and shout your cry of victory!

A spear went through his abdomen from the side. He stood up holding its handle.

The black specks on the field were increasing in number.

On the corner of the pine forest where Shingen was, there still stood the flag of Furin Kazan, and surrounding the flag many other flags of the Takeda remained standing. The troops of Takeda Yoshinobu must be protecting the camp well. In this melee, the arrival of 12,000 soldiers promised only victory. The victory was approaching by the minute. He had to live, Kansuke thought.

"Yamamoto Kansuke, I shall have your head," Kansuke heard a very young voice. He tried to look in that direction, but he could not. Holding the handle of the spear that had gone through his body, he wielded his long sword. There was no reaction.

My Lord! Shout out our victory! They will be here in no time.

Piercing pain shot through his shoulder again. Kansuke stumbled several feet, as if someone were pulling him with the spear handle, which was sticking out of him and banged against a pine tree. He was leaning against the tree, still holding his sword ready to attack.

The quietest hour of his whole life arrived. Thoughout the battle shouts and cries were filling the sky between heaven and earth, it gave him a sense of quiet. The face of Itagaki Nobukata appeared. He said, "You have lived for a long time. Ten years after I died!"

Then, Princess Yuu's face appeared. She laughed the way she used to when she was happy. The laugh was approaching like a pearl rolling toward him.

"Look at your wounds. You were born with such an ugly face to start with, and you added more scars to it!" Princess Yuu's typical way of reproaching him sounded pleasant, and Kansuke was enraptured by it.

"I believe it is Yamamoto Kansuke, but give your name anyway," Kansuke heard a young voice, breaking his sense of euphoria. For no reason, Kansuke was satisfied with being killed by the young samurai.

"Yes, indeed, I am the war strategist of the Takeda Clan, Yamamoto Kansuke."

The moment he said it, he felt the cold blade that would end his life run through his neck.

Blood splashed. The distinctive head of the war strategist Yamamoto Kansuke left its short body.

At that moment, at one corner of the plain, the group of the mounted force of Kosaka, Baba, and Obu, which had crossed the river, was dashing forward to attack the rear of the Echigo army.

And, at the same time, the commander-in-chief of Echigo, Uesugi Kenshin, who had wrapped his gold helmet with white and soft silk material like a priest[98] pulled out his two and a half foot sword and was about to whip his slightly brownish white horse. It was to attack Shingen single-handedly and decide the winner at a single stroke.

There was still more than two hours till the hour of the Sheep when Shingen was to raise a cry of victory, as he had prophesied.

From around that time, the appearance of the field started to change. The sun vanished behind the clouds, and in the south-west sky, black rain clouds started to gather.

TAKEDA SHINGEN'S ARMIES sustained approximately 4,600 fatalities and 7,500 injuries, whereas Uesugi Kenshin's troops sustained 3,500 dead and 9,400 injured. Uesugi Kenshin withdrew from the battlefield.

According to the records of Takeda sandai ki, three generations of the Takeda family history, Yamamoto Kansuke attacked the enemy head on and is believed to have killed thirteen opposing warriors before succumbing—this at the age of 69.

Takeda Shingen, who dreamed of the unification of Japan, died due to illness in Shinano district in 1573 without achieving his dream. For the warlord whose passion was to fight until his death in the battlefield, his death from illness must have been hard to accept.

Takeda Shingen's legitimate son, Takeda Yoshinobu, survived the battle of Kawanakajima. The emnity between Yoshinobu and Katsuyori was well known, particularly due to Takeda Shingen's obvious preference toward Princess Yuu's son, Katsuyori. The real truth is unknown, but it is believed that Takeda Shingen put Yoshinobu in prison, when his secret attempt at treachery was discovered. One theory says that he died in prison at the age of thirty, whereas another suggests that he died from illness.

Takeda Shingen's illegitimate son, Takeda Katsuyori, assumed leadership after his father's death. In spite of his dream to be a better daimyo than his father, Katsuyori eventually faced his fate to fight against the two strongest unifiers of Japan, Oda Nobunaga and Tokugawa Ieyasu.

Betrayed by his own vassal while facing Oda's army, Takeda Katsuyori killed himself, slitting his abdomen in the style of the cross along with his wife and sixteen-year-old son, thus bringing to an end the Takeda Clan of the warring era.

The unification of Japan was not to be complete for several decades. In 1560, Oda Nobunaga defeated the Imagawa at the battle of Okehazama. Unification was then pursued for many years through the efforts of Toyotomo Hideyoshi and consummated, in 1600, by Tokugawa Ieyasu, who established the Tokugawa Shogunate which lasted for close to 300 years until the opening of Japan and modernization in 1868.

—Yoko Riley

Notes

1. Warlord.

2. The way of the samurai; unwritten code of conduct for the samurai such as loyalty and obligation between lord and vassal, self-discipline such as self-denial, self-control, the way of handling swords, etc.

3. Masterless samurai. A samurai who has either lost his lord in battle or left his master.

4. The capital city of the province of Suruga where the Imagawa Clan was situated.

5. Samurai: A member of the class or warriors of feudal Japan who served their territorial lord according to the code of Bushido, representing loyalty, honor, and self-sacrifice, among other values.

6. A wooden sword used in practice and in tournaments.

7. Empress tree.

8. The name of the Imagawa family's fiefdom or domain.

9. Name of the era from 1533 to 1553.

10. The province of the Takeda Clan.

11. Nettle tree.

12. Lord of the fiefdom.

13. Takeda Harunobu, or Takeda Shingen, held different values from his father, Takeda Nobutora. Whereas Nobutora had, under feudal tradition, cruelly taxed and exploited the poor, Shingen was well read and sympathetic to the weak and the peasants. Shingen was supported by his father's samurai and successfully overthrew and exiled his father to the Imagawa's fiefdom when he was only twenty-one years of age.

14. A long sword.

15. Denomination of currency. 1 kan = 1,000 mon.

16. Zelkova tree or American elm: a large deciduous tree imported to the U.S. from Japan.

17. Fumadai: Japanese houses, in those days, had one step up from the ground before stepping on the floor of the house.

18. −san is a polite suffix to a person's name in Japanese, equivalent to Mr. or Mrs. or Ms. For example, Mr. Iohara is really addressed as Iohara-san in Japan. −san is the same for men and women. Use of somebody else's first name is uncommon and overly familiar in Japan, unless you now that person well. You do not use −san when referring to yourself, just as you do not use Mr., Mrs., or Ms.

19. Later called Takeda Shingen.

20. Capital city of the province of Kai where the Takeda Clan was situated.

21. Imagawa Yoshimoto (1519–1560), a warlord in central Japan.

22. The southwest island, one of the four major islands of Japan.

23. The southern district of Honshu island, the larges island of Japan.

24. The southern most island, one of the four major islands of Japan.

25. One of Suwa Yorishige's castles near Lake Suwa.

26. Japanese rice wine.

27. Zen-influence drama in slow and symbolic form.

28. Japanese samurai carried two swords, one long and one short. The short sword was called a wakizashi during the Muromachi Period (1333–1573) and later also was called the shoto.

29. A method of suicide, consisting of disembowelment with a sword. It was originally reserved to men of samurai rank in disgrace or condemned to death, but subsequently became an honorable and, in some cases, required form of suicide. Also known in the West as hara-kiri.

30. It was common for the children of a warlord to commit seppuku when their father was killed.

31. Sanskrit word meaning Titan.

32. Eight o'clock in the morning. See the chart on page 209 for all the Japanese hours of the day.

33. The origin of Suwa. The Suwa shrine deifies the god of war.

34. Fourteen characters are selected from Sun Zsu's *Art of War* written in two lines.

35. One of the war deities of the Japanese indigenous religion, Shinto.

36. The flag's content is taken from the *Art of War* by Sun Zsu, Sonshi is a Japanese pronunciation of Sun Zsu.

37. This was taken from the *Art of War* by Sun Zsu, a shorter description of this is Furin Kazan and was used in the title of this book.

38. Denomination of gold: one kan is about 8.3 pounds of gold. Takeda Harunobu frequently gave several handfuls of gold to samurai who made a great contribution to a particular battle.

39. Takeda Shiro Katsuyori, better known as Katsuyori. Shiro means the fourth male child.

40. This name means the third male child.

41. Eastern central provinces.

42. Mountain ash.

43. The god of war, a protective god of Buddhism.

44. The god of fire, a protective god of Buddhism. Fudomyoou in Japanese.

45. A compact formation.

46. A Japanese blue flower which blossoms on a tree.

47. Protective diety of the Suwa district.

48. Zen-influenced traditional and graceful dance form.

49. Later called Uesugi Kenshin.

50. Kawanakajima is situated between the fork of the Chikuma River and the Sai River in Nagano Prefecture.

51. Noon. According to the actual hours of the day, the hour of the Bull is 2 a.m.; however, the author specifically indicated noon in parentheses.

52. Original text by the author is written Oyamada, this could be a mistake of Yokota Takatoshi.

53. A baton with a fluffly moplike fabric on one end. It was used to direct a large army.

54. The flag carriers who ride horses flat to the horse's neck like a centipede. In Japanese writing centipede is written as one hundred legs.

55. 2.286 acres of land.

56. Japanese grass similar to, but shorter than, pampas grass. The plant often represents fall in traditional Japanese poetry. Officially called Japanese silver grass or Mascanthus sinensis.

57. A term used to call an old man who has served the family for a long time.

58. Spring.

59. Summer.

60. Rice paper sliding door.

61. Japanese traditional dance. Main actors wear a mask to hide human expression and feeling.

62. Shinshu and Shinano are synonymous. The modern name is Nagano Prefecture.

63. Takeda Harunobu and Nagao Kagetora (later Uesugi Kenshin) maintained a respectful relationship although they were enemies. A well-known story is that, at one time, when Takeda faced an embargo of salt from other provinces, Uesugi Kenshin sent a large amount of salt to Takeda saying that the samurai should always be fair and sincere to others. When hearing of Takeda's death later, Uesugi lamented with tears saying that he had lost a worthy opponent.

64. Area along the Kiso Mountain Range and Kiso River in Shinano Province, which is west of Takeda's province of Kai.

65. This was a common practice for samurai to get out of the secular life strategically, for whatever reason. This did not mean giving up life as a samurai.

66. Daisojyu is the highest rank of Buddhist priests.

67. Takeda Shingen held good relations with both the Imagawa Clan in Sugaru and the Hojo Clan in Sagami through the use of hostages.

68. This title is given by the emperor in Kyoto.

69. Up until the Tokugawa era (1868) high ranking samurai received new names on various occasions, such as reaching adulthood, receiving new rank, renouncing the priesthood, at the time of death, and so on.

70. Province of Sagami; territory of the Hojo Clan; Odawara is the headquarters of the Hojo; today's Kanagawa Prefecture.

71. North of the province of Shinano facing the Japan Sea; Uesugi Kenshin (Nagao Kagetora)'s territory; today's Niigata Prefecture.

72. Sanskrit word meaning Titan.

73. An alcove made in the wall of one side of a room to view a garden, a hanging screen, a flower arrangement, etc., originated in the fourteenth century.

74. Princess Yuu's name after death, chosen by the Buddhist priest.

75. Area east of Kiso along the Tenryu River.

76. Area in the province of Kouzuke, today's Gunma Prefecture.

77. Area in the province of Musashi, today's Saitama Prefecture.

78. The name of the Japanese era changed after the death of every emperor.

79. New imperial era from 1555 to 1557.

80. One of the three large rivers in the province of Shinano. The Tenryu River runs parallel to the Kiso River. It runs into the Pacific Ocean via the province of Totomi.

81. New imperial era from 1558 to 1569.

82. Japan was conquered by the first Shogun (military commander) in 1192 (Kamakura Period), Minamoto Yoritomo. The Shogun's position was hereditary and had to be legitimized by the emperor. The government run by the Shogun was called the Shogunate. Japan was managed by the Shogun and the Shogunate for about 700 years, except during the time of the warring era up to the time of unification.

83. The thirteenth Ashikaga Shogun, Yoshiteru, resided in Muromachi, Kyoto. The era under Ashikaga Shogunate was also called the Muromachi era. The last Ashikaga Shogun (the fifteenth Shogun) was exiled by the first unifier of Japan, Oda Nobunaga, in 1573.

84. During the warring era the Ashikaga Shogunate (1338–1573) existed, however, it did not possess any particular power at all except ceremonial power, such as nominating daimyo (rural lords) at the request of the emperor.

85. Peasant rebellions led by the group of the Buddhist believer, Ikko, were a common incident in the warring era. Peasants were not happy at being taken advantage of by the samurai, and, using weapons picked up from the battlefields, they rebelled against them.

86. Kai means ocean and zu means where the water flows.

87. Many Japanese shrines bear this name. It means that the shrine was built for the Oujin Emperor (fifteenth emperor of Japan according to Japanese mythology, Nihon Shoki). Under his era (270 to 310 BC), the power of Japan improved dramatically; therefore he became a protective god of the samurai.

88. Kongo is the location where the best-known Hachiman Shrine exists. This is where the spirit of the protector of the samurai comes from.

89. Capital of the province of Sagami. Takeda's daughter was married to the son of the Hojo family in Sagami.

90. Central districts of Japan such as Kai, Shinano, Sagami, Suruga, etc.

91. North of Kanto district.

92. This was done to support his daughter's family in Sagami.

93. Both Tomikura Sunset Point and Iiyama are close to the border between the provinces of Echigo and Shinano, along the Chikuma River.

94. Signal Flare Mountain.

95. The Five Mile Mountain Range.

96. Takeda Shingen's brother was guarding the forefront at the main camp, Yahatahara.

97. Shingen's legitimate and eldest son.

98. Uesugi Kenshin had renounced the world and entered the priesthood at a young age and stuck to his principles not to associate with women.

Chronology of Key Events

Some dates are subject to debate by historians, and in some cases the author of the novel has taken liberties with the historically accepted dates.

ERA	YEAR	EVENT	
Tenbun	**1532**		
	1540		
		1541	Kansuke employed by the Takeda
		1545	Attack on Suwa Yorishige (Princess Yuu)
		1546	Attack on Murakami Yoshikiyo
			Attacked by the Uesugi Clan (Fiefdom of Echigo)
		1548	Second attack on Murakami Yoshikiyo
			Death of Itagaki Nobukata
	1550		Encounter with Nagao Kagetora at Kawanakajima
			Entrance of Princess Ogoto
		1554	Attack on Kiso
Koji		1555	Nagao Kagetora re-enters Kawanakajima
			Death of Princess Yuu (25)
		1556	Attack on Ina
Eiroku	**1560**		
		1561	Battle at Kawanakajima
			Death of Yamamoto Kansuke (69)
Ganki	**1570**		
		1573	Death of Takeda Shingen (53)

Japanese Hours of the Day

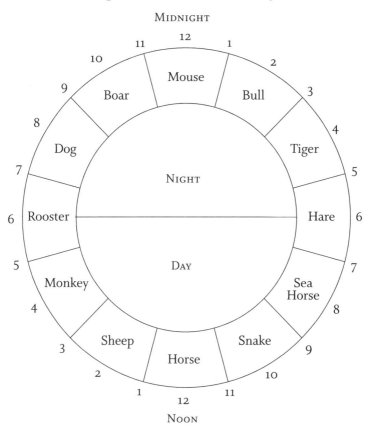

About the Translator

Yoko Riley teaches at the Department of Germanic, Slavic and East Asian Studies at the University of Calgary, Calgary, Alberta, Canada.

She has specialized in the area of Japanese Civilization and, in particular, the recent Sengoku Era (Warring, 1467-1563, and Unification Era, 1560-1600) and the Tokugawa Era (Shogunate Era 1600-1868) periods and their developmental influence on today's Japanese culture, society, and economic and organizational structures. This explains her interest in the works of Yasushi Inoue.

She has developed and teaches courses on Japanese Civilization, Japanese Film, and the Japanese Language. She has co-authored two Japanese language textbooks: *Interactive Japanese 1 & 2*, UTI, and was a contributing author to a collection of Faustian articles titled *Faust as Icon of Modern Culture* (Helm Information, 2004). Her essay, "Faust through the Eyes of a Japanese Cartoonist," deals with the great Japanese cartoonist/ Manga writer Osamu Tezuka's three little known, yet successful, attempts at interpreting Goethe's Faust to Japanese audiences.

Yoko Riley has two adult children and lives in Calgary, Alberta, with her Japanese Shiba, Sachi, and her husband Mike.